# THE STRUGGLE

## From Kenya to Jamaica

BROWN REFLECTIONS

# THE STRUGGLE
## From Kenya to Jamaica



ISBN:
9781944440152

Library of Congress Cataloging-in-Publication Data on file.

Editor: Tonya Williams

# THE STRUGGLE

From
Kenya
to Jamaica

KAREN SLOAN-BROWN

# Table of Contents

# Priscilla and the Stranger

I had lost track of time, and it was obvious that the uninvited guest was not going to leave until he finished his story. My perfect setting and best-laid plan had been irreparably disrupted. Now I was woozy and nauseated from all the wine I'd drunk, and the once-pleasant September air had become chilled. What was even more clear was that the stranger's monologue was nowhere near finished; and if I wasn't going to be able to take myself out of my misery anytime soon, I needed to go inside and get some food.

"Look, mister, can I trust you to come inside?" I asked, knowing it was a silly question at this point. "I'm a little uncomfortable."

"Of course, Priscilla," the stranger answered. "I've told you, I'm not here to hurt you."

With the throw still wrapped around me, I scooted to the side of the lounge chair and stood up. One of my legs was slightly stiff, and the other was asleep, as I limped to the patio door and led the man through the den into the kitchen. Unconcerned about being a perfect host, I rummaged through the refrigerator without exchanging any pleasantries with my uninvited guest.

I took my time making a roast beef sandwich and then grabbed a bottle of ginger ale. I took a large bag of barbecue chips from the cabinet, opened it, and tossed it on the table. I couldn't help but smirk at the irony, realizing that if I were on deathrow right now, this would have been my exact choice for my last meal. I sat at the table and motioned for the stranger to have a seat across from me.

"Would you care for something to eat," I asked offhandedly. Even now, my home training wouldn't allow me to be completely rude.

"No, thank you," he responded. "I'll continue if you're ready."

"Yes, go on," I told him, my mouth full.

"Let's see, where were we?" he mused, looking toward the dishwasher, as if the words were written there. Yes, so far, the Israelites had come out of Egypt, led by Moses and Aaron, and his descendants had been designated as high priests. They had gone into the Promised Land with Eleazar and his son Phinehas. Zodak had served as high priest under King David and Solomon. His son was Ahimaaz. And then there had been Azariah and his great-great grandson, Shallum. Then Azariah IV, Seraiah, and Jozadak had served during the Exile in Babylon.

Jozadak had traveled across the Arabian Desert, more than 1,200 miles, to Saba—modern-day Yemen—where the queen of Sheba had reigned five centuries before. Two of his sons, Rabin and Tobiah, and his grandson Nathan, who had migrated to Axum—modern-day Ethiopia—after Marib was flooded. Then there was Deron; followed by Abbott, who was high priest when Jesus was born; his son Myron; his son Ismael; his son Malachi; Malachi's two sons, Phinehas and Herschel; and then Herschel's sons, Yonas and Simeon.

The year was AD 490, 14 generations after the birth of Jesus Christ. In this era, Axum was among the top four super powers on the globe, along with Persia, Rome, and China. Axum controlled close to one million square miles, which included Eritrea, northern Sudan, southern Egypt, northern Djibouti, Western Yemen, and southern Saudi Arabia.

The Axum kingdom was culturally diverse, with more Arabs and Persians crossing the Red Sea and settling among the Axumites, Kushites, and Israelites. Although world trade had declined after the fall of the Roman Empire, Axum continued to prosper due to its control of the traffic on the Red Sea and its increased trade of ivory, glass crystal, brass, copper, and slaves. The kingdom attracted partners from all over the world to its cosmopolitan trading center, and only Axum ships were allowed to sail to the Far East.

# Chapter One

# Yonas and Simeon

Herschel's grandsons, Yonas and Simeon, were as different as night and day, but they were close friends as well as brothers. Ephrem taught them to respect the other's position: Simeon as king and Yonas as chief priest. Despite their father's traditional teachings of Moses and the laws handed down by God, the Israelites, now known as Beta-Israel, remained divided in their religious beliefs. What unified the people was their loyalty to both brothers.

Simeon was magnetic. He was tall, dark, and muscular, a vision of vitality that drew the people to him. He exuded a zest for life that was as effervescent as the morning dew. Only his wife, Zoya, rivaled him for physical comeliness. Zoya was the daughter of Ephrem's assistant priest, Titus. Zoya had been privileged since the day she was born, and her father doted on her.

Titus had optimistically anticipated that Zoya might be a queen someday. He taught her to read, and he made sure that she was educated on world history and the Scriptures. He wanted her to be intellectually equal to any man and to be able to advise her husband, a future king. With Ephrem dead, Titus approached Simeon with the prospect of marriage to his daughter. One glimpse at Zoya, and Simeon readily accepted. As king and queen, they dressed themselves in the finest of fabrics and regalia, and hosted huge royal banquets where they could entertain and celebrate God's blessings of peace and prosperity.

Yonas, on the other hand, was more common in his appearance. He was average in height, weight, and good looks; and he had a calm and comforting aura that made those he met feel peaceful and secure. Indifferent to the wealth and status of chief priest, he was modest in his dress, wearing only the unadorned white linen garb, except on the Day of Atonement. He was practical and thoughtful, the voice of reason necessary to balance his brother's exuberance.

Yonas first saw his wife, Subira, selling spices with her mother at the open market. Her face was partially covered with a shawl, but the cloth couldn't hide how stunning she was. Out of respect, Yonas didn't speak to her. He asked another vendor which tribe the women belonged to. Yonas was delighted to hear that they were Levites. He quickly arranged a meeting with Subira's father, and a dowry was agreed upon. Although several members of Yonas's extended family griped and gossiped that he should have selected a woman with a higher status, Yonas knew that there was no other woman who could catch his eye.

Yonas's marriage celebration was the one occasion when he didn't try to convince his brother to be less extravagant. Many oxen were slaughtered, and the guests drank countless jugs of honey wine. Yonas considered Subira his dream come true, and he wanted her to experience the best he could give her.

But Subira was intimidated by all the opulence. Instead of luxuriating in it and enjoying it, the rich extravagance of the celebration made her feel as if she didn't belong there. And when she looked across the table at her new sister-in-law, Zoya, Subira felt as if she didn't measure up. Yonas did his best to build his wife's confidence, assuring her that she was the most beautiful woman in the room. Unfortunately, she saw herself as a pigeon next to a lovebird.

***

A year later, the people rejoiced again at the birth of Simeon's first child, Opal, and again the next year at the birth of his second child, Ruby. Yonas and Subira prayed every night that they would soon see their family enlarge, but the third child born was to Zoya, a son they named Jemal.

"You are blessed, dear brother," Yonas said half-heartedly after Jemal was circumcised.

Simeon gave Yonas a robust pat on the back. "You will soon be a father, too," he assured him, after seeing the fretful look on his face. "Spend less time in the temple and more time with your beautiful wife."

Yonas laughed at his brother's teasing, but he was anxious and disturbed. What had he done wrong? Why was he being punished? He'd been a faithful priest. He'd done everything he was supposed to do: He studied the Torah and the Holy Scriptures, he'd kept the commandments of the ark of the covenant, he married a Levite woman, and he prayed fervently. Still, he searched his heart daily to discover why God had not favored him, despite his devotion, for year after year passed without his wife bearing a child.

When Yonas got home, he didn't mention his disappointment to Subira, but she could feel the pressure of it in the room.

"You must divorce me, Yonas!" she begged, pushing her food away and standing to her feet. "I can't bear the burden of you not having a son to follow you as chief priest. I can't live with the thought of it being my fault."

"Stop that talk, sweet wife!" he said, jumping up to hug her close. I didn't choose you to have babies for me. I married you because I love you. That hasn't changed. We just have to be patient. God fulfilled his promise to Abraham and Sarah, Isaac and Rebekah, and Jacob and Rachel. We just have to stay faithful and keep praying."

"We've already been praying for a long time. You don't have to wait for something that may never happen. You can get another wife while you are young."

"Hush, now. I believe it is in God's power to bless us with a child. Another wife for me is not the answer. You will always be more important to me than anything. Besides, Simeon has enough children for all of us to love."

His words seemed to appease Subira for the moment, but he knew it wouldn't last. He lay awake in the darkness repeating Psalm 123:3 in his head, "Thy wife shall be as a fruitful vine by the sides of thine house: thy children like olive plants round thy table."

***

It was after the Passover celebration that Subira told Yonas the long-awaited happy news: Finally, she was pregnant! More than happy, they were both relieved that Yonas would have an heir and possibly a son to follow him as priest.

On the Sabbath, Yonas stood and gave praise to the Lord for blessing them with a child. "Moses gave us this word in Deuteronomy 28:11, 'And the LORD will make you abound in prosperity, in the fruit of your womb and in the fruit of your livestock and in the fruit of your ground, within the land that the LORD swore to your fathers to give you.' Today is a day of thanks," he told the people. "It can be very difficult to wait on the Lord. We get frustrated and we don't understand why we have to wait. But when the Lord blesses us, it is most assuredly a time to rejoice. So I encourage you all to be patient in your petitions. In Jeremiah's Lamentations 3:23-23, the prophet said, 'The steadfast love of the LORD never ceases; his mercies never come to an end; they are new every morning; great is Your faithfulness.' We thank thee, O Lord!"

The people felt his exhilaration and shouted thanks to Jehovah!

***

During his wife's pregnancy, Yonas was protective of Subira. He handled her as carefully as he would a delicate glass vase. He hired two more servants to see to her every need. On the Sabbath, he made sure she received the prized cuts of meat. When she was too tired to sit at the table, he sat at her bedside, dipped enjera bread in stew and an herbal broth, and fed it to her.

Though he wasn't a carpenter, Yonas crafted a crib from a single piece of wood. Into it he carved small birds and trees and stained it blue and gold. Subira loved to watch him work, as she rubbed her belly and sang to the baby inside of her. At night, Yonas hugged Subira close, hoping to feel the motion of the baby while she slept. But when he allowed himself to think about it, Subira's belly had been growing much slower than Yonas had anticipated.

At last, the time was near. In November, at the end of the rainy season, Subira's pains began. Yonas sent for the midwife.

Unable to bear his wife's screams, Yonas went to the temple to fast and to pray. Subira's agonizing labor went on for days, despite the herbs the midwife gave her to ease her pain and push along her labor. Yonas pleaded with the Lord for mercy, as he became more frightened for his wife and the baby. There were a few hours when the pains would stop and Subira could rest. During those hours, the midwife encouraged Yonas, telling him stories of the long births of other young women with their first child. He was comforted and returned to the temple to pray.

In the early morning hours of the fourth day, Subira was exhausted and dehydrated. She pushed and pushed until her body went into shock. She screamed and then fell back lifeless on the floor. The midwife did everything she could to revive Subira. But when she couldn't do that, her instincts were to save the baby. With her knife, she cut through Subira's belly to the womb. Blood gushed from the gash, and the midwife swiped through it, feeling for the child. She gasped and covered her mouth at the sight. There was no baby.

The midwife rushed out to the courtyard wailing, with the servants running behind her. She refused to tell them what happened to their mistress or what happened to the baby. The midwife was terrified that she might be blamed for the dreadful thing that had come upon Yonas. The whole house was frantic. The cook sent one of the servants to run to the temple to bring Yonas home. The servant found him on his knees praying.

"You must come home now, master!" he said, gasping from his run.

Yonas could see that the servant was visibly disturbed. He jumped to his feet. "What is the matter? What is wrong?"

Yonas shrieked, grabbing his cloak and shaking him.

"I'm not sure. Something with the baby," he said, trembling.

Yonas took off running ahead of him, so nervous and sick to his stomach that he had to stop for a moment lest he choke. He leaned against a tree, dry heaving, for there was no food or drink in his body.

"Come, master!" the servant said, catching up to him. He wrapped Yonas's arm around his shoulder and ran, half carrying him.

"Where is my wife?" he asked the midwife, who stood dazed in the courtyard. "Why aren't you with her. How is the baby?" The woman's mouth hung open, speechless. Yonas moved past her and went into the house. He saw Subira lying lifeless in a bloody heap on the bed. He rushed to her side, fell to the floor, and began to moan Psalm 13:1, "How long, O Lord? Will you forget me forever?"

The midwife gathered herself and returned to the house. "Forgive me, my priest!" she said, falling down and groveling before him.

"Where is the baby?" Yonas asked, confused. "Is he dead?"

"There was no baby, my priest," she whispered.

"What are you talking about?" he shouted, anger replacing his grief. "Of course, there was a baby. I watched it grow in her belly all these months."

"I'm sorry, my priest, I know of this happening before."

"Speak plainly, woman! My wife is lying here dead before me, and my child has disappeared."

"No, sir. Some women want to conceive a child so badly that after a while the mind fools the body, and it is as if they are carrying a baby. All the signs are there of a normal pregnancy, except there is no real baby to give birth to. Subira struggled as if it were a difficult birth. It took all of her strength trying to push out a child that wasn't there."

"You are telling me that my wife died for no reason?" he asked, dumbfounded.

"To her, the baby was real."

Yonas was heartsick, devastated with grief and guilt. He would do anything to have one more chance to convince Subira that having a child was so much less important to him than having her as his wife. The pressure on her had come from him, and he was sorry for that. He wished he could turn back time. He had only wanted to make her happy, treat her like a queen. But the more he lavished her with love, the more Subira felt deficient. Maybe she was right. Maybe he should have divorced her. At least she would have still been alive.

***

The wailing of the mourners who came by the house only served to make Yonas feel worse. Their cries reminded him of how Subira had suffered in her futile labor. He never told anyone that there was no baby, except his brother, Simeon. He didn't want to bring shame on his wife. He buried her a few yards behind their home, under a papaya tree, which had born them much fruit.

As a priest, Yonas knew that he should have hidden his grief, but he wasn't concerned with decorum. Tears flowed like a river down his face and into his beard. He sat in the same chair in the same clothes for a week.

Simeon did his best to comfort him. "Come and live with me, brother," he said, pushing against Yonas's shoulders, trying to shake him out of his stupor. "We are family; my children are your children."

"I don't need children to be happy," he muttered. "I would have been happy living my life with Subira, growing old together, without any children to fulfill some legacy."

"You are hurt now, I understand that, but you must pull yourself together. Aren't you the one who says we have an obligation to those around us. The people need you. I can't fill your shoes. Remember the Scripture that father always said to us when we were young, Deuteronomy 31:8: 'The Lord himself goes before you and will be with you; he will never leave you or forsake you. Do not be afraid; do not be discouraged.'"

"Yes, I remember that Scripture. But I have been forsaken. I have been hurt beyond measure. All that I had is gone. Do you expect me to act as if none of that has happened? I'm sorry to disappoint you and anyone else, but I am flesh and blood. This wound will never heal."

"Your faith is strong, I know this, Yonas. You will recover. 'Though he brings grief, He will show compassion, so great is his unfailing love. For he does not willingly bring affliction or grief to anyone,' Lamentations 3:32."

"Simeon, how can you say these things to me? You don't put much account into God's word. You have never wanted to study the Scriptures with me. You seldom even bother to worship on the Sabbath. You know nothing of what you talk about!"

"I know that I love you, brother. I love who you are and what you do for our people. Being a priest was my birthright, but it wasn't my nature. You are a good and righteous man. I admire that in you, and it would hurt me to see that change. My faith in the word is not what it should be, but I have faith in you."

Yonas let his brother's words seep into his soul. "Thank you for that. It means much to me, probably because today that is all I have."

***

Simeon's marriage to Zoya continued to be fruitful, despite his nonchalant observance of his faith. They were blessed with two more daughters, Iris and Abeba. Simeon was a loving father and indulged all his children, but he saw his son as a pure reflection of himself. From the time Jemal learned to walk, Simeon kept him close in his tutelage to follow him as king. And much like Simeon, Jemal was adventurous and inherited his father's love of the hunt. From the time he was tall enough to mount a horse, Simeon and Jemal would ride off before daybreak in search of sport. Many of the men in their territory hunted for their livelihood, but Simeon and Jemal hunted for the game.

"That child is too young for you to drag around in the forests!" Zoya said, vexed. "Why won't you let him rest?" She detested the days Simeon would take her son hunting for long hours that sometimes stretched through the night.

Simeon laughed heartily, putting his arm around Jemal's shoulders as they walked out to their waiting horses. "He can rest all day tomorrow while Yonas fills his head with Scripture."

Zoya followed them into the courtyard, the dogs barking as Simeon and Jemal prepared to depart. Zoya was always nervous when her husband went out in the evening. Most likely, he would be hunting lions.

"What kind of man leads his boy into danger?" she argued hopelessly.

"I am a king raising a king," Simeon responded, grabbing his spear, which was leaning against the wall. "The only luxury he cannot have is fear, my love. When he can face a lion, he will fear nothing and no one, and the people will respect his power."

"He has plenty of time to become a man," she said, calling after them.

"We don't know that," Simeon said as the horses trotted away, with the hunting dogs running beside them.

Zoya shook her head with worry, watching her husband and her son until they were out of sight. While she adored Simeon for his strength and bravery, she didn't understand why he felt the need to prove himself over and over again.

At the edge of the forest, Simeon, Jemal, and his two attendants, met his cousin Hakim and six warriors who were waiting to accompany them. The horses and the dogs were left with the attendants, while Simeon, with Jemal on his heels, and Hakim led the warriors into the forest.

They hadn't gone 50 yards when Simeon stopped. "Can you spot the fresh paw prints, son?" he asked Jemal. "Which way should we go?"

Jemal said, "Yes, Father, I see the prints. He is not far."

"That's right," Simeon said, pleased. "We have to stalk him like he stalks his prey. The hunter becomes the hunted." Simeon looked for any movement across the tall grass blowing in the light breeze. He motioned to his cousin. "Hakim, take your group, and go east. We'll go in this direction. Maybe we can head off our lion and run him into the pit."

They had walked for about an hour when they saw a huge male lion with a black mane chasing a young zebra separated from its pack. Simeon and Jemal rushed behind them, peering through the dust kicked up by the pursuit. The zebra lacked the speed to outrun the lion; and soon, the lion pounced on the back of its prey. Simeon darted closer, and Jemal scurried just behind him.

"Now, son," Simeon said to him. "Take aim and throw your spear."

Jemal couldn't believe how close they were to the massive lion, they were close enough to see the huge cat's nose flare as he tore away at the carcass. Jemal took a deep breath and threw his spear as hard as he could. It fell short, and the lion stared in Jemal's direction.

"Are you going to kill him, Father?" Jemal asked anxiously.

"Another day," Simeon said, staring back at the lion. "We've done enough today. Let's go home and ease your mother's worries."

***

Zoya sat in her chambers with all four of her daughters. Opal and Ruby were taking turns styling each other's hair, while Iris and Abeba were asleep beside her. The girls always knew when their mother was troubled by how fast her hands moved as she weaved the straw into baskets. More often than not, Zoya's hands flew through the straw when their father went hunting.

"I don't know if I want a husband, Mother," Ruby said, twisting Opal's long, thick hair. "They are more work than caring for a child, and they keep your nerves upset."

"That's not the whole truth, child. We need them, and they need us," Zoya said, setting aside her weaving to stretch her arms. "Women are the earth, and men are the rain. We are sturdy, reliable, and constant. They are impulsive and volatile, and their presence can be too much or too meager." She leaned over and affectionately rubbed the faces of her younger girls. "As God planned it, we need each other for our beautiful flowers to grow."

"I want a husband just like father," Opal said. "Except, I'll make sure he listens to me."

Ruby laughed, and Zoya couldn't help but smile. Then she heard the sound she had been waiting hours to hear: horses approaching. "Thank you, merciful God," she said, pressing her hand against her heart.

"See there, Mother," Opal said cheerfully. "You worried and prayed for no reason."

"No, dear daughter, your mother's prayers were answered yet again."

Zoya hurried out to the front to meet them and to make sure that they had come home in the same condition that they left.

"We're back, my love," Simeon said, grinning proudly. "Your son is quite the hunter. He stared straight into the lion's eyes without a flinch."

Zoya grabbed Jemal by the arm and looked him over for scratches or broken skin. She breathed a sigh of relief when she found none.

"I'm not hurt, Mother. I can take care of myself," Jemal said.

Simeon proudly patted his son on the back. "He's a brave young man."

Zoya grunted at his words. "He is not brave. He is a naïve young boy."

***

Zoya's instruction and guidance from her father served her well. She managed many of the fiscal matters of the kingdom and settled small disputes among the people. Simeon trusted her judgment completely, and it allowed him the privilege to indulge in his many amusements. He participated in military exercises with his army, but his greatest thrills were in the hunt. He sometimes grumbled that he was a wartime king serving in a time of peace.

Zoya also took the lead as mediator in the arrangement of marriages for Opal and Ruby. The wedding celebration for Ruby had just ended, and Simeon had gone off on one of his adventures with some of the guests. Zoya sat in the courtyard with Yonas, resting after the festivities.

"Have you ever thought about taking another wife?" Zoya asked Yonas. "You are not an old man, and you are worthy of being loved."

"It has taken so long for my wounds to heal that I dare not wrench them open again. The little love that I have left to give will be poured over my brother's family, not lost trying to search for something that I won't find again."

"I wish I could convince you otherwise; but in truth, we need all the devotion that you have afforded us. Simeon withdraws from me and our daughters more every day. He's more in love with chasing that black lion across the grasslands."

"My brother is just like that lion he hunts. He is more comfortable protecting his territory from another adversary. His freedom is everything to him, and he must prove his prowess to himself more than to anyone else."

"As a king and as a husband, his recklessness is irresponsible!" Zoya said.

"For most men, manliness is exterior. They give from their body, not so much from the heart."

"Why can't I show him how important the heart is to a woman?"

"I'm not sure you can, dear sister. He's set in his ways. Jemal is the one we need to teach. He will have to be all things to the people. The time for him to marry will be upon us soon."

"I've spoken to Simeon about that, and he doesn't want Jemal restrained until it's time for him to be king."

"He must be readied regardless of when he takes the throne. Noah was warned by God to prepare for an event that others could not see. It was his obedience that saved the lives of his family. The changes all around us will creep inside our perimeter. Our greatest threat has not changed. It is still religious opposition. Jemal must be equipped to stand tall against the influences of outside forces."

"There isn't much I can do about that. Your brother feels he can fight our battles as well as the Lord can."

Yonas shook his head. "I could preach to you about the destruction our people have suffered in war because God wasn't with us from now until dawn, and I would still have more to tell you."

Zoya stared off in the direction where her husband and son had ridden. "I know that, Yonas. That's the one thing that terrifies me each time they go out looking for a fight in the forests."

***

Without a son of his own to succeed him as chief priest, Yonas was determined to complete Jemal's priestly training, despite Simeon's indifference. King or not, Jemal was a Kohanim, a direct ancestor to Aaron. But, as dedicated as he was, it was not an easy task tying him down for his studies. He had always been a restless child. Even though he could sit quietly during his lessons, his right leg would jump nervously to a rapid beat, indicating how anxious he was to spring from the confined space. More often, Yonas found himself reading and speaking in an accelerated pace, knowing that Jemal's attention was quickly waning and that the boy was more focused on escaping from his lessons than learning.

Nevertheless, despite Simeon's nurturing and Yonas's teachings, Jemal wanted to be unrestricted and free more than he wanted to be a king or a priest. Even the hunting adventures had lost their luster in his eyes. He wanted to see what was on the other side of the sea. His favorite pastime was hanging around the coastline, watching the ships come and go.

Once Jemal reached the age of accountability, he asked his father to let him explore the world away from their city. Simeon had been able to put him off for a few years, but Jemal was becoming more insistent, begging his father to let him sail on the next Axum ship that traveled out on the Silk Road to China for trade.

On his sixteenth birthday, Jemal sat at the table between his father and uncle, asking for permission to explore some of the countries outside Axum. Simeon had pondered his request and had arrived at a compromise he believed would satisfy them all.

"I understand your yearning to see more of the world, son. I would take the trip with you if I could. Nonetheless, I will give you my consent on one condition. When you return, you must settle down, assist your uncle at the temple, and take a wife."

"You have my word, Father!" Jemal said, overjoyed.

Simeon chuckled at his son's enthusiasm. "Arrangements will be made with your cousin Hakim to join him and his group."

Jemal jumped from the table and dashed out of the room to share his good news with his mother.

"What if his ship is wrecked?" Yonas asked, objecting. "Even if he is not to be king, he is the direct descendent to Jozadak, Zadok, and Aaron. He has an obligation to protect and administer God's word. It is his birthright. If he doesn't return, what will you do?"

"Where is your faith, Yonas?" Simeon asked defiantly. "Does not God hear your prayers? Jemal should see what's out there in the world. It will make him a better king."

"He has a responsibility given to him by God, and it's bigger than being king. You've heard of empires that have collapsed or been seized, but the kingdom of God is everlasting. The Scriptures tell us of the wrath we provoke when we are disobedient."

"Well said, brother. That will be the first lesson for you to impart when he returns."

Chapter Two
# Jemal

Jemal was ecstatic that he could finally begin his adventure! He would set sail at the beginning of the year and have at least 12 months of total freedom. He dressed in trousers and shoes under a tunic, as Hakim had directed; and with his baggage in tow, he joined his cousin in his meetings with merchants on his way to Zanzibar. It took them a week to get to the coast for the short ferry ride to Zanzibar, where they would board the large ship. From there, they would sail with the winter monsoon winds northeast to India and then to China.

When Jemal set foot in Zanzibar, he was buoyed in his heart and soul. He felt as if he could take flight and make the trip high above the seas, soaring on the clouds. The huge vessel amazed him. It was solid wood held together by iron nails. The ship was 70 feet long, with 14 oars on each side, benches for the rowers, and a large sail made of animal hides. He watched anxiously as the vessel was packed with grain, silver, salt, ivory, and other goods.

Jemal's belly quivered as the ship moved further away from the shore. He was transfixed, unable to move. His wish had finally been granted; but never having been on the water without land in sight, Jemal now felt a tinge of fear for the first time in his life. That evening, he laid down without eating. The next night, and for several more, he barely slept. Sometimes he was seasick; other times, he wanted to experience all the things he had only heard about. He had never been around men like those who worked on the ship. They spoke and behaved without reservation. While they rowed, a few of the oarsmen teased him about ships sinking and other mishaps and disasters at sea.

Standing on the deck of the ship, Jemal pulled his damp cloak tighter around himself in the cool air. With the oarsmen's stories still ringing in his ears, he grew more anxious as the first week passed. He surprised himself when he began to pray and call upon the Lord. He thought of his uncle, Yonas, who would be proud that his lessons had finally taken hold. He became more comfortable as the weeks went by, and he felt more secure in the company of hundreds of other ships of all sizes on the water around them. He even grew bored after a month, as they sailed across the Arabian Sea.

Jemal's excitement was reborn when the water quieted near the sight of land. It was his first glimpse of Madras, India, in the bright sunrise. The statue of the emperor welcomed them, along with the smell of spices and the day's catch at the dockyard. He thanked God when his feet touched the ground, not for safe passage, but for the freedom he felt again from being off the ship. Merchants and traders sat lined against the walls, surrounded by piles of various goods, as they conducted their business, much like they did on the port of Zanzibar. There were vendor tents of all colors where craftsmen sold their wares. The different languages clashed together in a cacophony of shouts, as they beckoned buyers.

"I won't be long," Hakim told him, as he strode away, "The hump-back cattle are traded just beyond the bend there. Look around. You might see something that interests you."

Jemal nodded, as he ventured toward the tents. The dock workers were bare-chested and dressed similar to those workers in his own city. They were brown, with narrow features and straight hair. On the other side of the wall, he saw a temple carved out of stone. He listened as men leaving the port prayed for fair winds. He smelled hot food, and his stomach rumbled. He hadn't eaten a decent meal since he had left home. Warned by his mother, he dared not eat anything he had not seen cooked. He went back to the wall to find Hakim.

"My business is done for now," Hakim said, with a look of satisfaction. "Follow me. I'll show you to an area where we can find a meal and a warm place to sleep."

Accompanied by two of his assistants, Hakim hired two-horse driven chariots to carry them. As they traveled away from the harbor, the ambiance and the character of Madras changed. Trees lined the narrow roads, with stalls for street vendors, who were selling all kinds of things. He saw military squads of cavalrymen and foot soldiers, who guarded the towns they passed through to protect the inhabitants from thieves and invaders.

The people seemed content as they walked about busily, carrying out their daily activities. They wore loosely wrapped garments, and the men wore turbans on their heads. Lots of animals—dogs, goats, and cattle—moved about freely among them. The homes were rectangular one-room huts made of wood or bamboo, with thatched roofs. Much like the villages around Lake Tana, the homes encircled a common courtyard.

In less than an hour, Hakim and Jemal arrived at a village with larger two-story wood houses with balconies. Prancing in the courtyard was a magnificent peacock that proudly spread its wings when they stopped. The two men climbed down from the chariots, and Jemal was surprised when a host of people who looked like his own people rushed out to greet them from the largest house. They welcomed Hakim with warm embraces.

"This is my cousin, Jemal, a Levite. He is the son of our king, Simeon, and nephew of our chief priest, Yonas."

The people bowed in respect to salute him. Then a beautiful brown-skinned woman dressed in flowing fabric, embroidered with silver threads, and embellished with precious gems rushed over into Hakim's arms with tears running down her face. Several young children followed on the tail of the woman's skirt.

"This is my wife, Rina," Hakim said, turning to Jemal. "These are my children."

Jemal nodded politely, showing no hint of his astonishment at the announcement. Even though he and Hakim were as close as brothers, Hakim had never divulged his secret life or family across the seas.

"Come, we have food prepared for you," her father said, ushering them into the tall house.

Inside, the walls were plastered, and the floors were paved with bricks. Ornate sculptures decorated the hall. In the room at the end of the hallway, Jemal followed suit, as they sat down on the floor cross-legged. Servants placed more flatbread, goat cheese, and stewed lamb in front of them. For the most part, they ate the meal in silence.

"This is my cousin's first voyage away from Axum," Hakim said when they had finished the meal. "Please tell him about life here in Madras."

Rina's father spoke up. "We are Jews, children of Israel, as you are, young prince. Our forefathers came here many generations ago as merchants and traders. We have our own community here, where we live in peace under the Gupta Empire. We are free to live and worship in our way. We have a good life here."

Jemal was amazed at what he heard. "I would like to explore and learn more about this place and your life here."

"Very good. My son, Ram, will be glad to take you to the university tomorrow. There is much there to see."

***

As Rina's father had said, there was much to experience in the city. Jemal learned that most of the people were Hindu and that Hinduism was more of a way of life than a religion. There was no specific holy book to read, no prophets, or any singular religious authority. Hindus can have one god, many gods, recognize all gods, or believe in no god. They gave gifts of land to their priests, the Brahmins, and their other gods. For Jemal, coming from a people who focus so much of their religion on the sacrifice of animals and the eating of meat, he found it unusual that most of the people there only ate vegetables, grains, breads, fruits, and milk.

Though most of the people were not educated, the city was renowned for its university. He marveled at the diversity of its student body. There were students there from all over the world. They wrote poetry and told stories that entertained him for hours. The scholars, writers, and artists of the country were encouraged to exhibit their talents and were paid handsomely by the Pallavas Dynasty.

At the end of their time in Madras, Jemal thanked the family for being gracious hosts and Ram for showing him around the city. He said a prayer of blessing and then waited in the chariot while Hakim bid his tearful wife goodbye. Jemal wasn't quite ready to be on the water again; but if Mahaputu, the port in Sri Lanka, had as much to behold as Madras, he was anxious to get there. He wanted to see the great mountain, Adam's Peak, where legends say Adam first touched his feet when he fell from heaven.

***

Their ship arrived in Mahaputa a week later. As in Madras, the goods were unloaded by slaves, and Hakim went about his business of buying and selling. Jemal accompanied him as Hakim sold gold, silver, and coral. Then he bought precious gems, pearls, cinnamon, and horses.

The people in Sri Lanka were Buddhists, and there were magnificent sculptures and drawings of Buddha everywhere Jemal turned. He was impressed with the tall buildings and religious monuments. There was no doubt that these were spiritual people. The monasteries were full of thousands of monks, and the temples were full of Hindu priests.

It was late in the afternoon when Hakim had finished his business for the day.

"There is a community of Jews west of here at the port of Galle, where we can lodge for a few days while the men refresh themselves," he said to Jemal.

"Am I to meet another of your wives here?" Jemal asked, half-joking.

"No, cousin, I'm not a king," Hakim laughed. "You must understand, she chose me. It would have been shameful for me to deny her hand."

"Why didn't I know you were so charitable," Jemal chuckled.

"There's quite a bit more to learn about me," Hakim said, smiling.

"I have no doubts about that, cousin," Jemal said, wide-eyed. "What other secrets are you keeping here?"

"Well, if you spent a bit more time studying the Holy Scriptures instead of running through the forests, you would know that the port of Galle is believed to be Tarshish, the source of King Solomon's metals to finish his palace. The Scripture says, 'Once every three years the ships of Tarshish used to come bringing gold, silver, ivory, apes, and peacocks.'"

"How can I argue with you, Hakim. You are certainly more educated than I am in more ways than I ever knew."

Hakim laughed again. "I believe you will surpass my low level."

"I hope that I can," Jemal said, grinning.

They spent a week in Sri Lanka before the ship sailed along the Indian Ocean to Quanzhou, the central port of China.

***

The pungent smell of pepper met Jemal before his feet touched the shore at the port of Quanzhou. He wrapped his cloak tighter around his shoulders. He had never felt temperatures this cool before. On the shore, there was the now familiar sight of traders shouting around mounds of goods stacked high above their heads.

It was the distinctive features of the people that fascinated him. They were shorter, with wide faces and small eyes, and the sound of the language was like nothing he had ever heard.

They dressed in different clothing and wore wide hats. Jemal chose to sit in the center market while Hakim handled his business.

Hakim returned there to find Jemal when he had finished trading. "Come, let me take you to the synagogue," he said, grabbing Jemal by the arm. "I'll introduce you to some friends."

"Your life is much bigger than I would have ever imagined, Hakim. Would you consider trading places with me and be king?"

Hakim chuckled. "I'm glad that I don't have to think about that."

Jemal marveled at the intricacies in the carvings on the synagogue. It was a glorious sight to behold. A rabbi invited him inside. He breathed in the incense and prayed at the altar, as he had seen Yonas do on so many occasions. Near the synagogue, there was a small village. The village had an inn, where Hakim introduced Jemal to more merchants who were also children of Israel.

After a pleasant meal with Hakim's acquaintances, the men drank rice wine.

Up to that point, Jemal had been holding his tongue, but he couldn't any longer. "Pardon me," he said, looking around the table. "But you don't look like my people."

One of the men, Jakob, nodded and answered. "There has been much intermarriage among our people over the generations."

"How long have you lived here?" Jemal asked, still curious.

"We were all born here," Jakob said. "There were many Jews who traveled here from Jerusalem many generations ago on the incense route. My family traveled here with a group that came along the Silk Road after the Bar Kokhba Revolt."

Jemal was astounded to see how far their people had migrated to Madras. "Do you have any thoughts of leaving this place?" he asked.

"This is my home. I have no other," Jakob said. "They don't interfere in our lives here, and we govern ourselves under our own rules. We couldn't do that in Jerusalem because it is now ruled by Christians."

"What is this place ruled by?" Jemal asked.

"A few are Buddhist, but Taoism is the religion of the people here, although it is more of a philosophy. They believe in a natural balance of the earth and embrace the wonder of nature. Tao teaches one to follow your breath and experience the joy of life. Their gods are their ancestors. They have no need for temples or monasteries, they have private altars in their homes, where they worship and honor their ancestors, spirits of their houses, and those of their village. Public rituals and festivals are not mandatory. Most never attend them."

The men talked into the late hours of the night, with Jemal finding more similarities with them. He and Hakim attended worship with the Chinese Jews at the synagogue in the village several times, but it was nothing like their service to the Lord back home. Oddly enough, more than his own religion, Jemal identified with Taoism. That was the way he wanted to live. More than the jade, porcelain, paper, cinnamon, spices, and fine silk fabrics, he wished he could take the newly discovered lifestyle back home on the ship.

***

The feeling of freedom was wonderful. Jemal had seen so many different places and met other descendants of his people. Separated by the seas over the centuries, they were bound together as Israelites. He thought more about the Scripture that he had read with Yonas, Deuteronomy 4:27, "The LORD will scatter you among the peoples, and you will be left few in number among the nations where the LORD drives you." He had seen for himself that the word of God was not void, but real. His perspective was forever changed because it had been proven true.

It was late in the spring when Jemal and Hakim set sail back to Axum. Jemal stared out into the horizon, while the waves of the water relaxed him. The anxiety of drifting on the sea was gone, as the winds carried the ship southwest. Jemal certainly wasn't ready to go home. What he had seen had only served to convince him that there was much more in the world for him to see. Nevertheless, he had made a promise to his father, and he would keep it—at least for a while.

## Jemal, Part II

The skin on Yonas's knees was thick and rough, like that of an old elephant. His skin had been toughened from spending most of his waking hours bowed in prayer. That's how it had been since his older brother, Simeon, the king, had been killed by the black lion. His prayers were not for his brother, for himself, or for the people; instead, they were for his nephew, Jemal, who returned home from his voyage a week after the horrible attack.

The travels that Simeon thought would have settled his son

only served to make him more restless. The news of his death changed everything for Jemal. The inner bubbling of joy that had always flowed through him was replaced with an anger that boiled beneath the surface.

Yonas kneeled before his nephew on the day he was crowned king and prayed for calm to come into Jemal's being; but his prayers weren't answered, for Jemal searched the forest every day for the lion whose head was framed with a thick, black mane. For more than a year, it had become his mission and then his obsession to slay the man-killing beast. Yonas had done everything possible to distract his focus, but without any success.

Yonas repeated the same plea each morning before the sun rose: "Jemal, come with me to the synagogue for the morning prayer. As the king and chief priest of the people, you must consult with your Creator. Show the people that you are obedient to God."

As usual, Jemal was sitting up in bed as if he had been awake for hours. "I'm the king. That's all the people need to know," he replied with disdain.

Yonas's tone became stern. "God is the only true King, and you must exalt Him. You are a Levite priest, so you must know God's word. You must memorize the Torah and the Holy Scriptures."

"God isn't in a book!" Jemal shouted at his uncle. "He's not quiet and still. He's high in the sky, deep in the sea, and vibrating in the muscles of the antelope when he runs. His powers can't be confined to the corners of the synagogue or locked in the ark of the covenant."

Yonas softened. "That may be true, but the priests have been instructed to keep His word."

"Then you look for Him between words. I feel Him when my lungs fill with air."

"But you're not searching for Him out there among the wild. That's revenge that sits on your heart. God's word says, 'It is mine to avenge.' It is for Him alone to punish. You are only questioning His will, and that is wrong, Jemal."

"Where was God when the lion killed my father, Uncle? Why didn't He send His angels to shut its mouth, as He did for Daniel?"

"It is not for us to question God's will. Let it be, son."

"I'm not asking anything. It is not my intention to struggle with God. The lion will pay with his life for the life he took."

"What if you are killed because of your defiance? You have not taken a wife. You have no heirs to carry your legacy. If you die, it ends with you."

"Then I won't die."

"You are foolish!" Yonas roared, pointing his finger at Jemal. "Your life is in God's hands, as was your father's."

Jemal turned away. "Then you must pray harder for me."

Downhearted, Yonas trudged to the temple alone with his thoughts. Flashes of the day Simeon was mauled to death still haunted him. He would never forget the sight of his brother's body ripped and torn, the flesh exposed, his regal robe tattered and covered in blood, his soul missing and gone forever.

Squalls heavy with anguish flooded the palace. As harrowing as all of that was, it was the tearful expression of grief on his nephew's face when he told him the awful news that crushed the broken pieces of his heart. Yonas had never felt as useless as he did at that moment. He could not fill his brother's shoes while he lived, and now that he was gone, it was even more impossible. That was the first day he dropped to his knees and began to pray for Jemal.

Yonas remembered the funeral ceremony and the sight of Iris and Abeba tearfully clinging to their mother, Zoya, as she struggled to maintain her dignity and composure. The people wailed and thrashed on the ground with sorrow. When Jemal returned from his adventures, Yonas took him to the burial site. They were there for only a minute before Jemal walked away without a word—past the temple, past the palace—and kept walking. Yonas stared at his nephew's back as the young man walked away. When Jemal was out of sight, Yonas fell to his knees again and prayed for the safety of his headstrong nephew, for he was the only direct descendant left from the line of Aaron, Zodak, and Jozadak.

Yonas knew that when he died, Jemal would be the only rightful one to protect their heritage and adhere to the covenant God had handed down to their people. The problem was that Jemal's faith was weak. He believed in his own invincibility instead of almighty God's. Fearing for Jemal's safety and the security of the Beta-Israel kingdom, Yonas decided that a wife would be just the remedy to exhaust his nephew's surplus of energy and preoccupation with retribution.

***

Her name was Layla. Yonas and Zoya had carefully chosen her. She was strong enough not to be crushed by Jemal, yet she was demure enough not to wrestle power away from him. Jemal was agreeable and respected Layla as his wife. He enjoyed the attention she lavished on him, but the love she desired from him was missing. He allowed her to love only a portion of him; the rest, he guarded. She bore him a son named Koji and a daughter named Jamila; but as time went on, he seemed less interested. She often cried on Zoya's shoulder about the emptiness she felt.

"He's already tired of me, Mother! He leaves me alone most of the time, and he barely talks to me. It's like I'm not even here."

"How can you complain that he ignores you?" Zoya fussed, chastising her daughter-in-law. "He has given you two beautiful children to love."

"The children are no substitute for my husband's love," Layla cried.

"That is selfish thinking. You are married to a king. He belongs to the people, and they to him. I explained that to you."

"I know that, but I thought he would love me as I love him."

"Jemal has never needed anyone. He is like his father was. You must remember that you are the queen. You are privileged. Be thankful for your blessings."

Layla tried hard to tame Jemal. She hated the days and nights he spent away from her, but it was no use. He was as wild as the animals he hunted. The more tightly she tried to hold him, the more he yearned to be free.

Layla wasn't the only one pulling at Jemal. All his responsibilities as king pulled at him, too. Jemal felt like the lion he tracked, causing him to feel that he was the one hunted. There were days he wished the lion would come out of the darkness and kill him, too, and take him out of his misery.

***

It had been 14 generations since the birth of Jesus Christ, and new wars over religion were beginning to rage. While others shook with terror over the brutal battles, Jemal welcomed them as a reprieve from the confinements of his duties as king. Most of the skirmishes were about power over trade and less about convictions. Jemal knew there were Christians among his people, and his travels influenced his belief in religious freedom. But as long as he was king, Beta-Israel would never be ruled by any extension of Rome.

Whenever he and his army weren't squashing rebellions in their territory, Jemal and his two trusted officers, Ebo and Ajani, resumed their hunt for the lion with the black mane. The three of them had become closer than brothers. Having fought in several battles together, each of them trusted the others with his life. With spears in hand, they trotted out of the grasslands into the forest. They had been tracking the lion for weeks. They knew the general area where they could find him.

"We will split up to surround him and draw him into a human trap," Jemal directed, examining the large, fresh paw prints.

Ebo hesitated. "Should we strike if we have the chance, or would you prefer to be the one to take vengeance for your father?"

Jemal's fist tightened around his spear. "It is my responsibility; it was my blood that this beast spilled. My father would want me to take this lion down with my own hands."

"All right, brother," Ajani said. "We'll take the sides. The center is yours."

Jemal nodded in agreement. "If either of you see him, chase him toward the pit."

Stepping cautiously in the lion's tracks, Jemal's heart beat faster with expectation. The woods were unusually quiet, except for his own movements against the brush. He paused and crouched down. The call of a bird was all he heard for several tense minutes. Then a bellow and a growl clashed in the air, and then there was silence again.

Jemal stretched his neck, his ears straining for the direction in the stillness. He waited. Then there was the sound of a limb cracking under the weight of a footstep. He creeped toward the sound without breathing. He heard another growl and a blood-curdling scream that hung in the air. He dashed into the clearing. The sight snatched his breath. Ebo was tossed into the air like a bird taking flight. Jemal shouted to get the lion's attention, hoping Ebo could escape.

The lion turned toward him, and the king's eyes locked with the beast's eyes. They were large and cold, like golden gem stones. Jemal stared deep into them, and like the sea, there was no ending. He was lost in them.

And then Jemal saw his reflection inside those cold, golden orbs. There was a flash of understanding between him and the lion. He too had fought to survive. Now, at this instant, they could try to kill the other, or they could leave it be. Jemal looked up to the sky, and the lion slowly stepped away into the thick brush.

Jemal rushed over to aid Ebo, but he was dead. He searched for Ajani and found him dead, too. No one ever asked what took place in the forest that day, and Jemal never spoke of it again.

***

In the year 511, Christian king Tezena ruled Axum. Although he respected the independence given to Beta-Israel, there were still skirmishes between them and the Christians who sought to infiltrate southern Axum.

With a sizable military, Jemal opted to lead his men in limited battles instead of waiting in the palace for them to win the latest conquest. Because of this, Yonas had seen no respite from the hours spent on his knees in prayer. He went by the palace on his way home from the temple to check on Jemal, who had just returned from another clash with missionaries.

"Why must you play with fate, Jemal? You know firsthand what can happen. Does not your son deserve time enough to be a man before he has to take your place? You must set the proper example for him to follow. You must bring Koji to the synagogue to honor Jehovah."

Jemal laughed loudly. "I've defended your right to worship in peace. What more do you want from me?"

"You must thank the Almighty; your victory is God's glory."

"From whose hand did the spear fly?"

"Don't be insolent! You must know who guides your hand."

Jemal waved his hand and changed the subject. "There is a council meeting today, Yonas. King Tezena will be visiting with us, and we must pay homage to him. It seems he visits us more often lately."

Yonas grunted. "That's just another name for the taxes he comes to collect from our people. Still, what he takes is well worth the exchange. When we don't have to pay with the blood of our people, the price for peace is meager. Thank the Lord we have plenty of gold."

"Surely you know our people pay a high price with their blood and sweat in the mines to bring out the gold," Jemal added.

"You're young, but you will learn. It's better to bleed and sweat for yourself and sacrifice some than to bleed and sweat for another man and have nothing."

"Maybe so," Jemal said, leaving the hall. "I'll be here to eat with King Tezena after the morning hunt."

***

"Welcome, my king," Jemal said, bowing slightly to Tezena. He motioned for his attendants to guide Tezena to the head of the table. "How can we serve you?"

Tezena sat down and smiled across the table. "Jemal, your gracious support to Axum has always been appreciated, and it will become even more important in the days ahead. We must band together for our greater strength. As you know, your people crossed the Red Sea and came here from Saba many centuries ago because of conflict. We have lived in peace all of these years, and that is the way it should always be."

Jemal nodded. "I agree. We are more than friends. Our households have blended. My sister is wife to your youngest brother."

"I trust you, as I trusted Simeon before you," Tezena said, his voice becoming more serious than congenial. "However, we are a Christian state, and you govern Beta-Israel. We need your loyalty, as Saba has resisted conversion to Christianity, and the people practice Judaism."

Furrows of worry creased Jemal's brow. "Why does their religious practice concern you?" he asked.

"It is because they have become aggressive in their persecution of Christians in their land. If that trouble continues, we may have to take a stand."

Tezena wanted assurances from Jemal that the military of Beta-Israel would not interfere in any conflict that might arise between Axum and Saba on the other side of the Red Sea.

"You have our loyalty, my king. We are no threat to you. We have Christians among our people who live in peace and are free to worship as they choose."

King Tezena raised his glass in salute, and his smile returned. "Our bond will never be broken, Jemal."

"May Axum rule forever!" Jemal said, smiling, knowing that as long as his men toiled in the mines, their bond would be as good as gold.

King Tezena stood up to leave, and Jemal rose from his seat. The door opened, and members of the king's entourage, who had waited outside, joined him. Tezena walked over to Jemal and embraced him. "You must be my guest at the palace. I'll expect you as soon as possible."

"I'll be there," Jemal said.

***

In truth, Jemal had lost his taste for the hunt after staring the black-maned lion in the face. Restless and bored, he and his entourage went to the capital of Axum on Tezena's invitation. When they arrived at the palace, they found themselves at a huge celebration, with hundreds of guests. It was at the fabulous banquet that he noticed an enchanting woman sitting at a table across the room. His passion was ignited like oil poured on a flame.

Jemal asked the king to introduced him to the mysterious woman. Her name was Mimi. She was the sister of one of Tezena's wives and a member of the inner court at the palace. Yes, she was beautiful, but that wasn't the only attraction between them. It was her free spirit. She was dressed in fine, bright silks from China and wore golden jewelry like the women from India.

Jemal stayed at Tezena's palace after the banquet and spent the better part of a week wooing Mimi. She talked a lot, laughed loud, sang, and danced as if each day were another celebration. Jemal felt more alive from the energy she brought when she walked into the room. When he returned home to Lake Tana, she rode beside him.

Tezena was more than pleased. His plan had worked perfectly. Mimi's family had come to Axum from Saba with other Israelites, but they had converted to Christianity during the reign of Ezana. Surely, she would be a guarantee that Beta-Israel wouldn't revolt against Axum.

***

Yonas was enjoying the peace of mind he had received when Jemal stopped hunting for the killer lion; but as a precaution, the chief priest had moved into the palace to keep an eye on his nephew. He had not long returned from teaching his morning lessons at the school of the synagogue and was in the middle of a relaxing meal when the hysterical cries of a woman disturbed his tranquility. His head bowed when he saw Layla's face streaked with tears.

"My priest, he has betrayed me!" she sobbed. "He has brought another woman into the palace and declared her his second wife."

"Calm down, dear heart," he said, trying to comfort her. "I know nothing of what you're talking about."

"It's Jemal, my husband. He has returned from Axum with a concubine, passing her off as his new wife!"

Yonas's stomach churned with disagreement at the disturbance and the news. "Settle down, dear. I will speak with Jemal."

Yonas called for his assistant to take Layla to Zoya's quarters. Then he went to find out about this latest calamity his nephew had created.

"What is this I hear about you taking another wife?" Yonas asked, storming into the king's quarters.

Jemal was eating his meal and turned to his uncle and answered casually, "That is true."

"What is wrong with you?" Yonas yelled, pounding his fist on the table. "A priest cannot have sexual relations outside of his marriage. You know that! You are supposed to be the example of piousness for the people."

Jemal continued eating nonchalantly. "Dear uncle, those rules don't apply to the king."

Yonas reached his arms up to the ceiling. "You are held to a higher standard! You are the chief priest. That is your first birthright."

Jemal grinned as he greedily gnawed the meat from the bones. "Should the king not be satisfied! I'm a man with strong appetites."

"You should hunger and thirst for righteousness, nephew. God's word will nourish you. Bow down and ask for forgiveness."

"I haven't done anything wrong. Abraham and Moses had more than one wife. Need I mention King David and Solomon?"

Yonas took a deep breath and closed his eyes. Certainly, as king, Jemal should have the privilege of having all the wives he desired, but he was also the spiritual leader of the people. This was the main reason Yonas objected to priests serving as kings.

"We are in a precarious time. Our beliefs are confused, and our faith is being tested," he said urgently. "There are many who fight against us. We must stay independent. It's time to cleave closer to God. 'When a man's ways please the LORD, he makes even his enemies to be at peace with him,' Proverbs 16:7." Yonas then knelt on the floor. "Pray with me, nephew."

"When my enemies come for me, I won't be on my knees. I'll be on my feet. My God is not weak. Why should I be?"

Yonas stood up slowly and shook his head in dismay. "Who is this woman Layla complains about?"

"She is Mimi, and she is also my wife."

"There will be no peace in this place with two women under one roof."

"Then I will build a place for her."

"Running between two women? When will you have time to counsel your people."

"Since you have no son of your own, that is your job, Uncle."

Yonas turned and walked out. He had no more regrets about not having children of his own. He lacked the patience to reason with his impetuous nephew. Dealing with him was enough.

***

Layla became bitter watching the construction of the house Jemal commissioned for Mimi. Years ago, Layla had accepted that Jemal could not love her as she desired, but she could not accept him loving another woman with all the love he had denied her. Conversely, Mimi came from an environment where men had many wives who lived as sisters, so she tried to befriend Layla; but Layla refused to meet Mimi and cursed her. Ignoring the advice Zoya had given her, Layla allowed her jealousy and argumentative nature to push Jemal further away; and he spent the bulk of his time with Mimi.

Anger replaced the hurt in Layla's heart, causing her to want to hurt Jemal in the way he had hurt her. Pretending to be afraid to stay in the palace alone, she requested that Ezera, Jemal's military general, stand guard. Ezera hesitated to accept the post because of his loyalty to Jemal, but he eventually accepted.

Once Ezera began serving as Layla's personal guard, she seduced him and carried on a secret relationship with him. Servants, afraid of keeping her confidence, whispered to Zoya of her daughter-in-law's infidelity. For the time being, Zoya kept the information to herself.

Jemal soon had a son with Mimi. They named him Dula. Zoya decided it was time to bring the family together for the sake of her grandsons. She entered Layla's private quarters after the children had left for their lessons.

"I've arranged for Mimi to come here this morning," she said. "It's time for the two of you to talk."

"I don't have anything to say to her," Layla said.

"Yes, you do," Zoya insisted. "This isn't only about your feelings and the competition for Jemal's attention. This is about the leadership of our people."

"I refuse to sit in the same room with her. She isn't my equal."

"Oh, but she is, Layla. There is nothing you can accuse her of that you haven't done yourself. There are no secrets in this place. I know how you spend your nights."

Layla's trembling hands betrayed her, and she dropped her cup. "Forgive me, Mother! I was sad and lonely!"

"Hush, I don't want to hear it," Zoya said. "Come with me. Mimi is waiting."

Zoya led Layla outside to the terrace and pointed to the empty chair beside Mimi. Layla obediently, though sullenly, sank into the chair.

"Today we put aside any animosity between the two of you. We can't afford bad feelings to be handed down to your sons, for they are brothers. They will have to support each other to cover and protect Beta-Israel."

Mimi spoke up. "I bear no ill will toward you, Layla. I understand your hostility toward me. Please believe me when I say that I will love your children as I love my son."

"I do not trust you," Layla said. "You are as any thief. You stole the love of my husband from me."

"I stole nothing from you. He offered his love to me."

"Enough!" Zoya said, interrupting them. "If either of you were certain that you would never want to share your husband, you should have married a poor man with no power."

Layla stopped talking for fear Zoya would reveal her transgression, and Mimi had no further objections. In the days ahead, Zoya brought the children together as often as she could, knowing they would need to love and respect each other. She made sure they were well-educated, as her father had done for her. There was only one difference between the sons. While Yonas raised Koji to be the spiritual leader for Beta-Israel, Jemal was raising Dula to be king.

***

When Tezena died, his son, Kaleb, was crowned the Axumite king of Ethiopia. Kaleb had been educated in the Ethiopian Church School and was a devout Christian. Religious wars were escalating across the Red Sea in Arabia, and Kaleb was primed to defend his Christian faith. It had been his father's ambition to invade southern Arabia for commercial interests, so the motivation for his intervention was two-fold. First, it was his goal to bypass and compete against the Persians in the silk trade. Second, imperialism and the engagement in religious wars cost Axum money and men, lessening their power and influence.

Just across the Red Sea in Saba, now called Yemen, King Dhu Nawas, who was born an Arab and converted to Judaism after his father's life had been saved by Jews, heard of the persecutions of Jews by the Byzantine emperors of the Eastern Roman Empire. He retaliated by attacking Roman merchants who traveled to Saba for trade. As a result, trade declined in the area. A neighboring king unhappy with the situation attacked Dhu Nawas, but he survived that war and was not deterred from inciting another, as he destroyed churches and turned them into synagogues.

During the winter, when the weather tethered Dhu Nawas's naval force, Kaleb plotted his military attack. Kaleb planned to lead his men in the attack and encouraged the neighboring kings of the Axum Empire to fight alongside them. Jemal consented to join the alliance and shared his plan with his uncle.

"My greatest nightmare has come to life," Yonas said, turning over in his bed. "I prayed I wouldn't live to see this day."

Jemal rested his hand on his uncle's arm to soothe him. "I know you don't want to see our people at war, but it can't be avoided. If we don't defeat them, they will one day cross over into Axum. Then it will be our fight. They are not Israelites."

Yonas was still agitated. It seemed Jemal was always anxious to do battle. "Then you go and fight," he argued. "Leave Dula here in your place."

"He must learn to fight, Uncle. He needs to go with me. I don't want my son to be weak."

"You're being a fool! Fear of God is not weakness; it's reverence to the Almighty. If you stand firm in your faith, He will give us the victory."

Jemal stood up. "I have the power in my own hands and limbs. I can fight my own battles."

"You're going to bring down the wrath of God on our people."

"Why would God breathe life into my body and strengthen me and expect me to sit down and wait on Him?"

"We must pray, nephew," Yonas said, pulling at his robe.

Jemal stepped back. "We must fight."

"Somebody has to rule if you are killed," Yonas told him. "Will it be Koji or Dula?"

"It will be Dula," Jemal murmured as he walked out the door.

***

In the winter of 523, Dhu Nawas, the Jewish king, led a brutal attack in the Christian city of Najran, near Saba, against Arab Christians who refused to convert to Judaism. Men and women were tortured and thrown into burning pits. More than 12,000 Christians were slaughtered, and over 11,000 were captured. The king's booty included 290,000 sheep, cows, and camels. Word of the massacre reached King Kaleb of Axum; and in the spring, when the winds shifted, he assembled a powerful fleet of 70,000 naval forces, including Jemal and the Beta-Israel military, and crossed the Red Sea to defend the Christians.

That summer, with the same zeal as Dhu Nawas used against Christians, Kaleb ruthlessly attacked and killed the army of Dhu Nawas and other Jews in Saba. Finally, Dhu Nawas's revolt was squashed. Rather than be taken as prisoner, he rode his horse to a ridge and jumped into the sea. Kaleb's victory gained him more respect and power as a defender of Christianity. After the conquest, Kaleb abdicated his throne and entered the monastery for the remainder of his life. He was canonized by the Ethiopian church and was the first Ethiopian to be recognized as a saint by the Greek and Roman Catholic churches.

There was no firsthand account of what exactly happened during the melee and intense fighting, but there were many rumors bandied about. Some whispered that Kaleb himself had struck the fatal blow. All they were told in Axum was that Jemal was killed in battle.

## Chapter Three
# Koji and Dula

All of Beta-Israel mourned Jemal's death. The wailing went on for days. Zoya took the lead in orchestrating the splendid funeral ceremony in his honor and had him buried next to his father in the palace garden. At the end of seven days, Zoya made a pronouncement.

"Children of Israel, my heart is filled with sorrow as we grieve for my son, but we must stand as one in this hour. We must maintain our sovereignty as a people. Before his death, Jemal declared that his second son, Dula, would succeed him as king. My grandson is young and unprepared to assume the responsibilities of king. Therefore, as queen, I will serve on the throne until he reaches the age of accountability."

The people cheered and waved their arms in approval, but Zoya knew it would be difficult to maintain the delicate balance among them as Christianity spread beyond the borders of Axum.

Unsure of who she could trust, she sent for Ezera, the military general, who had always been at Jemal's right hand but who had also betrayed him with Layla.

The general stood nervously before the queen, awaiting his fate. "What are your orders, my queen?" he asked, his head bowed.

"Ezera, my son believed you to be his top general, completely loyal. He trusted you with his life and the well-being of our people." At her words, Ezera's head hung lower.

"I'm not unwise to the ways of this world or the weaknesses of men. I don't condemn you for your betrayal to him, for you are no more guilty than the prey that found itself spun within the spider's web."

Ezera dropped to his knees. "Forgive me, my queen. What must I do?"

"Your insult was to my son, not to me," Zoya said calmly. "You can redeem yourself by taking Layla as your wife. She will leave the palace, and you will provide for her."

Relieved, Ezera stood. "Yes, I will," he said humbly. "I will gladly care for her and her son."

"No, general. Her son will remain here at the palace. She will be allowed to see him once a week. There are many serious problems for our people, but Layla is not to be one of them."

"You will have nothing to concern you, I promise you," he said, bowing in thanks.

"Then go, find your wife," Zoya said, dismissing him.

Zoya felt better with that matter handled. Layla had done everything she could to keep Koji isolated from his brother. Once Mimi and Dula were moved into Layla's living quarters, the two of them would no longer be divided.

***

As decrepit as Yonas was, he prayed for more time to stabilize the people. As queen, Zoya was a uniting force; but what she couldn't unite was the divide that was growing between the Jewish Christians and Beta-Israel. That task would be up to Koji as the spiritual leader and the chief priest. Yonas pressed him with that directive whenever they studied together.

"My time in this world is growing short, nephew," Yonas told Kofi on his twentieth birthday. "You are young, but you are ready to bring the word to Beta-Israel."

Koji paced across the room, thinking before he responded to his great-uncle.

"The question is, What word shall I bring? From the Scriptures, I'm convinced of the new covenant. I have no doubt that Christ is the Messiah."

Yonas clasped his hands to stop them from shaking. It seemed as if he couldn't escape his fears. "Why can't I die in peace!" he exclaimed. "Koji, do you understand the greatest challenge to our people from the time Moses brought them out of slavery?"

"I believe it was the disobedience of the people," Koji answered confidently.

"More than that, it was the divisions among the people, divisions that pulled them apart. That is why God instructed them not to mix with other peoples. That is why they were to kill all the occupants before they took possession of a city. We are in danger as a people because the foundation that was given to us—the word handed down to Moses, the word that is kept secured in the ark—is being challenged."

"Why can't we accept the new covenant along with the word given to Moses? What is the wrong in that? Our prophets told us it was to come."

"If we mix those covenants, we will be dissolved. As a people we will cease to exist."

"Then how can I bring God's word to the people and not speak of my convictions?"

"You have to determine if we are a people because of our blood or because of what we believe and how we worship."

"Uncle, we have intermarried. Much of our blood is already mixed."

"Then the answer is that we are a people because of what we believe."

"Why can't we be a mixed people with mixed beliefs who want to prosper and live in peace?"

"It's what I told you before: We will cease to exist."

It was a difficult decision for Koji. He was a believer of the new covenant given by God and in Jesus as the Messiah. But he was also persuaded that he had to keep the people united to maintain their independence from Axum, which was solely Christian.

"You have made your point, Uncle. I will do what you expect from me. You can die in peace."

Yonas chuckled uneasily with relief. "Not until you have a wife, and Dula is on the throne."

***

Yonas didn't have the time or the strength to travel far to select a wife with a pedigree for Koji. He selected the daughter of a Levite scribe at the school. Her name was Beca, and she was younger than he preferred; but he was assured of her purity. After Koji was married, the young man was consecrated as the high priest and gave his first message to the people.

"Children of Israel, we are a holy nation, and we will always be a holy nation. The Lord spoke to us through Abraham and Moses saying, 'Now if you will indeed obey My voice and keep My covenant, you will be My treasured

possession out of all the nations—for the whole earth is Mine,'
Exodus 19:5.

"He has promised us that our enemies are His enemies.
He promised to be merciful and gracious to us and to forgive
our sins. We have been blessed here in Axum because we have
kept this covenant. We must continue to obey His laws, or we
will suffer His wrath. Though there are differences among us
in wealth, status, and beliefs, these laws bind us together. The
words of the disciple John say, 'If a man say, I love God, and
hateth his brother, he is a liar: for he that loveth not his brother
whom he hath seen, how can he love God whom he hath not
seen?' John 4:20. Children of Israel we must love one another."

Koji's message was well received; and when Beca gave
birth to their son, Melku, Yonas died in his sleep, in peace.
The people of Beta-Israel also benefited from the peace in
Axum. Taxes on the people had lessened, and their resources
increased. More than love for one another, prosperity kept the
peace for Beta-Israel—at least for a while.

***

With each passing year, Dula looked more and more
like Jemal. Zoya doted on him, thankful for the miracle God
had given her as another chance to love her son. There was
nothing Dula desired that she denied him. When he was finally
enthroned as king, there was a great celebration. Guests from
kingdoms far and wide were invited to attend. Zoya, Dula, and
Mimi donned golden crowns with luxurious regalia and sat
at the head of a long table, where they drank honey wine and
feasted on lavish food.

Influenced by his grandmother, Dula loved to parade around in his royal dress and entertain the elite of Beta-Israel. He enjoyed dramatic plays, dancers, singers, and musicians. Concerns of state bored him, so he left most of those duties in Koji's hands. While his brother conferred with their alliances and stood in for him as judge, Dula preferred the company of traders and merchants who amused themselves making bets on sporting matches of boxing and racing. For the most part, Zoya was dismissive of the king's behavior. However, it was his increasing fascination for a variety of women that signaled to Zoya that it was time to select a queen.

Mimi was instrumental in making the match. Her name was Sheila, the sister of the Axum king, who was also Christian. Her thinking was that it would consolidate their alliances and make war less likely. What she couldn't control was the second wife and the numerous concubines that Dula welcomed into their orbit.

Koji worried about Dula's lack of discipline and humility. Like drops of rain seeping down into the ground, carried to the water, and then spread to the creeks and rivers around them, Dula's behavior would begin to seep throughout the kingdom and then spread to all of those around him. Soon all the people would be polluted. With this weighty matter on his mind, Koji went to the palace to have a serious talk with his brother.

"Things must change, brother, or there will be consequences," Koji told Dula. "Life is not a continuous banquet for you to feed on."

"Why isn't it?" Dula said, laughing. "That is my privilege as the king."

"You have responsibilities to the kingdom. You must lead the people with reverence to God."

"That is your position, dear brother," Dula said, raising his cup of wine in a salute.

"This can't continue. You are putting the kingdom and yourself in danger."

Dula frowned. "What are you talking about?"

"The lesson of another great king, David. Like you, he had many wives and many children from his wives. His sons weren't taught obedience, and they eventually turned on their father. It split the kingdom and caused the people to fight against one another."

"My sons are young boys. We won't have to worry about that for a long time," Dula said, brushing off his brother's warning.

***

Yonas's words of obedience woke Koji up each morning, and he shouted a warning message on each Sabbath. "And then you say in your heart, '"My power and the might of mine hand have gained me this wealth." And you shall remember the LORD your God, for it is He who gives you the power to get wealth, that He may establish His covenant which He swore to your fathers, as it is this day. . . . As the nations which the LORD destroys before you, so you shall perish, because you would not be obedient to the voice of the LORD your God," ' Deuteronomy 8:1-20. God destroyed Canaan and gave it to our people because of their sin and corruptness. His judgment of us will be even more harsh."

Later in the afternoon, Zoya spoke to Koji about the gloom in his words.

"Why must you dishearten the people when they come to worship? You should try to lift their spirits with your words."

"Those are God's words to our people, Grandmama. I must tell them the truth. How can you expect me to ignore Dula's behavior and the corruption of the people?"

"You worry too much. That is Yonas's influence over you. Beta-Israel will be fine."

"How can you say that when the people are becoming less faithful in their worship?"

"Maybe you should change your message. I think you should focus more on God's goodness and how he has prospered Beta-Israel."

"Not all the people are rich. Some of the farmers are struggling with the land. They envy the money that is wasted here."

"Then you must encourage them."

"If you are charging forward toward a cliff, should I encourage you to keep running, or should I warn you of the danger ahead?" Koji asked pensively.

"Possibly over that cliff is the sea, and I will survive the leap."

Koji surrendered the argument out of his respect for Zoya, but he knew she was blinded by the reflection of Jemal in Dula's face. In her eyes, he could do no wrong. Koji disagreed with the notion of ignoring the wrong path down which Dula led them. Instead, Koji chose to follow the example of Jeremiah, and he kept up his messages of repentance.

More and more, he realized why Yonas had worked so hard to impress upon him the importance of staying grounded in the Scriptures. He understood why the Lord handed Moses the Ten

Commandments. The people could not survive without laws and rules. He spent long hours with his son, Melku, to see that he understood the gravity of leadership.

Each night, Koji and his son kneeled together and repeated Psalms 1:1-3: "Blessed is the one who does not walk in step with the wicked or stand in the way that sinners take or sit in the company of mockers, but whose delight is in the law of the LORD, and who meditates on his law day and night. That person is like a tree planted by streams of water, which yields its fruit in season and whose leaf does not wither—whatever they do prospers."

***

However, Dula focused his thoughts on containing Koji. He was suspicious of his brother's intentions. He wrongly assumed that Koji was jealous and wanted his power. He requested that Koji and his family move out of the palace. He ordered that new synagogues be built throughout the kingdom in order to end centralized worship. Dula explained that it would limit conflict; but it was more to silence his brother's voice, lest he speak against him.

While Dula was focused on a potential challenge from Koji, he was oblivious to the animosity circulating among his wives. They were in a fierce competition for his favor and attention. As he spent the bulk of his time with his younger and newer wives, his older wives felt threatened and insecure about the succession of their sons. Whenever Dula was asked for assurances about the order of succession, he gave none and made no promises. That was a tragic mistake.

On the morning after a huge feast celebrating Dula's thirty-sixth birthday, Zoya found him dead in his bed, poisoned. She screamed and collapsed on the floor, devastated. The loss was too great to bear. First her husband, then her son, and now her grandson. Dula was buried at the palace in the garden beside his father and grandfather. The period of mourning went on for weeks. Unable to determine which of his wives poisoned him, Zoya banished them all from the city without their children.

Zoya took off her crown and all her clothing of fine silks. She removed all her jewelry and face paint. She dressed in sackcloth woven from camel's hair and rarely left her living quarters. After three months passed, she sent for Koji.

"Where have you been?" she asked him sternly.

Unsure of how to respond, Koji said, "I have been trying to preach comfort and confidence to the kingdom for the coming days."

"I've heard the general is considering a takeover."

"The people are restless, Grandmama. Maybe we should bring them back to the temple for centralized worship again, make sacrifices to God, and atone for our sins."

Zoya smoothed her hair back from her face and locked eyes with Koji. "Worship won't unite the people. We need a king now!"

"Benaim is only ten years old. He can't rule."

"I'm telling you, Koji. You will be king until Benaim is of age."

"I'm committed to serving as the spiritual leader for our people. It isn't possible to be king and priest. I would be ineffective in both charges."

"Then you must rely on Melku, because you must be king.

If this kingdom doesn't survive, who will care about your laws and worship?"

"Grandmama, the people love you. You were a great queen when Grandbaba died. You can rule as you did before."

"No, my wounds are too deep, and my pain is unbearable. My hope is that with your wife's help, we can raise Dula's children."

Koji knew Zoya was right. He would have to be king and priest like Melchizedek was in the days of Abraham.

***

Koji moved his family back into the palace, and a new general was chosen to lead the military. Mimi and Beca helped Zoya raise Dulas's children. Koji urged Melku to find a wife at 19, a few years younger than he thought he would, but it was preferred that all chief priests be married. Five years later, when Zoya became deathly ill, at her request, Benaim was crowned king at 22 years old.

Benaim was a noble young man, much different than his father. He hadn't been spoiled and required to become a man early. Both he and Melku married women from their own province. With war on their fringes, they did their best to isolate themselves. Benaim and Melku were blessed with many children. As one decade rolled into the next, the new king of Axum required more taxes from Beta-Israel to finance their struggle to hold on to power in Yemen. The easy times for the people became harder.

Five decades later, the war between the Axumite Empire and Yemen was reignited by combat campaigns conducted by the Persian Empire. It was the goal of the House of Sasan to expand into South Arabia to take control over the lower Red Sea and trade with India. The Axum army had been defeated, and the Yemen king, Abraha, was killed. The Axumites were then expelled from the Arabian Peninsula.

After Saifu, the grandson of Kaleb, was crowned king of Axum, he was determined to regain power in Arabia. He sent for Benaim to request that Beta-Israel fight alongside them in the war. Benaim had not given the Axum king any promises, only the assurance that he would discuss it with his council.

Koji, who had been their valued adviser, was too old to give counsel. Melku sat in the room with the other council members but offered no opinion. It would have to be Benaim as king to make the decision; but he was reluctant, knowing their children would be the ones who would have to live with the consequences.

"I don't want war for our people," Benaim said to the council. "We have paid with our resources, and now they want our blood. But there are times when we must fight with a rival to keep him from becoming an enemy."

Melku had to speak up and object. "We must not participate in this war, Benaim! We have been down this road before. Our grandfather was killed fighting for a cause that wasn't our own. Isn't it enough that our people have to take food from their own mouths?"

"Maybe sending a few troops would be a show of goodwill," Benaim said, hoping for a compromise. "It is in our best interests to have good relations with Axum."

Melku stood firm. "Axum has a Christian king. They want our help, but they would fight us as well. The Persians want to take over our trade on the Red Sea. There is no benefit for us. They are both enemies of Beta-Israel. Let them fight."

Benaim was still worried. "Saifu will question our loyalty to the Axum kingdom."

"It won't end with this war; it will only be the beginning," Melku warned. "If Axum can reclaim Yemen, they will have to fight to keep it. If the Persians are successful, they will cross the Red Sea."

"If we choose not to fight, then we still must prepare our sons to fight."

***

By the end of the sixth century, after several attempts to retake Yemen, the Persians had invaded South Arabia and defeated the Christian Ethiopian king. They took control over the sea trade with the East from the Axumites, cutting them off from their international trade network of the Silk Road. Yemen became a Persian province, and the Axum presence and reign there ended. Melku's oldest son, Gebreal, succeeded him as chief priest; and Benaim's eldest son, Alemu, would follow him as king.

Gebreal and his wife had several children. His oldest son, Mekonnen, succeeded him as chief priest. Alemu also had a large family. His oldest son, Tewodros, became king of Beta-Israel.

# Chapter 4

# Mekonnen and Tewodros

Along with Axum, Beta-Israel suffered financially when the kingdom was cut off from the Silk Road by the Persians; but they still had the gold mines, their fields, and goods to trade. Merchants and traders who wanted to conduct business with them had to travel beyond the port once they were on the other side of the Red Sea. All the changes caused an air of unrest in their territory around Lake Tana. The inhabitants of Beta-Israel wondered what the future might hold for them as the invasion moved closer inland.

As chief priest, Mekonnen was a traditionalist. He had kept with his father's and grandfather's teachings that Beta-Israel was, first, a people before they were given the laws and rules that bound them together in religion. It was important to him to preserve the lineage of priests, so thoughts of love and lust were secondary when he married a Levite woman named Eliana shortly before his father died. Counseled by his father, Mekonnen felt the weight of the survival for Beta-Israel rested on his back. He was grateful for Eliana, who became the calm confidant that relieved his stresses, encouraging him to refer to Psalm 119:98: "Thou through thy commandments hast made me wiser than mine enemies: for they are ever with me."

However, Tewodros enjoyed all the accoutrements of being king. The mundane responsibilities of war and the problems of the shrinking market for his people were annoying complications that distracted him from the pleasant pageantry of his position. Composed and lighthearted, he considered Mekonnen to be a worrywart. He married Adina, the most beautiful girl in the province, and he took immense pleasure in her appearance on his arm at all times. Members of the Beta-Israel council objected to her presence at critical meetings, but Tewodros ignored them.

There was a small degree of competition between Mekonnen and Tewodros, which developed when they were being educated together. In 614, both their wives gave birth to sons. Mekonnen and Eliana named their son Miruts. Tewodros and Adina named their son Negasi.

The people of Beta-Israel were celebrating the cousins' continuing legacy when they received word that followers of the prophet Muhammed, including his wife and daughter, had crossed the Red Sea, seeking refuge in Axum. They also learned that King Negus Kaleb had welcomed them and offered his protection.

Mekonnen spent another night walking the floor. "This doesn't bode well for us," he said to Eliana, while she nursed their son. "It will only divide our people more than ever."

"Possibly, but the few of them may only be in Axum temporarily until they find a place where they can worship in peace," Eliana said casually.

It upset Mekonnen that she was so relaxed about the matter. "Are you not aware of the wars and how many men have been killed trying to take over and defend the coast? This place is the door to the rest of the world. If we let this group get a foot in, they will never leave."

"Haven't our people been in that same position? Weren't we welcomed into Axum? To this day, we haven't done anything to harm anyone."

"This isn't just about migrants looking for a place to lay their heads; this is about the creation of a new religion. Like the Christians, they will be looking for converts."

"Each man chooses his own faith and what they want to believe," Eliana said, rocking her son to sleep.

"It is my obligation to protect our people, lest they be deceived."

"Do what you will, husband. You have made up your mind," Eliana said, rising to place the baby in his crib.

Mekonnen didn't usually dismiss the explanations from his wife, but this situation was different. From what Mekonnen had heard about Muhammed—the revelations he had received and his teachings—Mekonnen was sure that the Muslims would be another group with a new faith that could cause problems in Beta-Israel. It was hard enough to maintain the peace with Christians, and this would only add more fuel to the fire.

Mekonnen sent his servant out with messages for an emergency meeting of the council at the palace. It was urgent that they speak with Tewodros about what the presence of the Muslims could mean for Beta-Israel.

***

"Cousin, we have reasons to worry," Mekonnen told Tewodros. "Negus has offered protection to Muhammed's followers. You must speak to him."

Tewodros motioned for his attendant to pour more wine. "As usual, Mekonnen, you are being an alarmist. You know Negus as well as I do. He is a righteous ruler. He has offered us the same protection that he has given to the Muslims. He has always refused to allow the religious oppression of anyone. Besides, he is only providing safety from the Arabs for less than a dozen people, including the wife of Muhammed. You know how vicious those pagans can be."

"That was only the first group," Mekonnen said, looking around the table. "The word is that nearly 100 have already joined the first few. Certainly, in time, there will be conflict, and we will be drawn into the fray. You must speak to Negus for assurances that there will be no interference on our territory."

A member of the council spoke up. "There is no need for that, priest. The prophet has ordered his followers not to bring harm or danger to the people in Axum while they are here."

Mekonnen shook his head in disgust. "Is that all it takes to gain your trust?"

"The king has already sent a message to us," Tewodros said. "He is also convinced that they mean no harm to Axum."

"He is just as gullible as you are," Mekonnen said, glaring at Tewodros. "All they did was read to him from their Qur'an, quoting that they believe Mary the virgin conceived Jesus from the spirit of Allah, as he created Adam. To that, the king picked up a stick and said, 'I swear the difference between what we believe about Jesus, the son of Mary, and what you have said is not greater than the width of this twig.' Can't you see that we are the outsiders here? They will line with them against us!"

"Why do you fuss so much?" the council member said. "Some of our own people believe the same thing."

"If we do nothing else, God requires that we separate ourselves from other nations. You may dismiss this now, but more will come, and decisions will have to be made."

"Then trouble me when that time comes, cousin," Tewodros said, waving Mekonnen off. "I have enough worries today that I don't need to look for those in the future.

***

Mekonnen recited the history of Israel to his son each evening, while Eliana held the infant in her arms.

"He's only a baby. He doesn't know what you are telling him," she said.

"He must always be reminded of our struggle for independence and land that God promised."

"You are wearing yourself out for naught, Mekonnen. I have met some of the Muslim women. They are kind and God-fearing."

"You must avoid those people!" he shouted. "You must not allow your thinking to be polluted by the teachings of their prophet!"

"You think that all of us are weak in our faith and you are the only one loyal to God. Maybe you should concentrate less on the Scriptures and more on the people. You don't give them credit because you don't know them very well."

Mekonnen grunted. "I guess I know how they have behaved in the past."

"Then how do you judge the Muslims of whom you have no knowledge. If it were up to the women, we would have no problem living in peace. It is men who play dangerous war games."

Mekonnen didn't get much sleep that night. Early the next morning, he walked to the run-down temple for the morning prayer. From a distance, he could see his assistant priest, Dan, was outside waiting for him. When he caught sight of Mekonnen, he ran out to meet him.

Panting, Dan said, "The Persians have armed the Jews in Nazareth and Galilee and have captured Jerusalem from the Christian Roman Empire. They have killed 60,000 Catholics, and 35,000 have been made slaves. The Persians are willing to fight alongside us; they recognize that we have a common enemy. It may even be possible for our people to return to Jerusalem."

"Don't be naïve, Dan. There are few Jews living in Jerusalem. We have to be wise enough to know that we can't keep aligning ourselves with kings and empires and sacrificing our people in their wars. One year, we fight with Christians; the next year, we fight against them. This isn't about religion and worship; this is about power and money."

"We have to keep our minds open, my priest. The appointed ruler, Nehemiah, has said that they will build a third temple. He plans to search family lineages and reestablish a new high priest. We are the direct descendants, so we should serve in that temple."

"I doubt that will come to pass," Mekonnen grumbled. "We are scattered, and we don't have the military strength to go against the Persians. They would only use us to achieve their goals. How many times have I said this? You can trust no one except God."

Mekonnen was right. Two years later, the Persians had changed their stance and were supporting the Christians over the Jews. The churches were rebuilt, and the small synagogue on the Temple Mount was destroyed. Although the Jews currently living there were not run out of Jerusalem, there was a ban on new settlers.

***

Axum's protection of the family of Muhammed was remembered by the Muslims. For a while, the Axumites were spared during the invasions of territories in the holy war by his followers. Nevertheless, when the prophet Muhammad died in 632, Islam had spread across the Arabian Peninsula, the land southwest of Asia. Jerusalem fell to Islam in 638, and Persia was defeated in 651.

Beta-Israel had fought steadily to maintain its independence and territory under King Tewodros' son, Negasi. Mekonnen's son, Miruts, was now chief priest. Thirty-five years had passed since the civil war had begun in Axum, but the religious conflicts and wars over trade on the Red Sea still raged on. Miruts spoke to Negasi's council in the words his father had spoken to Tewodros on so many occasions.

"The Islamic Empire has quashed all the rebellions and united the Arabian Peninsula. This new religion threatens our people more than any other. While missionaries spread the word of Christianity, armies spread Islam. They are not motivated by religion; they want power. We have lived under the protection of Axum for many centuries. We have been independent, free to worship in our own way. The only cost has been taxes to the kingdom. Now that Axum is losing territory and the Islamic Empire is expanding, our way of life is in grave danger."

"What options do we have?" Negasi asked, glancing around the room. "Can we join together with the Axum military to hold them off?"

"The Axum military has been weakened from decades of fighting," his general added. "While we fight amongst each other, the Christians are united against us."

"We have fought too long to give up our land so easily," Negasi told them.

"Time will tell us how to proceed," his general said. "The Axum naval fleet is doing all it can to defend the aggression on the coast. The port is the livelihood of the empire. For now, we stay out of the conflict. There's no need for us to create an enemy."

***

War and blocked trade stifled growth of the Axum Empire and led to an extended period of decline. Over the next decade, the Islamic Empire had seized control of the Red Sea and the largest part of the Nile. Power gained by Islam eventually reached into Axum, pushing the Axumites back from the coastline and the valued trading posts. Axum quickly became overpopulated. Forests were cut down for the construction needed to accommodate the growth. More crops were planted to provide for the ever-growing influx of people. The once fertile land was worn down, and rainfall became irregular. The soil was eroded, the land was degraded, and Axum agriculture began to collapse under the strain.

In 700, the death of the second King Kaleb of the Axum Empire, Qwestantinos, triggered a religious civil war in the kingdom. The king's two sons—one Jewish and the other Christian— fought each other for control; and the violence between them split the army and divided the nation. This division and the rise of the Persian Empire accelerated the deterioration of the Axum Empire.

With the troops weakened by continual war, Axum was easily invaded. In 710, Muslim Arabs moved into Adulis and destroyed it, taking over the coast and the ports of the Red Sea. Axum slowly lost control of its natural resources and the trading posts. Beta-Israel gradually moved to ports further south to continue to trade. But eventually, Islamic expansion cut off the major ports and trade. More depots were built to accommodate the growing population, and the increase in construction caused the similar problems of deforestation that led the Israelites to leave Saba so long ago.

Axum, once a powerful kingdom, was isolated from the world. The people spoke Greek less frequently and stopped minting coins. The land, over-cleared, overplanted, and overgrazed, suffered as much as the people did. There were agricultural costs to the environment having been altered. One consequence was less rainfall, which limited the growing seasons. Revolts spread throughout the country, as Axum struggled to hold onto its identity. Despite their fierce warrior culture, powers began to shift, as their global presence diminished.

# Chapter Five

# Tariku and Ras

Beta-Israel felt the pressure as the Arabs pushed against King Wasan Sagad and the capital of Axum moved further south, closer to their territory. Negasi's youngest son, Ras, was the king of Beta-Israel; and Miruts's youngest son, Tariku, was the chief priest. Neither had been first in line to succeed their fathers; but the older sons of Negasi—Hassan and Zere—and of Mirut—Samuel and Palus—had been killed years earlier fighting with the military in skirmishes on the fringes of their province.

Tariku was the color of rich soil. He was average height and as wide as two men. All muscle, he was an intimidating sight, save for the warm, steady smile above his long beard. He dressed in the traditional white robe of priests; and under the white turban he always wore was a thick head of wooly hair that he twisted into a large knot. He had been a dutiful son and a righteous man, internalizing all the worries of Beta-Israel as his father had done. For two years, he had been married to Jalene, the daughter of another Levite priest. She had just given birth to their first child, Frew.

A couple of years younger than Tariku and bronze like an old coin, Ras was tall and thin like a palm tree and just as rigid. Whether it was unintentional or deliberate, he was the opposite of his cousin Tariku. He kept his head shaved, dyed his beard, dressed in layers of fine fabrics, and was never without shoes.

He married Emnet, the daughter of the wealthiest merchant in their territory. Despite his status, he was cranky most of the time, insecure, and unsatisfied with his standing as king. He was always comparing himself to Wasan, so when the king started encroaching on his territory, he was livid.

The crisis developed when Wasan ultimately crossed their boundaries and was making demands for land and resources. Tariku feared the presence of the Christian king would spark clashes among their people. Almost daily, outside the palace and the temple, the tribes gathered and called upon king and chief priest for relief. Ras sent for Tariku and his military general, Abel, for an emergency meeting.

They sat anxiously across from one another in a secluded room at the palace in an effort to come to some kind of resolution.

Abel opened the discussion. "As you both know, the conflict in Axum has spread to our territory. Decisions must be made very soon. The solidarity we have established can easily be torn apart when we are surrounded by invaders."

"This isn't only about loyalty," Tariku interjected. "The people are distraught. There isn't enough food to feed their families as it is, and Wasan is confiscating the meager provisions they have. I'm certain it won't be long before the situation becomes violent."

Upon hearing this, Ras frowned. Once again, he was at odds with Tariku. His cousin was always preaching misery and doom, with no answers except turning to God. "I see your prayers for heavy downpours have not been answered," Ras sighed, mocking Tariku. "The rains are dwindling more every season, despite your endless pleas and petitions. Now there are more mouths to feed in our region and one harvest. Of course, it is no wonder the people are starving. Do you have any other suggestions besides prayers?"

"We have to do something, Ras. Our people are desperate," Tariku said, ignoring his cousin's usual scorn and mockery. "Many have been forced from their homes, and they are hungry."

Abel took in a deep breath, weary of their constant bickering. "Should we prepare to fight or not?" he asked impatiently.

"Waging war with the Arabs is impossible," Ras answered. "Our men are outnumbered, and they have control of all the ports. We are boxed in."

"What other choices do we have?" Abel asked, becoming agitated. "If we do nothing, they will take everything we have, and the rest of the food out of our mouths."

Ras's chest began to swell with anger. "Has God not spoken to you?" he demanded of Tariku. "What are we to do? Have you no guidance for our people?"

"We have been in this position before," Tariku reminded them. "We have gone from Egypt to Babylon to Saba and to Axum to escape from our enemies. Now Christians, Muslims, and pagans surround us. There is no other sign to look for. It's time for us to move south."

"Speak with sense!" Ras yelled. "We have prospered here; the gold mines are here."

Tariku ignored Ras's tantrum. "With God's blessing, our forefathers built this kingdom for us. God will help us build another."

"How can a king tell his people to surrender? I won't do it!" Ras shouted.

"It's not submission to the Arabs or Wasan; it's obedience to God," Tariku said, glancing between the two of them.

Ras abruptly pushed back from the table with such force that his chair fell to the floor. "Then you tell them, chief priest! It won't come from my mouth!"

Ras then stomped out of the room, and Abel soon followed. Tariku bowed his head in supplication at the table and asked God to cover the children of Israel as he had done so many times before. Then he left the palace, returned to the temple, and directed his assistant priests to circulate word to the people that there would be a special announcement at the Sabbath worship service.

***

Instead of riding his donkey, Tariku walked beside it as he made his way home that evening. He needed the extra time alone with his thoughts. Along the way, he observed the village that he was so familiar with that he barely noticed it anymore. He watched the vendors in the market selling their wares, and he watched the children stirring up dust as they ran and played under tall trees in the fields nearby. He walked further under the birds that flew high above him in the sky. He hesitated for a moment to gaze at the tall rock cliffs that stood majestically in the distance while he meditated on David's words in Psalm 121:1-2: "I will lift up mine eyes unto the hills, from whence cometh my help. My help cometh from the LORD, which made heaven and earth." Then he continued his walk, taking it all in with the donkey leading the way.

When Tariku arrived at home, Jalene was sitting at the table having supper with her son, Frew, in her lap.

"You are late today," she said while she placed a piece of bread dipped in spicy bouillon into his mouth. "Is everything all right?"

"It will be," he said, lifting the baby from her arms.

"What did you and Ras decide to do?" she asked. "Is there going to be a war or a compromise with the Axum king?"

"Neither," he said, staring into his son's innocent eyes. "God's has spoken to my spirit, and it is clear what Beta-Israel must do."

Jalene waited to see if he would tell her. When he didn't, she asked, "Well, what is that?"

"We as a people will move south until we find a place where we can be a sovereign nation, independent from the influences of other religions and laws."

"Have you told that to Ras?" she asked, skeptical that he had done so. "I'm sure he won't agree with your plan."

"He doesn't agree, but he doesn't have a choice," he said, tickling Frew's belly. "We don't have the power to challenge King Wasan, and he is too weak to go against the Arabs. There are instances when might beats right. The wildebeest eats grass, and the leopard eats the wildebeest. For Beta-Israel to survive, we must find new territory. We have done it many times before. I'll present it to the people on the Sabbath."

Jalene began to worry. She couldn't think of one person who would want to hear this option, including herself.

"It's possible that you are reacting hastily," she said, hoping to give her husband pause. "Why should we move so quickly? Maybe you should wait for God's message to be more specific in the time and place. This is a critical decision."

"Faith is demonstrated by moving without knowing all the details. There is no reason to risk the lives of our people by waiting.

Jalene felt much like Ras and Abel. In her mind, they should be bold and fight for their land, or at least wait until there was no other choice. She was happy in her home with her servants. Why should she have to give it all up? If they defended themselves and God gave them the victory, all of Beta-Israel would reward Tariku for his diligent prayers for the people. She watched him lift Frew in the air. Somehow, she would have to think of a way to change his mind.

****

The service began with all the traditional Jewish prayers, despite Ras and his attendants being absent. Abel was there with some of his men to quell the riot he felt was sure to come. Outside the temple, the choir prayed with words in African melodies. They had not practiced the sacrificial ritual for many years; but on this Sabbath, a dozen perfect sheep and goats were slaughtered, and the procedural preparation of meat to be eaten was done. Then Tariku raised his arms high to deliver the message they were all waiting to hear.

"We are the chosen people," Tariku exclaimed. Then he paused as the crowd cheered. "God has directed our path for thousands of years. When He tells us to move, we must move." There was a brief hesitation, and then the people began to groan. But Tariku kept speaking. "He has blessed the children of Israel. Do you think He will stop? We must be obedient. Whenever we have found ourselves in a place where we cannot worship our God in the way He directed, we have had to move. As God was with Moses, so will He be with us. Lands are promised to us for as long as they are useful to us. This land is overrun; it does not yield fruit or grains enough to feed us. There is another land promised to us. We will know it in time."

"How can you expect us all to leave our homes and land," a voice cried out. "We are not slaves as those who escaped with Moses."

Tariku nodded patiently while more protests were shouted at him. Then he spoke, "Certainly, we are not slaves, and that is the way we desire to keep it. The Arabs have conquered the Persian Empire and the Roman Empire. Their empire reaches to the borders of India and China. They are now moving into North Africa. As they encroach upon Axum, Axum will continue to encroach upon us. How many of you are willing to die for land that no longer provides for you?" The shouts quieted. Tariku nodded and said, "We will make measured shifts toward the south to keep the peace between us until God speaks and tells us otherwise."

There was an uncomfortable silence, then low rumblings of displeasure. Gradually, the crowd dwindled down until they had all gone home. Tariku stood there alone, reflecting back on the times when he had watched his father and his grandfather speak to the people in the same spot. He thought of the generations that had stood there before them and the reality that his son would never have that honor. So much had changed over the years. He whispered Exodus 23:20: "Behold, I am going to send an angel before you to guard you along the way and to bring you into the place which I have prepared."

***

Tariku began preparations to lead the first caravan of Beta-Israel migrants on their journey south. He was grateful that this trek would be a peaceful mission and none of the military would be traveling with them. He held Frew in his arms, while Jalene wrapped up her jewelry and personal belongings in cloth.

"It's not like you to hold your tongue," he said, noticing his wife's unhappy expression. "Speak your mind. No one else has spared my feelings."

Jalene answered slowly in an even tone. "I understand the burden you carry and that you are doing what is best for our people, but why must we be the first to leave? Why can't Dan go with the first group? I don't want to go. What if I never see my mother or my sisters again?"

"Dan is only an assistant priest. He is not a leader, and the people won't respect him. Furthermore, your family is welcome to come with us; there is room for all of them."

"Few of them are willing to leave all they have and all they have ever known."

"That is because their faith is weak, Jalene, and I pray they don't suffer for it. Our time in this place is short no matter what. We can walk away peacefully, or we can stay here and fight to the death. I want life for our people. I can't convince them now, but the Lord has told me to prepare a haven for them."

Jalene still wasn't content with leaving. "Frew is young. He could catch a disease or be bitten by some vermin out there in the wilderness."

"That is nothing for you to worry about. I'll take care and

protect you and our son. You know I wouldn't let anything endanger you."

"How will he get an education away from civilized society? He will be ignorant."

"Stop talking foolish, wife! I can teach my son all that he needs to know. Do you think we going to this place to live like animals? We will be among our own people. We aren't going to change simply because we live in a different place," he said, trying to reassure her.

"Maybe you should go first, and then Frew and I will come in the next group."

"Absolutely not!" Tariku said firmly. "You are my wife, and you belong with me, and there is no way I would be separated from my son."

Jalene turned away to hide her tears. If Tariku saw her crying, he would surely rebuke her for being selfish and only thinking of herself.

***

It was the less prosperous of Beta-Israel that were anxious to venture out of their shrinking domain. They had a lot less to lose by walking away. They piled their possessions on the backs of donkeys, herded their cattle, and rode camels south and east toward the coast. It was a long trek, over 175 miles, through thick forests, past dry desert land, along steep highlands, through valleys whittled by water, and finally to grassy plains.

The journey was painstaking, with hot days and cold nights in the mountains, dust from the dry ground filling their throats; but even through all of that, their trek wasn't completely unpleasant. Tariku was able to see God's presence each step of the way—above them in the blue sky and in the bending of the trees from the light breeze. He even laughed when they passed baboons and zebras that stared back at them, as if they understood their plight. He was much more optimistic than Ras. Though they would be uprooted from homes, the palace, the temple, and their land, at least their integrity as a people would be preserved.

Tariku saw himself as Jozadak on his journey out of Babylon with the ark of the covenant in tow. His only regret was leaving the ark in the temple. It was in bad shape and fused shut. Having been kept out of sight for centuries, priests had advised against prying it open or trying to lay eyes on God's word. Each generation had vowed to restore it, but the appropriate time never seemed to come. Maybe it was the idea that it should be returned to Jerusalem that caused the delay or that a great temple worthy of it had not yet been built. The fact was that they were still a nomadic people searching for a Promised Land.

"We've gone far enough," Tariku told them after seven days. "We can make a home here." The group faced him with questioning stares. "Everything we need is here. The river is close, and the land is fertile. There are fields for the animals. That means this place is soothed by the rain and kissed by the sun. Tomorrow we will begin to build huts."

"You've brought us to the middle of nowhere!" someone shouted.

"There's nothing here!" complained another.

"That was the point of moving," Tariku told them. "Here, we can create a new province, free from other kings and religions."

A woman spoke up, "God led Moses to cities, like you said, a place prepared for them."

"We don't need to depend on anyone but ourselves," Tariku said, dismissing the protests. "As soon as we set up our tents, we can start building homes for our families."

***

Tariku rose early every morning, recited Psalm 91, and began a song to ease the monotony of work. His cheerfulness was contagious, and after a few verses, the people joined him in singing. The men chopped timber, and the women and children gathered thin branches that could be weaved into wattle. They made walls that they covered in daub mixed from clay, sand, and hay. They were all busy building, turning the soil for planting, and getting settled, unable to reflect on their reduced living conditions.

Jalene missed her family and struggled to adjust. She was like a dolphin cast upon the shore, left to flip and flop out of range of its natural environment. She felt demeaned by the humble home made out of grass and mud. Her servants weren't available to tend to her or Frew's needs. Her resentment turned on Tariku, and she became distant, pining for the life left behind them. To punish him and vent her discontent, Jalene began to deny him conjugal rights.

Frustrated with the change in her temperament, Tariku said to Jalene, "The Scriptures say that a man has authority over his wife's body, and she has authority over his. You cannot deprive me of my rights as your husband. It only opens the door for Satan to come in."

Jalene was defiant. "You tell me that you prayed for the Lord to guide you in your decision to come here. I doubt that you love me, because you ignored my wishes. Now I am in prayer with the Lord and have asked him to help me remove that doubt and warm my heart toward you again."

"I have done nothing to injure you, wife, or to turn your love away from me."

"You may not have realized it, but that is what happened when you separated me from my family. I have no one here to talk to."

"That is because you spend your days sulking and isolating yourself from the other women. Stop putting on airs. I am not the king, and you are not the queen. 'Pride goes before destruction, and a haughty spirit before stumbling,' Proverbs 16:18. I am a servant of God, and so are you. You should be at my side, administering to the people who are working their fingers to the bone to raise a village."

Jalene listened, but she didn't reply. There was nothing Tariku could say and no amount of chastising her that was going to change her mind. For three months, she kept herself from him.

Tariku grew impatient with his wife. "It is your duty to lay with me as my wife."

"What about your duty to me, to provide a home for me, to care for me as my father did?"

"You are behaving as a spoiled child, and I won't tolerate it anymore!" Tariku said angrily.

He pushed her down on their bed and forced her to lay with him. "I should not have done that. I'm sorry," he said later, apologizing for his behavior. "It's the pressure and responsibility of making sure everyone is settled that made me lose control of myself. Please forgive me."

"Take it to God, and ask him to forgive you," Jalene said coldly.

Neither of them would ever forget that night, especially when they realized she was pregnant. Jalene gave birth to another son, Nebiyou. She was civil to Tariku, but she was never warm to him again, and he never forced her.

***

Increasingly, more and more of Beta-Israel followed the first group to their new village. Some who were Jewish Christians chose to stay closer to the capitol of the Axum king, believing he would better protect them from religious clashes. Ras had hoped to delay his departure until after Emnet gave birth to their first child, but the wait ended when King Wasan moved into his palace. Without a choice, he and his wife, his close attendants, and the military packed their possessions and left. There simply wasn't room for two kings in one castle.

Ras was bitter. It was hard for him to accept that Beta-Israel had been displaced. The number of Muslims had multiplied and pushed the Christian Axumites south, deep into their territory. Many days, Ras thought he would rather have been killed than put out of his palace. It was only the persuading words of Emnet—assuring him that he would build another, greater kingdom—that brought him temporary comfort. He stayed hidden in the large home that Tariku had built for him, ashamed to stand before the people in his humbled state.

"The people must see you, Ras," Emnet kept telling him. "Show them your head held high. They need encouragement from you."

Ras refused. "That's Tariku's job to give them false hopes."

"You are still the king, the leader of Beta-Israel. You can't abandon the people or your birthright."

"I refuse to stand before them without a real throne. Out here in the dirt, we barely live better than the laborers."

"We have to build the kingdom up from nothing, and that's a slow process. These times of trouble are when the people most need their king. It is now that your strength is visible to them. Only in easy times can you afford to be weak-willed."

"The people relied on me to protect them; I should have had a plan for the invasion. Our military had too few men. I kept believing Tariku that God would give us the victory."

"He has given us the victory, my love. We are here together, alive and well. We have not suffered; we have been blessed."

"What about our child that is about to be born? He will be a prince without a palace."

Emnet chuckled and rubbed her belly. "This child can't miss what he has never seen. He will be happy and loved."

"That is not enough. I want him to have what my father gave me."

"I'm sure you will. This place may only be temporary for our people. God has always kept his promises to us."

"You sound like Tariku," Ras said, lifting the goblet of honey wine to his lips. "I don't want to hear anymore."

***

It wasn't a difficult birth, and mother and baby were healthy. There was only one problem. Ras's son, Girma, was born with a clubfoot. Unable to accept his son's imperfection, Ras blamed his wife, he blamed God, and he even blamed Hasan for taking his province. He began to drink wine every day to wash down his disappointment. The more that Emnet tried to reason with him, the more he despised her. It became harder and harder for him to look at her and his son. He ordered that another home be built for her.

Tariku built Emnet and Girma a hut near his own, where he could look after her and the boy. Emnet bore no hard feelings toward Ras. She wished him the best when he took another wife. More than anything, she was relieved to be freed from the prison her life had become with him. But Ras's second wife couldn't make him happy, either, despite giving birth to two beautiful healthy daughters. He lived like a recluse in the biggest house in the village.

Chapter Six
# Gideon Dynasty

Raids and conflicts with Arabs and pagan tribes pushed Beta-Israel even further south, and they had to live like nomads in makeshift communities and military colonies. To survive, they traded with the Arabs and the Persians on the coast. They spoke to one another in Swahili, a mixture of the Bantu, Arab, and Persian languages. When Ras died, his belly eaten away with honey wine, the people refused to crown Girma, his only son, as king of Beta-Israel. Tariku's eldest son, Frew, served as king and chief priest. Frew's son, Gideon, succeeded him and began the Gideon Dynasty.

Gideon as chief priest and ruler of Beta-Israel was a spiritual king. The assistant priests officiated over Sabbath worship, but he spoke from the Scriptures when he addressed the people and blessed them as Aaron did. He understood that obedience was key to their survival.

In his first declaration, he said, "Children of Israel, I know that many of you are anxious about the pressures around us and are reluctant to put down roots. It is time to bury those worries. We must do what God has always directed us to do, the words he gave to Jeremiah to deliver to us: 'Build houses and settle down. Plant gardens and eat their produce. Take wives and have sons and daughters. Take wives for your sons and give your daughters in marriage, so that they too may have sons and daughters. That you may be increased there, and not diminished.' Our faith requires us to submit to God and follow His laws. 'When a man's ways please the LORD, he makes even his enemies be at peace with him,' Proverbs 16:7."

Under Gideon, the harvests were plentiful, and the cattle multiplied. The people reestablished trade on the coast. Schools were built to educate the growing number of children. Beta-Israel had regained her footing. Gideon II collected tithes and taxes from the people. He believed that it was important that they have sufficient resources, as well as strong faith. He also required that at least one male from each family train with the army and become a warrior to strengthen their military.

Gideon III followed his grandfather and father's examples, but he didn't put his trust solely in the Lord. He invested the tithes and taxes from the people into spears, javelins, bows and arrows, and knives. He wanted his military equipped with more than just the armor of God. Beta-Israel prepared for war; but, thankfully, they lived in peace with the Axumites on their fringes for over a century.

Gideon IV had trained with the Beta-Israel military since he was a young boy. His father wanted him to be prepared for the battle that would inevitably come. The disciplined child became a serious man, with little interest in amusements or celebrations. When his time as king and chief priest came after his father's death, he patterned his leadership after Joshua and King David. Without fear, he wanted to lead the people in every way, in worship and in battle. He emphasized the power they had, looking to God as their General.

When Gideon IV took a wife, together they were father and mother to Beta-Israel. Gideon IV was the protector, and Nishan was the nurturer. The people were strong and proud again. The men and women learned to trust and rely on one another. However, while they invested their time and energy into leading the people and solving their problems, Gideon and Nishan neglected their own son and daughter.

Growing up, Judith and Seghen struggled for the attention of their parents. Seghen was timid and feigned illnesses to get out of training with the military. He preferred to stay in the safety and security of their home, tending to his pets, which included a falcon and a monkey. Gideon IV, disappointed in his son's lack of valor, would often chastise him, call him a coward, and demand he join the young men training to be warriors. Nishan would always come to her son's defense, stating that his brain was just as important as brawn and insisted that he be given more time for his lessons. What neither of them understood about Seghen was that he was more afraid of not living up to his father's image than anything else.

Judith was bold. She challenged her parents and refused to fit in the mold of the virtuous daughter of the priest and king. As feisty and free as an African eagle, she ventured to taverns where merchants, prominent persons, and high-ranking military officers frequented for entertainment. For her impetuousness, she had been banished from the court of the royal family.

Having a rebellious streak, Judith had coaxed her lover, a man of high status in the Christian church, to show his love for her by bringing her cloth from the cover that laid over the ark of the covenant. When he did, she made shoes of the fabric, which she paraded around in public. Officials of the church punished Judith for her irreverence of the holy article by slicing her breasts. She was sold to a general who also was a prince. He fell in love with Judith and made her his wife. When he became king, she became his queen.

***

A few years later, Beta-Israel was pressed by another expansion of the Axum Empire into their territory. This time, they stood their ground and valiantly fought back. God gave them the victory they prayed for, but they were still heartbroken. Gideon IV, their beloved king and chief priest, was killed in battle. Nishan was distraught and went into seclusion.

The general and several of his officers arrived at the palace to confer with Seghen, as he was designated to succeed his father as king. The general stepped forward to speak, while the officers stood ready to proceed with the orders.

"What would you have us do?" the general asked Seghen. "Our enemies must pay dearly for the life of our king."

"My father was a warrior, a soldier, he understood that any battle might cost him his life," Seghen answered. "The important fact is that we have defeated Axum. We will no longer be tyrannized by our adversaries. There is no need for any more blood to be shed."

"This is not a time to be timid or show weakness," the general said. "Our triumph must be absolute. With Gideon IV dead, no man in Axum should be left standing."

Seghen did not have the charisma or the courage to lead or avenge his father's death, but he knew the person who did. "Go out and find my sister. Judith is the one you need to speak with."

The officers located Judith. Hungry for revenge for her father's death and the way they had treated her, Judith took command of the army. Determined to stop any future invasions, she formed a military coalition with the Agaw people, who also opposed the expansion of the Christian Empire.

A warrior queen, riding on horseback beside her husband at the head of the Beta-Israel army, Judith headed to Axum. She attacked the weakened kingdom with a vengeance, burning the churches and tearing down monuments. The military force was decimated and scattered, and Axum was conquered. Judith killed the emperor, slaughtered the princes, took the Axum throne, and reestablished Hebrewism as the state ideology.

So, in 960, 14 generations after the religious wars began, Queen Judith ended the perpetual tug of war between those Israelites who had converted to Christianity and those who remained faithful to the Jewish faith. She crowned herself empress, reestablished trade relations with their neighbors, and ruled for four decades. Seghen served as chief priest during his sister's rule, and the golden age of the Beta-Israel kingdom began.

***

Nevertheless, the Christians on the highland, the Muslims on the coast, and Beta-Israel in the southern interior and on the Swahili Coast were constantly fighting over trade routes. Kilwa, an island just off the coast joined to the mainland by a bridge, dominated the major trade routes and was one of the most coveted port cities. Its favorable position made it the optimal commercial center on the East African coast and attracted merchants and immigrants from Arabia and Persia.

After Empress Judith died, the Bantu king, Almuli, sold Kilwa to Ali ibn al-Hassan for a tremendous amount of colored cloth that supposedly was enough to cover the entire circumference of the island. Beta-Israel merchants were irate and rushed to make their complaints to Seghen. He was no longer chief priest, having passed the position on to his son Jember, but they hoped as Judith's brother he might still have influence with the king.

"Why do you men come to trouble me?" Seghen asked when they entered the synagogue where he prayed.

"We need you to speak to the king on behalf of the merchants and traders in Beta-Israel," one of them stated. "I'm sure you've heard about the sale of Kilwa."

"Yes, I've heard," Seghen sighed. "That is the king's business."

"The king has made a terrible decision," another of them added. "We have lost a valuable gate to our trade. It is bad enough to have our land taken by force, but to give it away in exchange for cloth is ridiculous."

"Possibly, he thought he should sell Kilwa before it was seized," Seghen replied dryly, wishing they would go away.

"You must speak with him," another merchant insisted. "Something has to be done about this. Obviously, he has lost his mind. What man of thought doesn't understand keeping your enemy out of range where he can hurt you?"

"I'll speak with the king about it," Seghen said to get rid of them. "But don't expect that to make any difference."

Seghen was still wary of confrontation. He was finally at peace. His mother had died years earlier and his wife not long after. There was no one left to criticize him and no one left for him to disappoint. His only motivation to get involved was to spare his son the headache. Jember had enough to worry about with the people and his own family. He sent his servant to find his assistant priest to go with him to see the king.

Almuli's castle was quite impressive. It was much grander than the palace his father Gideon IV had when he ruled. They waited outside the receiving room while the attendants announced their presence to the king.

"Come in. Welcome," Almuli said.

Seghen respectfully addressed Almuli. "My king. I will get straight to the point and not waste your time. I bring messages of distress from the people. They feel you have tied their hands. From your sale of Kilwa to the Persians, they will be shut out from the main center of East African trade."

Almuli raised his hand to end Seghen's petition. "Let me put your worries to rest. The Arabs and Persians have promised that we will have unfettered access to the coast, and trade will continue without change."

"What reason would you have to believe our enemies, your majesty?" Seghen said. "Please reconsider the consequences."

There was a long pause as Almuli thought about the exchange. Then he yelled, "Leave me!" realizing he may have been duped.

Seghen and his assistant quickly left the castle. They heard later that the king did decide to rescind the sale but that the Persians refused his proposal. To add insult to injury, the Arabs dug up and destroyed the land bridge to Kilwa, separating it from the mainland.

Although there were continuous skirmishes between the Jews and the Christians, Beta-Israel stood strong. The

Beta-Israel dynasty of Judith would last for 177 years. When Seghen died, his son Jember became chief priest; his son Fassil succeeded him, then his son Mulu, and then his son Lire.

# Chapter Seven

# Lire

Lire was a good-natured man, and he found fault in very few people. He had been born in a time of relative peace and great prosperity. He was thankful that God had blessed the Israelites once again with land and resources where they could worship and thrive. Even more, he was thankful for his beautiful wife, Durah. He knew it was God who had drawn her to him. He was enthralled and still somewhat in disbelief that she would have him for her husband. It wasn't that he was unattractive; it was that he was unassuming and reserved and thought she would be bored to be the wife of the chief priest.

Though Lire may have mistrusted his instincts, he was right. Durah would have preferred to have been the wife of a king. The blood of Sheba flowed through her veins, and she was ambitious. Day and night, she dreamed of living in the palace. She married Lire because of his status and the belief that with a push in the right direction, he could be king, which meant she would be queen. They would return to the capitol, and she would see Axum brought back to its former glory.

In the meantime, Durah loved to attend festive gatherings at the court and imagined that one day, she would not be a guest but instead the host. She was smart, and it was apparent that the Axum Empire was shrinking steadily into a smaller area, as the Arabs encroached on their territory, despite

King Dil Nead's useless skirmishes. She understood that the real threat came from the missionaries who came to spread Christianity among them. Lire thought the battle was about religion and worship, but Durah knew that it was about control and wealth.

It was also no secret that the people were battle-weary and afraid. From what she could ascertain, more of the army disappeared than were killed. She figured that all the military needed was a leader who could give them more to live for than to die for. With the loyalty of the people, Lire was in the perfect position to take that lead and then the throne. The one thing holding them back from achieving everything she wanted was Lire's indifference and lack of drive. They had the same conversation over and over again.

"Something has to be done, Lire," Durah told him for the umpteenth time. "Dil Nead has no right to the throne; he isn't even from the House of Gideon. He can't protect Beta-Israel from the Arabs, and he's leading us to certain death."

Lire answered her as he usually did whenever she got on the subject. "I have prayed, and God has told me to be still. Our enemies are fighting one another. He will give us the victory, and one day we will return to Jerusalem."

Lire's blasé attitude was always frustrating to Durah, but she refused to let it go. She had to get him to see things her way, or her dream would never be realized.

"I don't understand how you can believe that," she persisted. "The Christians have already taken Jerusalem back from the Muslims, but they don't offer to help us. Dil Nead can't be trusted. He claims to be the last descendant of Solomon but cannot even prove who he is. He favors the

Christians, and the Israelites come to you for guidance. You must take a stand, husband. Tell me whose side are you on?"

"Dear wife, first, I am a man of God; my allegiance is to Him. He fights our battles. The king has the military to fight his."

Durah let it go for the time being, hoping that her appeals would soon find fertile ground and her plans would come to fruition.

Weeks later, Durah made her argument again, without success. Months later, Lire remained steadfast and ignored her entreaties. A year later, in 1137, Durah took no joy in being vindicated for the accuracy of her prediction, because it wasn't Lire who took advantage of the situation. Dil Nead was overthrown by his own general, Mara Takla Haymanot. To establish some legitimacy, the general married Dil Nead's daughter, Masaba, ending the line of kings who had been part of King Solomon and the Queen of Sheba's lineage.

For Beta-Israel, this also brought the Gideon Dynasty to an end. Their problems were compounded when Mara Takla Haymanot converted to Christianity. Durah was incensed. If only Lire had listened to her, they wouldn't be in this predicament.

"How can you stand by and do nothing after Mara has betrayed our people?" Durah asked Lire, wringing her hands to keep them from encircling his neck.

In his usual unruffled manner, Lire answered, "Mara is the emperor. He is a politician. I can't condemn or second-guess his actions. He has done what he feels will unite us with a power to shield our people from the infiltration of the Muslims."

"How can you say that? He won't shield Beta-Israel! We'll be pushed out again."

"Be comforted, dear wife. God has protected and provided for His people. Rest assured, that won't change."

"I don't see how you can stand there saying that when everything has changed!"

"God has not changed toward our people. Nothing has happened to us. You must get on your knees and thank almighty God for His blessing."

Disheartened but determined, Durah did get on her knees. She prayed for a son who would have the ambition her husband didn't have. She deserved to be queen in the palace instead of Masaba. She believed it to be her birthright. If her husband didn't care to get her there, her son could. She would make sure of it.

***

Durah's prayer was answered when she gave birth to a son, Feruzi. From the day he was born, Durah told him he was a king. She dressed him in the finest clothes of royal colors. He was rarely out of her sight, and she supervised every aspect of his life, including how much he ate. When Feruzi was seven years old, Durah begged Lire to have him educated at the monastery instead of in the synagogue. She would miss him, but the sacrifice would be worth it for all of them. She had to get him away from the limited thinking of his father. Lire eagerly consented, pleased that the boy would get to breath air his mother hadn't exhaled.

Feruzi was overjoyed to escape the watchful eye of his mother. What he found in the monastery was a whole new world. He was able to see things in his own vision and not from his mother's view. He learned to read and write, and the monks discovered his artistic talents. Because of his standing as the son of a chief priest, he was permitted to read the Garima Gospels. He soaked in all the beauty of the illuminated manuscript. He was moved—more precisely, compelled—to paint. They supplied him with the skin of calves and sheep and plenty of pigments to mix. That's how he spent his free time when he had finished with his daily lessons and chores.

Feruzi painted images of Jesus and Mary, the wise men seeking the Messiah, Jesus washing his disciples' feet, and the Last Supper. The monks were so impressed with his gift that they implored him to return when Durah sent her attendants to fetch him. It was the first thing Feruzi spoke of when he saw his father sitting outside their home under a silk sunshade.

"Father, I want to go back to the monastery," Feruzi said earnestly. "I feel that's where I belong."

"That would absolutely break your mother's heart, my son," Lire said with apprehension. "You are our only child. Your home is here with us," he said, pleading with him to stay.

Feruzi shook his head slowly. "My heart and soul are at home there."

Lire could hear and feel the depth of sincerity in his son's plea, and it brought the sting of tears to the back of his eyes. Still, he had to ignore it. His son's responsibilities were the most important, even if it meant sacrificing his happiness.

"Son, you had an obligation before you breathed your first breath, as I did. It was given to us by God. We must serve the people and not ourselves."

"That is the old covenant, Father. The new covenant says that each man can find his own salvation."

"I didn't send you to the monastery to forget all that I have taught you, Feruzi! We are the children of Israel. Our covenant is the one that God handed down to Moses. There are no questions surrounding that. Our history tells the consequences of when we strayed from it."

"Father, I have read the Torah, the whole Bible, and the Qu'ran. I have spent weeks in solitary meditation. I know what I believe and what is best for me."

Lire was distressed. He knew he was losing his son as surely as he was standing there in front of him. Instantly, he regretted giving his consent for Feruzi to attend the monastery for schooling. He should have never listened to Durah. Now, having spoken in countless worship services and council meetings, at this moment, he could not find the words to sway his own son. He went to the single seam that had held the people together for centuries.

"We all pray to one God, son. We are Israelites. We must stay unified if we are to survive and return to our land in Jerusalem. Promise me you'll take time and give this more thought."

Seeing the desperation in his father's face, Feruzi nodded. It wasn't his desire to hurt his parents or endanger the people in any way. He only wanted to follow his own heart. So, for the time being, he decided to stay.

***

Feruzi stood by his father's side in service and supplication in the synagogue. He listened to his father's stories of the struggles of his people. He paid attention to his father's words when he preached to the people. He heard his father's message of submitting to God's word for survival. He never spoke of his desire to go back to the monastery with his mother. He was determined to do whatever was necessary to make her happy for as long as he could. When she chose a bride for him, without question, he acquiesced. Her name was Mumbi.

Durah chose Mumbi because of her quiet nature. Durah was friends with Mumbi's mother and was privy to the girl's behavior at home. Mumbi had always been polite and showed deference to Durah as the wife of the chief priest, which was a key quality for the woman who would be Feruzi's wife. Durah needed a woman who wouldn't quarrel with her for control of the family or steer her son away from his true destiny. The end goal was for her to be queen, not Mumbi. She was simply to be her son's wife and give birth to his heirs. Her hope was that Feruzi would want more for his children, that he would develop ambition. Then she could influence him to challenge Mara for the throne.

There was little for Feruzi to complain about. Not only was Mumbi pleasant to look at, she was a devoted and kind wife. Within a few months after their marriage, she was pregnant. When her delivery time came, it was a long and difficult labor. Finally, she gave birth to a daughter, Elene. Durah and Feruzi were disappointed, but for different reasons. Durah wanted a boy who would inspire her son to reach higher, to be king. Feruzi wanted a son who would inherit his birthright. Mumbi was the only one who was delighted with the birth of her daughter.

Durah refused to give up her plan. She hovered over Feruzi and Mumbi, encouraging them to have another child as soon as possible.

"It would be wise to have your second child soon," she said to Mumbi. "It is my greatest regret that Feruzi did not have a brother or a sister as a playmate. He was such a lonely boy."

Mumbi smiled down at Elene. "We will have another baby, but not right away. The midwife advised me not to have another child for a while. Besides, I don't want to share all this love I have for Elene for a good while."

"Feruzi, there is no reason to wait. There is more than enough love to go around," Durah said, taking baby Elene away from Mumbi. "You must remember that it is your godly duty to produce a son."

"It isn't me you have to convince, Mother," Feruzi added. "Mumbi is the one to carry the children."

"Give me a little time," Mumbi said, holding her arms out for her baby. "I haven't gotten over the strain of having this little one. Feruzi and I have only been married for one year. I'm sure we will have many sons and daughters.

"You're right, Mumbi," Durah said, stroking her daughter-in-law's hair. "We should take care of you and Elene for a while.

Feruzi looked at his mother. He could see there was something else on her mind. She always had a reason for everything she said or did. He wasn't bothered by it, whatever it was. It would serve his purposes as well.

***

A few months went by, and Durah grew more impatient. In her desperation, she sought out a shaman to give herbs to Mumbi to strengthen her body and to increase her fertility.

However, Durah wasn't completely honest with Mumbi about her motives. She began taking her meals with her daughter-in-law.

"These herbs with your food will give you more energy," she said, sprinkling them on her food and stirring them in her water. "Taking care of a young child is physically draining."

"You have been so supportive and good to me and Elene," Mumbi said graciously. "I have been blessed to have a mother-in-law like you."

"It is you who have been a blessing to me and this family," Durah said. "Feruzi has the light back in his eyes that had gone away. I thank you for that. The more of these herbs you eat, the stronger and more beautiful you'll be."

Mumbi trusted Durah and followed all her instructions for her health, her marriage, and caring for Elene. It was Durah she confided in when she suspected she was pregnant again.

"I'm worried, Mother," she said to Durah. "I don't feel ready to have another baby. I haven't gained all my strength back."

Durah was overjoyed with the news but did her best to hide her glee.

"You mustn't fret about it," she said, squeezing Mumbi's hand. "A child is always a blessing. The Lord will carry you as you carry your child."

The pregnancy took a toll on Mumbi. She spent most of the time in bed. In the fall, she gave birth to a son, Workneh, meaning "You are gold." Although her labor was easier than the first time, Mumbi never regained her strength. In spite of that, she nursed her son and was an attentive mother to Elene. Oddly enough, there was a strange bond between her and the children. It was if her life was connected to theirs, that her vitality was transferred into them. As they grew taller and stronger, her body curled and grew weaker. She died on Workneh's third birthday.

***

Mumbi had been buried for only a month when Feruzi told Lire his decision. "I have performed my obligation. I have produced a successor. Now, it's time for me to go back to the monastery. In good conscience, I cannot teach only the old covenant when I believe in the new covenant. There is no way I could unite our people when you and I can't find common ground. My life is there, not here. You must understand that. I have prayed and called upon the Lord, and He has given me a new mission as an artist. I will paint unto His glory until the day I die."

Lire could not argue. He had done exactly what he felt God wanted him to do in his life. He couldn't in good conscience tell his son to go against what God had called for him to do.

Durah cried for weeks after Feruzi left. Her beloved son had failed her. Then she woke one morning to find Elene and Workneh sitting at her bedside. It was then she realized her dream had not died but had only been delayed. Learning from her previous miscalculation, she decided to keep their education closer to home. She taught them how to ride horses, shoot arrows, and throw spears.

Lire objected to her obsession with the children, but there wasn't much he could do about it. His only consolation was that as Workneh got older, he developed an affinity for God's word and sought out his company. He wanted to hear about the history of the Israelites, and he wanted to study the Scriptures. When asked about fulfilling his legacy, Workneh showed no qualms about becoming chief priest when the time came. Lire shared with Workneh his dream of the day when the Israelites would all return to Jerusalem.

On the other hand, Durah introduced her grandchildren to "the right people," and they accompanied her as she frequented elite parties again in hopes of making a great match for Elene. There was a slight setback when a wealthy merchant proposed marriage to Elene. Ahmed had the means, but he had no title. Elene wouldn't give her grandmother any peace, insisting that she approve the match. Reluctantly, Durah gave in and hosted the grandest wedding seen in the province for many decades.

It was at the wedding celebration that Workneh met Zera, the daughter of the king's brother. Her beauty captivated him first. Then, when he learned that she practiced Judaism, it was her spirituality and commitment to their people that then captivated him. None of that mattered to Durah. What was most valuable to her was Zera's disapproval of her uncle and his allegiance to Christians. Her spirits were lifted, and her hopes revitalized when she successfully arranged their marriage.

***

On October 2, 1187, Lire's patience faded for the day when the Israelites would be delivered and united. That was the day he heard the news that the crusaders had been defeated. Jerusalem had again fallen into the hands of Muslims, and

Christian pilgrimages to the Holy City were ended. Lire threw up his hands, fell to his knees, and surrendered his spirit.

A week later, Durah's patience faded for the day when she would be recognized as royalty in Axum. That was when Mara announced that he had seen Jerusalem in a vision. He renamed the city river, the Jordan, and vowed to build a New Jerusalem as the capital of Axum. Her blood boiled hot and she had a massive stroke. The mourning period for Lire hadn't yet ended when she was buried next to his fresh grave.

Mara, known as King Lalibel, the man whose position she coveted for her husband, dedicated himself to the construction of replicas of the holy places in Jerusalem and Bethlehem. He hired builders and artisans, who literally carved out 11 churches from single rocks. The town he erected was known as Lalibela, with replicas of the crib of Nativity, the tomb of Christ, and its river was named the River Jordan. They were breathtaking monuments to Christianity.

# Chapter Eight

# Workneh

Islam's power was growing in the Axum region, although for the most part the kingdom remained Christian. However, both entities were pressing against Beta-Israel over territory and religion. Workneh was also concerned about the infighting within the Zagwe Dynasty over political control and which philosophy would ultimately prevail. The temporary benefit was the power struggles between the leaders kept them occupied from creating more conflicts with Beta-Israel over taxes and their expansion into Lake Tana and other lands deep in the south highlands. The long-term detriment was that the internal strife weakened the Abyssinian Empire, which served as a buffer between them and the Islamic Empire.

The situation proved more worrisome near the end of the twelfth century, when Suleiman Hassan, the ninth sultan of Kilwa, had also taken control over Sofala. Sofala was a mainland city-state and the oldest harbor in southern Africa. Persian Muslims used it to trade gold, ivory, iron, tortoise shells, and animal skins from the inland as far as Zimbabwe. Possession of Sofala and its goldmines contributed a huge amount of wealth to the Kilwa Sultans, which they used to finance the expansion of their rule all along the East African coast.

Slaves had also become a profitable export on the Indian Ocean after Muslim traders gained control of the Swahili Coast and sea routes. Later, they began to export slaves to Egypt, Arabia, Persia, and all the countries bordering the Indian Ocean, most as soldiers, guards, and domestic workers. The Africans suffered the brunt of it. It became so prevalent that some people of Beta- Israel adapted Islam as their religion to avoid being sold as slaves. Deprived of their source of income, the native people fled.

***

The morale in Beta-Israel sank as the problems of overcrowding surrounded them. Zera did her best to encourage the people and pitch in to help the families that lived near her courtyard. It had been a particularly rough day for her. Listening to the women who gathered at the well moan of their hardships was depressing, especially when she had no remedies to offer them. Tired, she rose to her feet and scooted across the floor to light the lamp, as the setting sun was growing dimmer. She stared at the small flame as it flickered. For some reason, it soothed her, even though she wouldn't be able to relax until Workneh returned home from his evening prayer at the synagogue.

Zera's tranquil moment ended when the door burst open. Startled, she turned around in an instant. It wasn't Workneh coming in. It was Elene breathing heavily, her eyes flashing frantically. Her baby, wrapped and tied to her chest, whimpered softly.

Zera rushed across the room. "What is wrong?" she shrieked, her eyes searching Elene for anything out of order. "Are you all right?"

Elene took a deep breath so she could speak. "I'm fine. It's Ahmed. He's in a rage, stomping through the house and breaking things."

She took Elene's hands in her own. "Why, what happened?"

"Every day, more of the cattle die. There isn't enough for them to eat with the land drying up. The crops are meager, and he had to let some of his loyal workers go. He says that the men are blocked from hunting in one direction and blocked from trading in the other. He says he'll be ruined if things keep going this way."

Zera gathered her frayed nerves and exhaled. "Ahmed is a rich man. He has nothing to worry about," she said, patting Elene's hand.

"Believe me, he is on the edge!" Elene said, still in a panic. "He's afraid that he will lose all he has worked for, afraid of what he will become."

Workneh walked in as Elene was explaining. "Is Ahmed violent with you?" he demanded to know.

Elene shook her head, "No, but he scares me. I've never seen him behave like this."

"Stay with us tonight," Workneh insisted. "I'll go home with you in the morning.

Workneh laid in the darkness, whispering to Zera. "The constant tension is overwhelming all of us. Never have we suffered like this since Pharaoh held us in bondage in Egypt," he said sadly. "After so many prosperous generations, large numbers of our people are being enslaved by the Arabs in Persia. We walked out of servitude, and now another is walking in on us to enrich themselves from our backs in fields that once belonged to us."

Zera could hear the hopelessness in her husband's voice. He grew more downhearted each day. She did her best to keep him uplifted, but she had run out of words to raise his spirits.

"God delivered us from that cruelty," she said, gripping his hand. "Pray that He will deliver our people from this offense."

"Will he answer while our people are disobedient?" he asked despondently. "Look at Ahmed. Our people are desperate. We have fallen so far that many are converting to the Islam religion to regain status. Others are adapting to keep from being sold as slaves."

"Pray, husband," was all Zera could say.

Just after daylight, when the baby was fed, Workneh walked the mile with Elene to her home. Ahmed was there, sitting outside on the ground. He jumped to his feet when he saw them approaching. His eyes were bloodshot, and his clothes disheveled.

"I thought you had left me for good," Ahmed said, wrapping his arms around Elene. "I'm sorry for showing you weakness when I should be strong for our family. It's not easy for me to be helpless. I've always been able to control my life and my livelihood. Everything is changing, and I don't know what to do."

"It's happening to all of us," Workneh said. "You mustn't let these circumstances break you. My sister and the baby need you to stay calm and composed."

"I will, I promise," Ahmed said, ushering them into the house.

Elene seemed relieved and happy to be home, but Workneh wasn't totally convinced. He would have to make it a point to stop there on his way home each day just to be sure. For so

many, the pressure around them was becoming too great, and
they were beginning to crack.

*****

Workneh did what Zera advised. He prayed for guidance
on leading the people. The answer came to him in an early
morning dream. On the ground in a dense forest was a colony
of millipedes. Above them, were two webs between trees on
the opposite sides, with spiders busy spinning their silk wider
and wider. They had spun near the ground with their sticky
webs when a ray of light shone through the forest. Attracted to
the light, the colony of millipedes began to march toward it,
escaping the unknown traps.

On the next Sabbath, standing before the people, Workneh
looked out into their faces. The gathering reached farther than
he could see; but it was quiet, save for the squawks and calls of
the birds that circled about them.

"My people, children of Israel, we face a new day!" he
declared. "It's a day that our forefathers have seen on more than
one occasion. It's a day for change, a day for trust, and a day for
survival. We have lost land, and we have lost trade, and because
of that, we have lost power. We have lost political power and
military power. In the conflicts with the Arabs, greater numbers
of our people are being captured and turned into slaves. Many
of them are being traded along the coast like goods. This cannot
continue. The Arabs have taken over our trading posts on the
coasts, and now they are moving further inland.

"I have prayed for God to speak to me on how to lead us
through this trial. He has finally spoken. We sit in the midst of

our enemies. They have depleted the land. We must move to land that will sustain us to stand against those who would harm us, to a place where we can maintain our independence.

"The Lord has directed us to move further south toward the city-states of Azania and Zanj, away from the Muslim immigration to the Land of the Black. There, we will build our own nation. We will educate our own children. We will establish our independence. We are a strong nation of people; our king will not be subject to another king."

Workneh stopped and waited for the complaints and protests that many other chief priests had contended with when they proposed migration. He was stunned when the people raised their arms in triumph and cheered. Kneeling to the ground and bowing his head, Workneh prayed that God would deliver them yet again.

***

The Israelites faithfully followed Workneh's directions. It wasn't the gradual move of Tariku, where they shifted south over time. Instead, it was more like the journey of Moses, where large numbers packed up their worldly possessions to make the trek.

"I don't know where I'm leading our people," Workneh said, beginning to panic when the day arrived for them to strike out. "What if I'm wrong?"

"You must do what Moses did. Trust God to guide you," Zera answered, her own voice trembling.

Workneh wasn't sure how far to venture on the journey, but he was sure it would be more than a three-day walk. His plan was to stay within one day's walk from the coast, being the sea was their only passage to the outside world. He led them from the front, prepared to be their shield come what may. At the end of each day's trek, they set up camp, and the men took shifts on guard. They were in unfamiliar territory and unsure what animals or enemies lurked about.

After the fourth day, Workneh thought that possibly they had reached their destination. He got up before dawn the next morning to pray. He walked a few hundred feet up a hill into the clearing. He fell on his knees and was about to close his eyes, when a huge snake slithered along the ground. It was a green mamba. It raised up off its belly and looked him in the eyes. He glared back at it as he reached for his knife. It reared back to strike. In a split second, as he felt the fangs against his skin, he chopped off the snake's head, and it fell down with a soft thud in front of him. Terrified, he checked his arm. There were two long scratches but no puncture wound. He rushed back to the camp and announced that they would travel further south for two more days.

After the sixth day, they set up camp near a commercial outpost city along the coast of the Zambezi River, near Kilwa in the highlands. The area had some of the highest elevations on the continent, with many plateaus. From the rainfall, there was excellent grasslands for grazing cattle. The land contained zebras, gazelles, lions, leopards, and elephants whose tusks were traded for ivory. Workneh was confident that this was the place where they would put down roots. The next day, on the Sabbath, he addressed the people.

"Children of Israel, we have traveled across many countries, the desert, and the sea in our commitment to survive as a people. The prophet Isaiah said, 'Forget the former things; do not dwell on the past. See, I am doing a new thing! Now it springs up; do you not perceive it? I am making a way in the wilderness and streams in the wasteland.' Here, we will form our own small autonomous kingdom. We will call this place Sena."

Workneh, Ahmed, and several warriors traveled to the coast to confer with the residents and dwellers for any opposition. They met with a group of Bantu and Swahili men who were seafarers who traveled to India, China, and Europe for commercial purposes.

"We have journeyed here from the perimeter of Axum," Workneh told them. "We are a peaceful people. Do you own the land to the west of here?"

"The earth belongs to God," one man said. He appeared to be the leader of the group. "We came here for better farming conditions, as have others."

"Our people would like to stake a claim for the territory that is two miles west. We can pay. We don't want to offend any natives."

"We don't begrudge any peoples for their motivation to thrive. What we ask from you is that your industry be mutually beneficial to all who live here. The land can support us all."

Workneh nodded his head happily. "We wholeheartedly agree to that."

***

With nothing else to rely on, the faith of the people grew strong. Inspired by the Scriptures, they hungered for the word, and God blessed them. They started with homes woven from sticks and twigs, with clay or mud, and then wattle and daub. They discovered that they could continue to provide for themselves with hunting and trading. Beta-Israelite men worked together with Bantu and Swahili men who were farmers and planted large crops.

The people were as fruitful as the land. Zera, who had tried for several years to have a child, became pregnant.

"All of our prayers have been answered," she said to Workneh. "I was afraid that it would never happen, that maybe something was wrong."

Workneh hugged her tightly, "It wasn't to happen in our time. It was to happen when God directed. A child might have changed everything. I might not have decided to leave Axum. Because we were obedient, God has blessed us. David said in Psalm 1:3, 'He is like a tree planted by streams of water that yields its fruit in its season, and its leaf does not wither. In all that he does, he prospers.' I'm so thankful. I wouldn't have had the courage to do any of it without you beside me."

Zera smiled at him. "Then you will accomplish many things, because this baby and I will always be here with you."

Their child was born one year after they set foot in Sena. They had a daughter they named Melesse. A few years later, they had a son named Jonah, and then another son named Reth. From the time they were all born, Workneh told them the stories of their long history, the journey of their people from Egypt to Babylon and then to Saba, Axum, and now Sena.

Being that Jonah was the older son, from the time he was five years old, he had to sit at his father's side. Workneh wanted him to see what it would be like when he took over as chief priest. Jonah was with him at council meetings, when he settled business disputes among the merchants, and when he sat as judge before the people. Jonah was exposed to the complicated issues of adults, things beyond his understanding, and it tarnished his childhood. He became a solemn boy with a suspicious nature.

However, Reth was shielded and indulged by his mother and sister. While they worked, he was on their heels. When they decorated cloth with embroidery to pass the time, he loved to sit at their feet and listen to them sing. Unlike Jonah, he was allowed to play, run with his dog, and enjoy the company of other young friends. Zera often took him on visits with the wives of the prominent men in their village, and they greeted him with smiles and treated him to apricots and gooseberries. Reth became an outgoing youth with an openhearted nature.

***

Nevertheless, the migration hadn't been such an easy transition for all of them. Ahmed was still suffering, impatient with their growth, especially after Elene gave birth to a son. He wanted to pass onto his son the same wealth that his father passed to him. He tried hard to remain positive, but he wasn't accustomed to any amount of struggle. His optimism morphed into regret. So, while many of the people had much to celebrate after their migration, he was one who felt most of his fortune was left behind.

Seven years passed, and he still didn't have another rock home like the one he'd built close to Axum, the number of his cattle had not gotten to the large number he had had before, and he wasn't able to trade and make the money he did in Sofala. He brooded so much that his dissatisfaction ruined his marriage. He blamed the weather, his neighbors, Workneh, and then Elene; and when he had no one else to blame, he blamed himself.

Elene had a bad feeling the day he slept late and then announced he was going hunting. None of his team were with him, and he left the house alone. She also noticed that he didn't have his weapons with him. She grew fearful by the hour and ran to the synagogue to alert Workneh. He sent out a team of men to search for Ahmed. They returned with his body just before dusk. They explained hearing the trumpet sounds from a herd of elephants, miles off in the distance. They walked for another hour before they saw Ahmed's broken body lying in the dirt near the pond, trampled.

It hurt Workneh's heart to tell Elene what she already suspected: Ahmed was dead. He didn't call it suicide; it was more that he threw his life away. It didn't matter that he had a wife, a daughter, and a son who loved and needed him. He was a victim of his own pride, blind to all the reasons that he had to keep living.

If only Ahmed would have given himself a few more years, he would have become richer than he ever thought possible. Sena became a metropolis rich from trade. Most important, a seam of gold was discovered running along its highest ridge. The men, women, and children were all miners of gold, despite the danger of mine shafts being at least 100 feet deep. But together, they extracted nearly a ton of gold each year.

Beta-Israel prospered exporting gold, ivory, rhinoceroses' horns, tortoise shells, leopard skins, and coconut oil. They maintained the iron smelting from the Cush. They imported cotton, luxury silks, wools, glass beads, rice, coffee, spices, silver, and Chinese porcelain. Some continued to live in the mud huts with thatched roofs on the plains, but the elite lived on the hills in stone houses with elaborately carved doors.

***

Instead of preparing them to be crowned as rulers, Workneh trained his sons to be priests, spiritual leaders of the people. He taught them to read and write. He taught them about the foundations of their religion and the importance of the ark and the word of the covenant. He was determined that they would have all the necessary knowledge to guide the people, insisting they read the Bible, although he focused their attention on the covenant given to Moses. It didn't occur to him that they would receive the information and the word differently. Jonah gravitated to the Old Testament that aligned with the Torah, while Reth overlooked it and preferred the New Testament and the expectation he felt in it.

Zera's lessons were more basic. She insisted that her sons love each other without jealousy or rivalry. She would always remind them, "When there is no one else you can trust, you will have each other. You all are bound by blood, so protect each other. Never allow anyone to come between you. Anyone who would do that has no love for either of you."

Workneh preached endogamy as the key to their independence, so he was disappointed when most of the men available for Melesse were not members of their tribe. Zera persuaded him to agree to her marriage to a well-established

Bantu man, but he struggled with the decision. How could he demand the people obey the laws that his children didn't abide by? He was determined not to have the same issue with their sons, declaring they would marry women from their own tribe and not intermarry with Bantu women.

Jonah and Reth were handsome young men and had their choice of women within their town and in the urban settlements, where they were known as heirs to the power of Beta-Israel. Several leaders who hoped to arrange marriages with them in order to forge bonds and make political gains approached Workneh. Knowing that that would be the end of Beta-Israel, Workneh used every last bit of his waning strength to concentrate on finding suitable wives for his sons.

The wives chosen for his sons were the two daughters of a wealthy farmer who had land near the property Elene and her children inherited from Ahmed. The older sister, Fana, would be Jonah's wife; and the younger sister, Berta, would be Reth's wife. The celebration of the weddings carried on for a week. They feasted, drank, and danced; and they received gifts received from merchants all around the globe. Many of those merchants wanted to show the ailing Workneh how much they appreciated his guidance and dedication to the people.

When Workneh died, the people buried him like a king. His sons, Jonah and Reth, were treated like royalty. They became rulers as well as spiritual leaders. Remembering his lessons, they were careful in their governance and teachings, and the Israelites remained resistant to the Swahili culture that had been created from the intermarriage between Arab men and Bantu women and characterized by the practice of Islam.

## Chapter Nine
# Jonah and Reth

Zera was the first to detect the precarious situation. It had been subtle at first, almost unnoticeable, but now it was unmistakable. Fana was more interested in her sister's husband than she was in Jonah.

Zera shouldn't have been surprised. She hadn't met many young women who weren't attracted to Reth. What gave her pause was the sense that Reth had given in to the temptation on countless occasions. She wasn't sure which of them, Fana or Reth, to speak to in order to end the folly before the situation got out of hand. After much thought, Zera concluded that Reth was the one who should have behaved better.

Reth always rose early each morning to feed his dogs and to take them running. Zera made sure she was waiting at the door.

"I'd like to join you this morning," she said with a smile. "I could use some exercise if you don't mind walking."

"You're always welcome, Mama," he said, leading the way to the pen. When they got there, he instructed the groom to feed and run his dogs after he was finished tending to the horses. "Now, we can spend time together like we used to," he said to Zera, taking her by the arm.

They walked for about a quarter of an hour without talking, taking in the fresh morning air and feeling the moist grass under their feet.

When she got to the tulip tree she admired, Zera stopped. "Let's rest here for a minute." Not one to dodge around hard subjects, Zera got straight to the point. "I need to talk to you about Fana," she said, waiting for a reaction, but Reth gave none. "She seems to be less attentive to Jonah and more infatuated with you."

"I haven't said or done anything to encourage that."

"You don't have to, son. Whether it is a blessing or a curse, women are drawn to you. This is dangerous because Fana is your brother's wife. It can poison this family and spread until it has torn all of Beta-Israel apart."

"Honestly, Mama, I have laid with other women besides my wife. That is my sin. And Fana has made advances toward me, but I have ignored them. Whatever my weaknesses, I would never betray my brother or touch anything that belongs to him."

Zera took a big breath and exhaled. "It comforts me to hear you say that, Reth. Don't mention this to anyone, not even Berta or Jonah. I'll speak to Fana."

"Thank you, Mama."

"Now, let me get back. I've worked up an appetite."

Reth laughed and took her by the arm, and they headed back to the house.

***

After Jonah left home, Zera went into his sleeping quarters. "Good morning, Fana. I trust you slept well," she said, surprising her daughter-in-law.

"Yes, ma'am. I am rested."

"I've been thinking about the time when I was a new bride in my husband's home and how uncomfortable I felt in the beginning. I want you to know you are another daughter to me."

"Thank you, ma'am, I have felt welcomed here," Fana replied politely.

"Good," Zera said, smiling. She touched Fana's hair. "Get me your comb." Then she sat down in the chair and motioned for Fana to approach. "Sit here, and I'll braid your hair. I loved to style Melesse's hair while she was at home."

Fana was a bit uncomfortable, but she dared not insult her mother-in-law. "Yes, ma'am. I would like that," she said, taking a seat on the floor in front of her.

"You know, sometimes it takes years for a man and a woman to love one another after they become husband and wife," Zera said. Fana didn't respond, but she was becoming more uneasy about Zera's visit. "Is there any reason why you may feel like you won't grow to love Jonah?"

"No, ma'am. Why would you ask that?"

"I have watched you since the wedding, and it seems as if you have eyes for your sister's husband more so than for your own."

"Forgive me, Mama. If I may speak frankly, I feel my sister and I have been mismatched. I would be the better wife for Reth. I sense something meaningful between us."

"Why would you believe that?" Zera asked.

"I can see it in his eyes when he looks at me. The smile he gives me is warm and loving."

"Listen carefully, Fana. Reth is my child, and I know him better than anyone, the way he is with you is the way he is with everyone. He was born with the charm of two men."

"That doesn't change the fact that Jonah doesn't seem to be happy with me."

"Probably you haven't shown him that you care for him. I pray he doesn't know you lay beside him thinking of his brother. Have you no loyalty to your sister?"

Fana tried to pull away, but Zera kept combing her hair, making it difficult for Fana to move.

"Because Berta is the youngest, she has always been spoiled," Fana said bitterly. "From the day she was born, she has been given first choice in everything, and I have to take second-best."

Zera kept a soothing tone, feeling some sympathy for the girl. "My husband arranged the marriages with your father. There was no argument raised then."

"It shouldn't have happened that way. Jonah and Reth weren't farmers who needed the dowry to take wives. They are like kings to the people. They could have chosen wives for themselves. I know he would have chosen me."

"I talked with Reth this morning, and he is happy with Berta," Zera told Fana sternly. "He has no interest in his brother's wife. You must find satisfaction with your husband. What is done is done."

With tears in her eyes, Fana objected. "It doesn't have to be. Jonah can divorce me, and Reth can divorce Berta."

"Listen to me, Fana. You are my daughter now, and I care for you. You will be the mother of my grandchildren—from Jonah. Don't ruin your marriage and life with fantasies about things that can never be. Jonah is a good man, and he will be a good husband to you. He doesn't have all the allure of his brother, but he is faithful. He deserves a wife who is faithful."

"How can I change what my heart feels? It's not a candle with a flame easily blown out."

"Ask God to forgive you, and pray. Be the wife my son deserves. The woman in Proverbs 31:10-12, 'a wife of noble character who can find? She is worth far more than rubies. Her husband has full confidence in her and lacks nothing of value. She brings him good, not harm, all the days of her life.' Learn to love Jonah, and you will be blessed. You will have a husband who belongs to you and no other woman."

"Thank you for coming to me, Mama," Fana said, wiping her face. "I will try to do what you have told me."

"Good, Fana. Your hair is done, and you look beautiful. Go find your husband and walk with him for a ways. It's a beautiful day!"

***

Fana did as Zera told her. She focused her attention on Jonah. She found that despite not having the boisterous personality of Reth, he was quite interesting and thoughtful. He talked to her as an equal, asking her opinion on important matters relating to religion and politics. It didn't stop her from having moments of jealousy when it seemed that Berta was having more fun attending social gatherings, while Jonah preferred the quiet of their living quarters. But she found love and contentment in her marriage. If Jonah was aware of Fana's earlier preference for Reth, he never mentioned it or allowed it to influence their relationship.

The two brothers always had a different view of the world, but it didn't affect their love or respect for each other. Jonah was the older and could have usurped authority over Beta-Israel as leader, except there was no rivalry between them. They worked well together, aside from their differences in the interpretation of the New Covenant. Both were secure in their responsibility to keep the people united. They agreed to bring the worship outside the synagogue, where all the people could participate. They also organized a council that consisted of a leader from each village, the general of the military, a representative of the merchants, and themselves.

As the years passed, the brothers were blessed with three children. Jonah had three daughters: Habesha, Kess, and Cheren; and Reth had three sons: Sarki, Petros, and Tangene. All of the children took part in Sabbath services. Reth's sons had great voices, and they led the choir in song. When Jonah's daughters danced, it was if angels had descended in front of the congregation. It was Zera's dream to see her sons and their families bonded in love and praise for the Lord. Once it was realized, she died in peace and was buried beside Workneh's grave.

***

At the start of the thirteenth century, Kilwa was still under the control of the Arabs. They had also seized gold trade from Mogadishu, making Kilwa the most wealthy and powerful city on the Swahili Coast. Because there was no agriculture in the urban settlements, Sena was a beneficiary of their great prosperity. The businesses of the Kilwa Sultanate were solely centered on external trade of raw materials from the interior. The provisions of grain, meat, and other supplies needed to feed the large-city populations had to be purchased from the inland Bantu and Beta-Israel highland market towns.

The wealth generated from the sales and trade created competition within the villages; and the division of commerce instigated squabbles between government leaders, businessmen, and spiritual chiefs under Jonah and Reth's authority. The same conflicts that had uprooted Beta-Israel so many times were threatening them again. Reth and Jonah called for a meeting with a small group of the council to discuss the problem.

The men gathered in their government building. Those present included Jonathan, the representative of the merchants; Ajani, the general of the military; Jonah; and Reth. The brothers agreed that having the leaders from the villages joining in the meeting would probably create more problems than solutions.

Jonah spoke first. "The Zagwe Dynasty has been defeated in Axum, and the Solomonic Dynasty has been restored. This shouldn't have a significant effect on us because there is still a Christian emperor in power. The difference is that there will be no capital city for the kingdom they now call Ethiopia. For now, there is peace. We are free from the religious wars between this restored Solomonic Dynasty and the Muslims. Even so, we quarrel among ourselves."

"Whenever there is money to be made, there will always be wrangling among the people," Jonathan offered casually. "That is part of it; conducting business can be ruthless. Why is that so serious that we must have this meeting."

"That isn't the sole purpose of this meeting," Jonah said. "The issue is the clashes between our people. It leaves us vulnerable when there is interference from other nations and their rulers. The people must be united, not absorbed in their individual ambitions."

Then Reth interjected, "Speak bluntly, brother. You are worried about a Christian emperor roaming around near our territory. That is unnerving and keeps you awake at night. Why? Because it has been well over a thousand years, and we haven't found a way to resolve the issue among our people about whether Jesus Christ is the Messiah."

"Yes, that does trouble me!" Jonah shouted. "Why? Because there are those who seek to divide and conquer us as a people. We are all Israelites! We were Israelites before Jesus was born, and that has not changed!"

Reth shouted back at him. "No, you're wrong, Jonah! Everything has changed! You read the Bible. Can you deny that the new covenant is real?"

"Look, I respect both of you," Ajani said, interjecting. "But don't for one minute believe we are fighting over religious beliefs. Myself, I believe in Jeremiah's prophesy and that Jesus is the new covenant. But the truth is, with Christianity comes control from the Byzantine Empire. It opens the door to invaders. Don't be fooled by the motives of the Arabs or the Christians. This is about power and money, gold and slaves."

Jonathan sat up straight. Ajani had gotten his attention. "For that matter, it's the Muslim Arabs who have trampled us for our treasure," he said, showing his resentment for their position on the coast. "They're the ones who make us slaves. Why shouldn't we join forces with the Solomonic Dynasty? They have made inroads in reclaiming Abyssinian territory from the Islamic Empire. That would be to the advantage of our people."

"We have been betrayed thinking that many times," Ajani broke in. "The emperor doesn't rule over all of Ethiopia. He only governs a small area. The Muslims still control the coast. We are here in the southeast highlands, but they hold the advantage to our economy. With no trade, we can't survive."

"There is no urgency for us to make alliances," Jonah reiterated. "As I said before, we will continue with our present strategy for as long as we can. We have no allegiance to either side. We will remain neutral. Let them spill their own blood."

Reth took a deep breath and reminded them of the reason for the meeting. "With all that said, we have not decided on how to bridge the growing divide between the people."

"It's clear that we have to separate the leadership. We must have a king and a chief priest again. The spiritual leader must be separated from governance. We will be united as a people, even if we aren't in our beliefs."

"I agree," Ajani said, standing up to leave the meeting. "Come along, Jonathan. Let's leave these brothers alone to decide which one will be king."

Jonathan laughed as he got up to follow Ajani. "I hate to go just when this meeting is getting interesting!"

"There's nothing to decide," Reth said after they were gone. "You are the elder brother, and you should be king."

"No," Jonah said. "You will be king. The chief priest must follow the covenant given to Moses, and I can't trust you to do that."

"I would follow the teachings of our father. I have no desire to destroy Beta-Israel."

"I'm glad to hear you say that, Reth, except there are other reasons why you should not be chief priest."

"What are they?" Reth asked, puzzled.

"Your weakness for women, brother. I doubt you will be the best example. Nobody cares if the king commits adultery."

There was nothing else Reth could say. He and Jonah had never spoken of his dalliances, and now he wondered if he had known Fana's feelings years ago. Though Jonah had never judged him or his behavior, he suddenly felt guilty. He wanted to tell him that he never betrayed him nor would he ever, but then he thought better of it. They had more important matters to tackle.

*** 

Jonah's decision was a wise one. Reth was a king for the people. Beta-Israel loved him and was loyal to him. He wasn't a perfect family man, but he held Beta-Israel together and quieted all the rumblings about war and religion. They stayed united and neutral, while the Solomonic Dynasty increased attacks against the Islamic leadership and military in 1290.

The emperor surprised them with an enlarged and transformed imperial army. Though they still relied on bow and arrows, his troops were now armed with swords, spears, and long shields. He divided them into regiments, swordsmen, and shield-bearers that guarded his archers. When the emperor attacked Zeila, the capital of the Ifat Sultanate, his forces were not prepared for the onslaught. This began a series of clashes between them for over 30 years that were successful for the Solomonic Dynasty in reacquiring territory that had once been part of the Axum Empire.

# Chapter Ten
# Petros, Sarki, and Tangene

Reth's sons were born a little more than a year apart and were almost identical in their physical appearance; but in almost every other way, they were distinct. Sarki was reverent and introspective, listening more than he spoke. Petros was shrewd and meticulous, outsmarting their tutor when they wanted to play. Tangene was self-confident and impulsive, constantly itching to show his strength and prowess. As young boys, they spent most waking hours together and were close. They knew one another so well that they could communicate with a look or a gesture.

When Reth died, Sarki could have demanded that he follow their father on the throne as the oldest son. Instead, he requested to be trained to succeed Jonah as chief priest and yielded the crown to Petros. Having been responsible for his younger brothers since they were born, Sarki knew he could better serve and safeguard them and Beta-Israel through his communication with the Almighty. He was convinced that the voice in his head that spoke to him belonged to God.

Petros patterned his leadership after Solomon, not as a lover of women like his father, but in his wisdom and his peaceful reign. He contemplated every decision he made to avoid unforeseen consequences. He was also intelligent enough to know that he needed Sarki at his right hand to intercede with the Lord for confirmation.

Tangene was a born warrior and an expert with the crossbow. He was as accurate as the archerfish that can target an insect on a tree branch with a jet of water from the surface of the lake. In his capacity as general, he personally trained the military and was confident they were ready to fight. In his opinion, they had been ready for years; it was only the word of his older brothers that held him back. He and his army satisfied their urge to join in the fight with the daily hunt. Still, no matter the catch or the value of the skins and ivory traded, he felt as if he was wasting time.

Jonah had taken most of the responsibility of arranging marriages for his daughters and Reth's sons, cognizant that intermarriage was not an option for the leaders of Beta-Israel and the preference that they not be related. He also had separate homes for Sarki and Tangene built outside of the castle, telling them that each of their families needed breathing room. He cautioned them to remember the tenth commandment: Thou shall not covet. He did not want any jealousies or confusion to crop up between the brothers or their wives.

Sarki's wife, Lilah, was the youngest of the women and, as such, the most impressionable. To bond with her, Sarki taught her to read. He gave her the Bible as a gift, and they studied Scripture together. Even though she kept it to herself, she was greatly influenced by the New Testament and the story of the young Mary who gave birth to the Messiah. She secretly believed that Jesus is the Savior of the people.

Petros's wife, Ranita, was the first to give birth; they had a son named Alamini. Tangene's wife, Penina, was the second to give birth; they had a son named Waitimu. A year later, Lilah gave birth to their son, Yaro. Over the next five years, all three wives gave birth to daughters—one for Petros and Tangene, and two for Sarki. Jonah's nervousness about envies were unfounded. The women got along well and raised their children together.

Lilah shared with her sisters-in-law Scriptures she had read, especially those about Mary. "All these with one accord were devoting themselves to prayer, together with the women and Mary the mother of Jesus, and his brothers" (Acts 1:14). She persuaded them that women can gather and pray for themselves. So, whenever the brothers met to confront the problems of the people, their wives had a ritual where they would come together as well. Their sisterhood grew deeper after Lilah initiated their prayer triangle, creating an unbreakable spiritual bond.

***

Jonah still lived on edge for the rest of his life, anticipating the day when the battles between the Christians and the Muslims would disrupt the peace and the prosperity they had worked so hard to achieve. He died six months before the Christian dynasty's expansion reached the outer lands of Lake Tana and the southern highlands. Jonah had no sons, so after his death, Reth's oldest son, Sarki, became chief priest.

The brothers met at least once a week to discuss any important issues pertaining to Beta-Israel, specifically the movements of Amda Seyon, who was treacherous enough to overturn his own father and was now the emperor of Ethiopia. Petros insisted that they be on one accord to deal with the ruthless Christian emperor regaining ground and authority. As usual, they had three different approaches to the intensifying aggression.

"We have to use our wits to outmaneuver them," Petros explained to his brothers. "Our weapons are no match for theirs."

"We should be out there!" Tangene fumed, whipping his sword through the air. "The gold, silver, metals, and livestock they've taken from Ifat belonged to our people. This is our land. We are the ones who built it up. What difference does it make if we don't pay them taxes? They still get to take what belongs to our people!"

Sarki shook his head, straining to hear the voice in his head. "Timing is more important than a million armed men, Tangene. Need I remind you of Joshua and the battle of Jericho?"

Tangene scoffed at him. "I don't want to hear about that ancient history! It does not have anything to do with this situation. Now is the time for us to move! The Arab army has been weakened. We can take back our ports."

"No, brother, that would be foolish," Petros said, dismissing all of Tangene's bluster. "Whether we like it or not, this is Amda Seyon's time. He is killing our enemies, which should not bother you. The strength of an army is not limitless. Regardless of how well trained they are, that strength runs out in due time."

Sarki nodded in agreement, and Tangene chopped the air with his sword in frustration.

"We will continue to wait," Petros told his brothers.

***

Less than a year had gone by before Tangene stormed into the receiving room of the castle, his chest heaving in anger.

"You should have listened to me!" he shouted to his brothers. "We had an opportunity to crush the Arabs, and now they are banding together."

"What are you talking about?" Sarki asked, confused.

"He's talking about the attacks from Emperor Amda Seyon that convinced the independent Muslim provinces that they needed to make alliances with one another to defend themselves," Petros said, answering before Tangene.

"That's right!" Tangene said. "The Sultanate of Ifat was nearly broken down from the skirmishes with the Solomonic Dynasty, except now he put together a larger army that has launched a full-scale religious war!"

"We've had this discussion repeatedly," Petros said. "This is not our fight. Why are you in such a rush to risk the lives of your men and yourself?"

"What do you think we'll gain?" Sarki added.

Indignant, Tangene shouted at them. "We'll get our self-respect back. If we're such a great people, God's chosen people, why do we slink back in the crevices of these highlands hiding from our enemies?"

"We have our way of life to protect," Petros answered. "We have families to protect. We all have sons. I wouldn't want their blood spilled unless it was impossible to avoid."

"I should have been king," Tangene said with resignation. "I wouldn't have ruled in fear or followed the voices in my head!"

***

The Ethiopian emperor was undeterred by the sultan's reprisals and stayed on the assault. The battles between them went on for years, with Amda Seyon maintaining the upper hand. In his boldness, he also attacked Beta-Israel and the northern provinces of Semien, Wegera, and Dembiya, where many had been converting to Judaism. In exchange for their safety and survival, he demanded loyalty and financial support.

"They've brought the fight to us. Now we can't back away," Tangene said to his brothers. "We have no choice."

"How many lives must be sacrificed?" Sarki asked. "Our sons are men, too. Will we put their lives in danger without thinking?"

"There's no decision to be made," Tangene reiterated. "The emperor settled that when he attacked our people in the north."

Petros sighed. "The Sabbath is in two days. I'll speak to the people then."

Tangene rushed out to prepare his men for war.

"What is that voice in your head telling you?" Petros asked Sarki.

"It's gone. I can't hear anything," he answered. "There's too much noise around the city. I'm going into the mountains where I can meditate."

All the people of Sena felt the tension in the air. They had been used to Tangene's rantings about getting in the conflict, but they were always followed by reassurances from Petros and Sarki that they would not be involved and would maintain their neutrality. The silence from their king and chief priest was deafening.

***

Sarki climbed higher into the mountains, thinking about the war between Israel and the tribe of Benjamin. Each time the Lord had told Israel to go out and fight, and twice they were beaten. He gave them the victory on the third battle, but the number of lives lost seemed so unnecessary to Sarki. Why should they have suffered such despair because of the actions of a few? He reached a plateau and found the spot he had come to several times before, the place where the voice had spoken so clearly to him. He knelt down, looked to the heavens, and began to pray.

"Lord, have mercy on your people. It seems as if our trials never cease. Now the enemy is close on our heels. What would you have us do, Lord? Our soldiers are ready to turn and face them in war. Speak to me, Lord, what is your will?" Sarki bowed his head and listened for the voice. He waited until his knees ached, but still silence. "Please God, we need your guidance," he pleaded without hearing anything. Sarki became angry. "Why would you choose the time when I need you most to abandon me?" he shouted, and then he wept. "Tell me what to tell the men who are willing to sacrifice their lives."

Sarki spent a sleepless night on the mountain, his body shivering from the cold. The only sounds he heard were the night howls and calls of the nocturnal animals moving about in the darkness. He climbed down when the sky began to lighten, despondent from the imminent tragedies that were sure to come.

*** 

After Sarki finished the prayers and blessings, Petros stood high on the outside podium to speak to the people of Beta-Israel. It had been his hope that this day would never come, the day he would announce that they would join in the war. From his studies, he understood there was no glory in war, not even in victory, only temporary jubilation when the killing ceased. There was always great horror of what was lost when the dust settled, the price paid for the spoils, but again underestimated. Even so, it never stopped men from entering into the absurdity of combat.

"Children of Israel, once again we are besieged by our enemies, who come to disturb the peace we have worked so hard to foster. Presently, we have been pulled into warfare over the land under our feet. We have no alternative but to defend ourselves against this aggression. So I say as Joel 3:9-10, 'Proclaim this among the nations: Prepare for war! Rouse the warriors! Let all the fighting men draw near and attack. Beat your plowshares into swords and your pruning hooks into spears. Let the weakling say, "I am strong!"'"

Tangene's army, standing aside the people, danced and chanted. Feeling their energy, the people joined in. After a few minutes, Petros raised his arms to quiet them. "Prepare yourselves," he said firmly. "Three days from now, our soldiers will meet the forces of the emperor."

The army chanted and marched away from the synagogue in formation with Tangene; his son, Waitimu; and his officers leading the way on horseback.

***

The brothers spent the next two days with their wives and families. The prospects ahead of them were a reality they wanted to avoid as long as possible. Petros sat at the table, but he had no appetite. He had encouraged his son and his nephews to train with the military as young men for the exercise and discipline, believing they should experience being followers before they were expected to lead. He had not foreseen the day when Alamini would insist on riding behind his uncle in the conflict.

Ranita slumped over the platter of Alamini's favorite meal, flavoring it with the saltiness of her tears. Their son had chosen to spend the evening at Tangene's home rather than sit in the gloom of his own. Petros had no false comfort to offer his wife; his own heart was heavy. He felt like a failure as a king who left his people exposed to invaders and as a father who couldn't shield his son.

Sarki's evening wasn't as solemn as his older brother's. His daughters fussed over him, entertaining him with stories and songs that kept his mind occupied. Having stopped straining to hear the voice in his head, he was somewhat relieved that he had no input on the decision to go to war. He and Lilah were also grateful that Yaro was too young to join the military.

At Tangene's home, the atmosphere was full of celebration. His officers sat with him at the table, and they ate and drank like warriors who had already claimed the victory. Penina listened to the ruckus as she lay in her sleeping quarters, tossing on her bed as if she were drowning. She had never agreed with her husband's thinking that fighting was the appropriate response for their people. Not every man needed to prove himself on the battlefield. Truth be told, she tired of all the uproar about their people remaining independent from everyone else. Her father was a merchant, and he did business with men of other religions, and it never did him any harm.

Penina cringed when she heard Waitimu join in with the boisterous bragging of the other men. He was barely a man.

The hair on his face was thin and soft like a baby's. He knew nothing of the world and was only adept at imitating his father.

And oddly enough, for all his bluster, Tangene had never fought an enemy, let alone another whose mission it was to kill him. He envisioned himself as a modern-day David, conquering one adversary after another, but he had never been tested. Penina knew that neither her husband nor her son felt the dread and anxiety that covered her in her bed. She cried out in desperation, unheard in all the noise, begging God to be merciful and to spare their lives.

***

Tangene and his officers had slept only a few hours, if at all, before they gathered outside the synagogue at dawn for their final blessing. Petros was there, dressed in all the finery of the king. He wanted to be the image of power. Seeing his son astride his horse and dressed in armor with his spear held high, Petros's head pounded under the crown. Sarki's belly burned with worry. He was uncertain about their strategy and perplexed that the voice hadn't spoken to him.

Sarki bowed his head, imploring the Lord to hear him. Then he raised his head and said, "'Hear, Israel: Today you are going into battle against your enemies. Do not be fainthearted or afraid; do not panic or be terrified by them. For the LORD your God is the one who goes with you to fight for you against your enemies to give you victory,' Deuteronomy 20:3-4." Then he blessed them in the way he did every Sabbath, "May the Lord bless you and keep you; The Lord make His face to shine upon you and be gracious unto you. The Lord lift up His countenance upon you and give you peace. Amen."

Tangene moved to the front and began the military chant, as they marched toward the edge of the city. They were headed to the northern provinces. Petros and Sarki stood and watched until the last man was out of sight.

***

Ranita and Lilah got up early that morning as well. They were there waiting to sit with Penina after Tangene and Waitimu left to join the army at the synagogue. Penina was so terrified, her whole body trembled.

"Sit down. You need to eat," Ranita said, guiding Penina to a chair and pouring her a cup of milk.

Penina shook her head. "I can't keep any food down; my stomach is upset."

"Join hands. I'm going to pray," Lilah told them. "Lord, God in heaven, comfort my sisters, and comfort our people. Help us not to be afraid, for we know You are God and that You will help us. I ask that You place a shield of protection around the soldiers, our husbands, and our sons from the enemy. Strengthen them in battle; and please, O God, give them the victory. Amen."

"Amen, amen," Ranita whispered, squeezing their hands.

The prayer seemed to momentarily ease Penina's fears, and she drank some of the goat's milk. "Thank you for being here," she murmured. "My nerves have been frayed for days."

"You shouldn't be here alone with only your servants for company," Ranita said. "Come to the castle with me. I'll take care of you. It will keep me from worrying about Alamini."

"You both are my true sisters; the same blood could not make me love you more," Penina said, forcing a smile. "God has blessed me."

"May his blessings continue," Ranita said.

***

Tangene had been thorough in his preparation for war. His men were fit and well-trained in warfare. They were well-armed with armor, shields, swords, spears, bows, and arrows. His strategy was to spread his army wide, surround the emperor's troops, and overtake them. The army was divided into three groups, with the first third leading the charge. Tangene had envisioned the attack in his head over and over. He would lead fiercely, running into the face of opposition, as if he were running into the sea, and they would fall at his feet like defenseless animals.

Except Tangene ran straight into a wall. Waiting for him was a well-armed force of men just as determined as he was. He had miscalculated the strength and resolve of the invaders. He assumed that the Christian and Muslim militaries had weakened each other. He was only half-right. The Muslims had been weakened, but Emperor Amda Seyon's forces had been fortified. Tangene's numbers weren't large enough.

Tangene refused to retreat. Bravely, he forged ahead with his men. They were engulfed in a battle from all sides. They fought fiercely, and it was only when a spear found its target on Tangene's neck, knocking him from his horse, that they withdrew.

Those who managed to survive the onslaught informed Waitimu that his father had certainly been killed in the battle. So Waitimu called upon his group to rush in to defend Tangene. Outmanned, they met the same fate as the first group, and Waitimu was killed as well. Petros's son, Alamini, insisted on leading the men but pulled back to regroup before they advanced again. His tactic was to wait until dark and then penetrate the enemy front on the far left with a small group to reduce one end.

Alamini and his men failed to surprise the enemy troops and suffered more casualties, and Alamini was one of them. It was the experience of the emperor's army that defeated them even more than their size. Tangene's general, who always led on the flank, survived and sent word back to the king that Tangene, Waitimu, Alamini, and more than 1,000 soldiers had been killed in battle.

***

The wailing that filled the city when the people got word of the deaths and defeats were something that this generation had never heard before. Ranita and Penina were there when Petros received the message. Penina collapsed and laid on the ground as if she were frozen. Ranita was inconsolable. Sarki and Lilah rushed to the castle to be with their family.

"I have to go to the front," Petros said in anguish. "I should have been there. Tangene was too impulsive. He should have been patient and let the fight come to him."

"I've heard that Amda's army has grown in power and skill," Sarki said. "Your being there wouldn't have made a difference. The people need you here. We have to regroup. Maybe we need to try to negotiate with them."

"Whatever happens, I'll be there," Petros declared. "I have no choice. A leader can't ask others to sacrifice if he won't sacrifice himself."

"I'll go in your place," Sarki urged. "Ranita has already lost her son. She needs you."

"Don't you understand?" Petros roared. "I can't sit on a throne in a palace after my son has died for our people! I am the king. I must take command."

All the while Petros prepared to go, Ranita begged him to send others. But he ignored her pleas. On the morning he was to leave, she grabbed his arms and clutched his cloak, sobbing until Sarki had to pull her away.

"Pray for me, brother," Petros said, ready to join his entourage.

Sarki put his hand on his shoulder and said, "In the words of David, Psalm 20:8-9, 'Some trust in their war chariots and others in their horsed, but we trust in the power of the LORD our God. Such people will stumble and fall, but we will rise and stand firm. Give victory to the king, O LORD; answer us when we call.' May the blessing of the Lord be upon you, brother, and no weapon formed against you prosper."

It seemed as if the grieving began when Petros rode out of the city. It is the frontline that suffers the brunt of the casualties, and Petros took his place there as the leader. His men proudly behind him, he fought valiantly in the battle, and they gave all they had to give. No one was surprised when the message came that the king had been killed. Beta-Israel mourned over their losses and questioned why God was punishing them. Beaten down, their conviction grew weak.

The faith of Ranita and Penina was shaken. They had prayed fervently for protection, they had trusted God, but their husbands and sons were dead. When Lilah came to pray with them, they rebuffed her.

"Go home to your husband and your son with your useless prayers!" Ranita said. "We have no use for them. We have no one else to lose."

"Sisters, we must not stop praying. God is our comfort. He will heal our suffering."

Ranita waved to her servant to usher Lilah out. "No, we won't listen to those empty promises again. Leave us alone."

"God's will is not always our will," Lilah persisted. "Many were struck down in war under the covenant given to Moses. Don't blame the Lord for the evil men do."

"Get out of here!" Penina screamed before slumping back on her chair.

Lilah hurried out, her face covered in tears. She still had her husband and her son, but she had lost the women who were her sisters. Unable to see past their pain, they never spoke to her again.

***

The emperor of Ethiopia continued to encroach on Beta-Israel territory, and they in turn moved further into the Simien mountains. The large battles downscaled into small skirmishes on the fringes. Sarki's only son, Yaro, had come of age and was eager to fight for the revenge of his uncles and cousins.

"They need to pay for what they took from us," he told his father. "I can rebuild the army better than ever; the general knows how to fight them now. I'm sure we'll triumph this time."

Sarki was tired of listening to his foolishness. "No, Yaro, not another life will be thrown away needlessly."

"The people will think I'm a coward if I don't stand up and fight."

"It doesn't matter what the people think. It's your duty to serve them. You don't have the luxury of dying as a hero. Prepare yourself to lead as king and chief priest."

Yaro resented the responsibility and refused to study God's word. His heart was hardened against any love, especially the love of God. Sarki arranged his marriage to soften his spirit, but Yaro was mean and bitter to his wife and struck her on many occasions.

Sarki and Lilah prayed for their son when he was crowned king. They weren't sure how he would wield his power. Both were afraid his anger might possibly lead the people to their destruction. Thankfully, when Emperor Amda Seyon died and his son, Newaya Krestos, took the throne, Beta-Israel was given a reprieve, as his focus was to continue to fight against the Muslims in Ethiopia and in Egypt.

Yaro had one son, Jaali. Sarki hovered close to the castle, teaching his grandson about God and governance. It wasn't his desire to come between Yaro and Jaali; he simply wanted to counteract the negativity spewed by his son. As time passed and Jaali grew, Yaro managed to turn his own son against him. Jaali despised his father for his abusive behavior and was determined to be everything his father was not. He became a righteous man, loved his mother, loved his wife, and loved God. He had no interest in being a warrior; he was a peaceful man. When Sarki died, he succeeded him as chief priest.

Yaro trained with the army regularly. He wanted to be ready for battle when the emperor or the Muslims attacked. In one of the exercises, he was accidently killed. It was the general's story that Yaro's horse stumbled, and he fell to the ground on his own knife. Most of the soldiers stated that they didn't see what happened. Those who witnessed the mishap corroborated the general's description of what happened.

Although Jaali inherited the throne, as chief priest, he kept the people in prayer. And while all around them seemed to be violence and death, they were in an oasis of tranquility.

On each Sabbath, Jaali said, "We are in God's hands, my people. He protects us. We are as Shadrack, Meshack, and Abednego; we are in the midst of the fire, but we don't perish."

Jaali had two daughters and one son. His young son died from a sickness; and his wife, Duni, refused to eat. He prayed for her healing, but she prayed for death. Her prayer was answered. He took another wife named Tish, and their son Gitonga was born in 1370.

# Chapter Eleven
# Gitonga

Large in frame but gentle and uncomplicated, Gitonga wasn't interested in hunting or participating in war games with the military. Having been spoiled as a child, he enjoyed the simple pleasures of life: eating and sleeping. Jaali, in his conscious effort not to be overbearing in raising Gitonga, had inadvertently neglected his son's education. As a result, he had a simplistic view of the world and preferred to ignore conflicts and controversy.

When Gitonga became a young man, Jaali took all of these things under consideration as he contemplated the perfect wife for him. He selected Eritha, the daughter of Ebo, his first officer. Not only was she trustworthy, she had been raised with might, means, and manners. He believed she would be an invaluable asset when Gitonga became king. Even so, Jaali opted to retain his position as chief priest and prayed for longevity to ensure the independence of Beta-Israel until the threats were resolved.

The only thing that Gitonga loved more than a delicious meal followed by a long rest was the company of Eritha. She made him laugh; entertained him with poems she wrote; and taught him to play mancala, a board game she learned from her father. She also intervened and solved most of the issues brought to the castle to be settled by the king. He also insisted she attend the regular meetings he had with her father, who now served as officer and general.

Gitonga ambled to the conference hall, dreading this meeting, since Eritha was heavy with child and chose not to come. It was the same matter every week. Ebo kept pressuring him to take some form of action on the Solomonic Dynasty, which had been conducting relentless raids on Muslim territory that had gone on long before he was crowned king. Ebo felt Emperor Dawit was not as strong as he seemed, being that he had been ineffective in taking control of the coasts.

Gitonga had no time to eat from the platter of food or drink from his cup before the general began his proposal.

"Our standing has increased; more of the migrants have converted to Judaism. This might be the right time to push back against the emperor," Ebo suggested after he sat down at the head of the table.

"What good would that do, Ebo?" Gitong asked dumbfounded, hating it when the general was always looking for trouble. "Then, next, we would have to fight the Muslims."

"Why shouldn't we?" Ebo asked. "We won't be a great people until we take back the ports. If we could gain clear access to the coasts, we would have wealth beyond your imagination."

"That reminds me of what my father always tells me," Gitonga smirked, looking at the food. 'Better is a dry morsel with quiet than a house full of feasting with strife,' Proverbs 17:1."

Ebo shook his head. "You may be able to avoid the battles for the time being, but there is the question of the monks who have left the monasteries and ventured among us into the Siemen Mountains."

"Why should I worry about that?" Gitonga asked, shrugging his shoulders. "I hear they have left the church because of their objections to the lewd behavior of the Solomonic kings. They say they have traveled south as missionaries."

"That does not explain why these monks are coming into our territory. They know we are Jews, I believe they are spies of the emperor."

"I've spoken with many of them, and that's not what they have told me," Gitonga said in the monks' defense. "They say they are religious men who detest the shameless depravity of the emperor."

Ebo shook his head again at Gitonga's naiveté. "My king, we can't trust them," he said, mustering up a bit of patience. "They practice the religion of the state. They must die."

"For what reason? They come as evangelists to share the word of the Gospels."

Ebo's eyes widened in shock. "Your father's heart would stop if he heard you utter those words! Don't you understand his objections to invaders among us? If they want to convert our people, how are they different than the emperor?"

"They don't come with the religion on the edge of a sword," Gitonga answered. "This isn't about gaining power. Christ was about love, not conquering."

"As king, you must be diligent. Something has to be done about their expansion into our provinces. We have always been independent. They hide behind the Christian religion, but it's only a façade. This is about politics. They want total power."

Gitonga wasn't convinced they were a threat and was tired of discussing it. However, he didn't think it wasn't worth a disagreement with his general. He gave Ebo permission to deal with the problem in the way he saw fit. Needless to say, Beta-Israel was pushed back.

***

The people of Sena celebrated when Eritha gave birth to her first child in 1400, a son they named Ochieng. Tish was joyful, and Jaali was thankful. His grandson would be the greatest hope for Beta-Israel to survive. For more than a decade, the people had been able to thrive as more migrants converted to Judaism, but the strain of the conflicts around them were taking a toll. The political winds had shifted after Emperor Dawit I died from a kick in the head by his horse and his son, Yeshaq, took over the throne. The delicate balance among them, the Christian kingdom, and Beta-Israel tilted, and they were in a race against time as the unrest surrounded them.

As soon as Ochieng learned to walk and talk, Jaali requested that he be brought to the synagogue to begin his lessons. Jaali began teaching him the history of their people from the time they were held in bondage in Egypt.

Ebo also took an interest in his grandson as he grew up. From the time the boy was ten years old, Ebo insisted that Ochieng train with the military when he finished with his studies. Ebo taught him to throw a spear, fling rocks with his sling, and shoot a bow and arrow. Ochieng, who was as energetic as a young cheetah, loved to hunt.

"I don't remember my father ever having that much interest in me," Gitonga complained to Eritha, as he lay beside her. He was beginning to resent the attention and focus that Jaali gave his son. Watching his father prepare his son to take his place made him question himself as a man. Did his father not think him capable or approve of him as king? "I guess I'm a disappointment to him."

Eritha rubbed his head. "Stop talking foolish, husband," she said. "You sound like you are jealous of your own baby."

"Ochieng is the son he wanted. He never bothered to teach me. He must think I'm stupid."

"End all that whining! Didn't Jaali put you on the throne? You need to begin doing what your father is doing. He's thinking about the future of Beta-Israel. Ochieng is your legacy, not your rival. Swallow your pride and encourage the relationship between him and your father. You should also do your part to see that he is prepared to lead."

Gitonga thought about it for a minute and began to see things in a different way.

"You are a wise woman, my love. How can I think ill of my father when he found me the best wife in all the world?"

"You can't. Now show me some appreciation."

Gitonga chuckled and took his wife in his arms.

***

Without capital cities, the Ethiopian emperor, the monarchy, and the nobles moved with the army, living in tents and huts. Requiring more area and resources, the emperors of the Solomonic Dynasty continually attacked the Jewish kingdom under the guise of a divine mission; but it was certainly a reaction to Beta-Israel gaining prominence and converting more to Judaism. Still, Sena was starting to crumble around the edges with their increased presence.

In their regular meeting to confer on their defense strategy, Ebo brought two of his officers with him. He surprised Gitonga and Eritha when he asked her to leave the room. Eritha wasn't happy about it, but she understood protocol and would never demean her father or husband by challenging them in front of the other men. She nodded demurely and excused herself.

"The time for peace has passed us," Ebo said. "The emperors of Ethiopia have raided us for 14 years. We have shown restraint, and our enemies have taken it for weakness. We must revolt against the political and religious expansion of the Christian kingdom. We have to push Dawit back, or the fight we have delayed will be on the door of the people. Our women and children will be raped and brutalized."

Gitonga gnawed at the inside of his jaw and looked around the room, as if the answer to his dilemma might be written on the wall. If his father taught him nothing else, he cautioned him against rushing into war. Confrontation with the enemy should be the last resort.

Sensing his reluctance, one of the officers spoke up. "The army is ready, my king. We can't sit and watch their abuse and not defend our people with honor."

"There was no doubt that this day would come," Gitonga said soberly. "Peace always seems to escape our people. I am ready to march with the army."

Ebo lifted his hand to stop Gitonga as he stood up. "It isn't necessary for you to fight, my king. I'm sure Jaali would not advise you to leave the throne empty. Ochieng can ride with the soldiers in your place."

"Absolutely not!" Gitonga roared. "Ochieng is only 14 years old." Now he understood why Ebo had asked Eritha to leave the room. "I would never send my son to take my place on the front."

"Pardon me," Ebo said. "I assumed that you had no interest in fighting."

"No man should want to take the life of another. I would take no pleasure in it. The fact remains that I am king, and I will lead the troops in this battle. Ochieng will stay in the city with his mother."

Ebo nodded. "As you say."

"Now go!" Gitonga commanded. "I must speak with my queen."

Ebo and his officers got up without another word. Gitonga sat there by himself for a while, pondering his position. Up to that moment, nothing seemed real. He was merely playing a game or acting in a play. He had never felt the responsibility of being king or an actual threat to his family. Everything had changed. There was no time left to waste. With long strides, he went to look for Eritha.

"What did my father say?" Eritha asked. "What didn't he want me to hear?"

"The time has come for our people to show their strength. We will revolt against the invasion. Either we push back on the emperor, or he will eventually take us over."

"This is the same thing my father has been saying for 17 years. Why is this so different?"

"We can't pretend anymore, Eritha. Those on the edge of the city are being persecuted. We can't let them bear the burden by themselves."

"So why couldn't he say that in front of me?"

"Your father wanted Ochieng to ride with him— Now, don't get upset. I told him that that was out of the question. I am the king, and I will lead the army."

"No, Gitonga! I see why he wanted me out of the room. He couldn't look me in the eyes and betray me. Do I need to remind you of your great-grandfather and your great-uncles who died in war?"

"No, my love, I am aware of my family's history."

"Then tie my father's hands. Don't give him your permission to attack. Wait. The conflict may blow over. It has before."

"You asked me to protect our son and the future. How can I do that if we don't fight?"

"Why are you going? You have never thrown a spear or shot an arrow."

"Now I will have that opportunity."

Eritha tugged at his robe. "We can't win! Can't you see that? The world has changed, and there are people and things we have to learn to live with."

"I know that, dear wife. Still, there are times you must fight, even if your chances are slim."

***

Jaali had no expectation that Gitonga would ever participate in war. Physically, his son was built for it, but he didn't have the mind for it. Thinking about the possibility of him being wounded or killed dug up the buried memories of Duni and the baby son they had lost. He didn't ever want to feel that pain ever again, and he didn't want that misery for Tish.

Early, on the day before the army would march, he went to the center market and bought a young sheep with no flaws. He returned home, sacrificed the lamb, and communed with God for hours. Then he took the meat and gave it to Eritha to prepare Gitonga's favorite meal, a spicy lamb stew and sour bread.

It was a joyous feast, with them all pretending the evening was no different from any other. At the end of the meal, Jaali asked Gitonga to meet him on the terrace with his cup of coffee so they could talk alone.

"Son, I have a confession to make," Jaali said wistfully.

Gitonga was already feeling melancholy and didn't want to bring anymore emotions to the surface. "It's not necessary, Father. I know that you love me."

"Let me speak my peace. I wasn't the father to you that I should have been. When you were young, there was so much I needed to prove to myself. I neglected you; and despite my shortcomings, you have become a good man and a good king. I am proud of you."

"That means a lot to me, Father."

"I need you to make me a promise," Jaali said, pausing.

"You only need to ask, and it is done," Gitonga said.

"Promise that you'll bury me, that you won't let them kill you on some battlefield."

Gitonga's eyes filled with tears. "How can I promise you that? It is out of my control."

"You said I only need to ask, and I have asked."

"You have my word, for whatever its worth."

"Thank you, son. I never pushed you to memorize the Scriptures, but I want you to read this and memorize it." He handed him a piece of linen cloth.

"Let me hear the words," Jaali said.

Gitonga read them, "'Through you we will push down our enemies: through your name we will trample down those who rise against us. For I will not trust in my bow, neither shall my sword save me. But you have saved us from our enemies, and have put them to shame that hated us,' Psalm 44:5-7."

"I want you to tie this around your head and read it every night."

"That I can promise," Gitonga said, taking the cloth in his hand.

Jaali wrapped him in a firm embrace. Then he turned away without making eye contact and said, "Go be with your family."

***

Gitonga rode clumsily beside Ebo, his heart thumping so hard against his chest that he could almost hear it. The armor he wore was uncomfortable and chafed the skin under his shirt. He could sense Ebo's misgivings about riding with a man with no experience in battle. They set up base a half mile from the emperor's military. The plan was to strike them after nightfall.

"When it's time to advance, you can bring up the rear," Ebo told Gitonga, preferring to be flanked by his trusted officers.

"You don't have to protect me, Ebo," Gitonga said, offended. "You advance with the cavalry, and I will lead the infantry." He felt he had at least half a fighting chance on his feet than he did on a horse.

"You can wait here at the base," Ebo murmured. "Your being here is enough to fire up the men."

"That is not enough for me; I will lead them as their king."

"It's your choice," Ebo said, as if his death were certain.

Gitonga sat alone in his tent, reading the words on the torn linen his father had given him. The army was eating, but for the first time in his life, the king had no appetite. His stomach bubbled with thoughts of what would happen in a few hours. He had never killed an animal, and now he had to prepare to kill as many men as possible.

Ebo sounded the horn that it was time to march to the enemy camp. Gitonga picked up his sword and shield; he had no aiming skills for a bow or spear. With his head held high, he marched ahead of his men. When they were close, Ebo gave the signal to charge. Gitonga ran as fast as he could in the darkness toward the light of campfires. It seemed longer, but only seconds passed before the scene around him turned ugly. It was pure pandemonium as spears and arrows whizzed by his head from opposite directions. He could hear the sound of swords clanging with grunts and growls in the background.

In his most vivid nightmare, Gitonga had never seen such terrors of blood gushing from severed limbs. Then a body fell at his feet and snapped him out of his haze. He began swinging his sword like a mad man. Smoke from the balls of fire thrown through the air clouded his vision. Mortified by his own actions, he closed his eyes and swung his blade in a circle around him as he moved forward. Then shouts echoed, "Retreat!" and a team of men on horses ran past him, galloping over the dead.

Exhausted, Gitonga tried to trot, but he staggered back among the injured. None of them stopped until they reached their base. In the midst of the mayhem, he searched for Ebo to get a report. He found him in a tent, lying on a mat, with a spear stuck in his belly. Ebo's personal servant cared for his other superficial wounds.

"My God, Ebo!" Gitonga stammered at the sight. He gathered himself from the shock. "Get the physician!" he ordered. With blank looks on their faces, his officer and the servant just stared at him.

"There's nothing to be done," Ebo said, straining to speak.

"We'll take you back to Sena. Something can be done there."

"Listen," Ebo said. "Tell my wife and my daughter that I didn't suffer."

"No!" Gitonga shouted. "Officer, you lead the soldiers back to Sena at daybreak. Gather a small team for me; I'm taking Ebo back now."

With Ebo stretched out in the wagon, it was a long, slow trek back to Sena. At that point, unknown to the small group traveling with Gitonga, the emperor's full army had invaded the Jewish army at their base in the Siemen province. Beta-Israel was defeated, and the revolt quashed.

***

By the time Gitonga got back to Sena, Ebo was dead. Gitonga hung his head, despondent over all that happened. It was hard enough returning without a victory; but with their beloved general's body in tow, it was much worse. Having been there in the midst of the battle, he knew his army was outmanned and that there was nothing he could have done to change the outcome, but that didn't stop him from feeling like a failure. Maybe Eritha was right. It's better to be voluntarily subjected to the emperor than to be beaten into submission.

A messenger sprinted ahead to the castle to announce that the king was en route. When she heard the news, Eritha shook nervously with relief. The she called for Ochieng.

"Come, son, we must greet your father!" she said, grabbing his hand.

"They are back soon. It must have been an easy fight," Ochieng said, running in front of her.

Eritha screamed with joy when she saw Gitonga and the small group of men approaching the castle. She was free from all her worries and fears. Her screams quickly turned to horror at the sight of her father's corpse.

Gitonga hated to see the anguish on her face. "Your father was a true warrior, but we had no chance against the emperor's army," he said, trying to soften the blow.

"Now he's gone! And how many more for no reason?" Eritha shrieked. "I begged you not to give your consent!" She covered her face, took Ochieng by the hand, and rushed back inside the castle.

The news of the king's return to the city traveled fast, and Jaali arrived a few minutes later.

"Praise God, you kept your promise to me, son!" he said earnestly. Then he looked him over from head to toe. "Were you hurt at all?" he asked.

"Not in my body, but in every other way," Gitonga lamented.

***

While Beta-Israel mourned its dead, Emperor Yeshaq built the church Debre Yashaq to commemorate his victory. He then divided the Jewish kingdom into three territories and appointed commissioners he controlled to govern them. He declared their status to be below that of Christians. All Jews were told to convert or lose their land. Yeshaq pronounced, "He who is baptized in the Christian religion may inherit the land of his father. Otherwise let him be a falasha, a wanderer."

Gitonga was unnerved by the presence of the commissioners, but he kept it to himself. He feared for Ochieng's safety and wanted him away from the intrusion.

"I think it will be best for Ochieng to be educated away from Sena. I don't want him to grow up like I did."

"Your father is teaching him," Eritha balked. "He will be educated."

"There are things happening outside of this city that he should know about. Here we are isolated from the rest of the world. I want to send him to a monastery. They are the only places where you can receive adequate religious and literary training."

"You must let the boy be a child," Eritha fussed, overwhelmed with shielding Gitonga and her son from the responsibilities of their birth.

"He will be a man soon. There's no time to waste."

On the Sabbath after worship, Gitonga told the people that he wanted his son to have as much knowledge as possible to be the chief priest and leader of the people. The council approved, and Ochieng was sent with escorts to northern Ethiopia to be educated.

Unfortunately, the emperor and his troops stayed among the residents of the cities draining the land and the residents of their food and supplies. Gitonga had no way to safeguard the people of Sena who were tormented by Yeshaq's overbearing authority. They came to the palace day after day and laid their complaints at his feet.

"Nothing has changed. God is still with us," Gitonga said, trying his best to reassure the people. "We are like Jonah, swallowed up in the mouth of a giant fish, but we must continue to pray. We will survive this."

***

Ochieng came into his own during his time at the monastery. An inquisitive young man, he read the Torah, the Bible, and the Qu'ran. He had learned from his grandfather that preaching about Jesus Christ being the Messiah had caused divisions among the people, but he was moved by the words in the New Covenant and the New Testament. When Jaali died, Gitonga sent for him to return to Sena and serve as chief priest.

Determined to remain true to his convictions, Ochieng taught from the Torah, gave lessons on Jeremiah the prophet and the New Covenant, and the Scriptures. Several of the priests protested. The last thing Gitonga wanted was a revival of the conflict in Beta-Israel. He called for Ochieng to come to the king's receiving room to have a talk with him.

When Ochieng arrived and saw no one else in the room except his father on the throne, he thought it odd.

"You sent for me, Baba?"

"Yes, I did. We need to have a serious conversation."

"Why are you being so formal," Ochieng asked, laughing.

"The life of the king is full of formalities. The responsibilities are great. You exist not only for yourself but for an entire nation of people. Everything you do must be carefully considered, and all decisions heavily weighed."

"What are you trying to tell me?" Ochieng asked, impatient and ready for his father to get to the point.

"One day, you may be king and possess the influence that comes with it. You will have to understand that your words sway people. I sent you to the monasteries to be educated so you would learn how to lead our people, not to wield it like an ax to create a wedge between them."

"That is not my intention, Baba. I only preach that we must learn about our adversaries to defend ourselves from them. The kingdom of God is the only true king, and we must exalt Him. I haven't said anything wrong."

"You make me proud, son. You have learned much from the monks, but you are not the first to believe in the new covenant. Many of our chief priests have embraced it. You must learn to balance what you believe with the foundation of the Israelites."

Ochieng's demeanor changed, and his shoulders drooped. "All right, Baba. You want me to uphold antiquated thinking to preserve the unity of the people. You want them to stay ignorant to the words given to the prophets of God."

"No, that is not what I'm saying. Understand that we are in a tenuous situation right now. Our survival is the most important thing for you to worry about. Internal strife right now will be the end of Beta-Israel."

"What do you want me to do?"

"You must be a man. Your mother and I have chosen a wife for you. Marry her, and then you will be consecrated as chief priest. When I die, you will be crowned king. I want you to remember that the needs of the Jewish kingdom come before your own."

***

Ochieng followed his father's instructions, he married Basha, the woman they chose for him. She was the daughter of another Jewish priest. Although she was young, she was feisty, with an independent streak of her own. Ochieng's parents hoped she would settle some of his divergent notions. Sadly, the marriage didn't last long enough. Basha died giving birth to twin sons, Omondi and Odongo. Ochieng, desperate for consolation and a mother for his sons, married his wife's sister, Nya.

Ochieng grieved for Basha for years, not for the great love they shared but for what he believed it might have been. With that mindset, he treated Nya more like a trusted servant than a wife. It didn't matter that much to Nya. Out of her love for her sister, she was a loving mother to the boys and would have no children of her own.

# Chapter Twelve
# Omandi and Odongo

When Gitonga died, Ochieng finally understood the complexity of being king. Keeping the Jewish kingdom united would have been a challenge under the most ideal circumstances, but under the supervision of outsiders, it was extremely difficult. With all his responsibilities, the education of his sons was his highest priority, and he was committed to instructing them himself. Every morning, Ochieng thanked God for two sons and the blessing that neither would have to juggle spiritual leadership and the politics of ruling. Even when the twins were boys, it was clear to Ochieng that one was wise and the other a warrior.

Omandi, who resembled Basha, was the prudent son. He preferred to spend the bulk of his time studying, and his interests weren't limited to religious Scripture. He was fascinated with history and the economics of trade. He believed that the survival of the Jewish kingdom would be determined by the wealth and the resources of the people. He felt the siphoning off of their resources for war was the reason for their weakness.

Odongo, on the other hand, resembled Ochieng. He was ambitious and spent his time strategizing with the general on how they could reclaim their land and their glory. He was intrigued by the legend of Hannibal and aspired to be as great a warrior. There was no doubt in his mind that the way to unite the Jewish kingdom was to conquer their enemies. To him, it was simple. They were weak because their army was weak.

Nya provided the gentleness in their lives. When they were home with her, the world and all its pressures were left outside. She taught them to laugh, love, and appreciate the small things in life, such as a beautiful bird, a lovely tune, and the taste of a sweet orange. The twins were devastated when Nya died of a stomach ailment when they were 19 years old. To fill the void left in his son's lives, Ochieng chose wives for both of them. Odongo married Lakiara, the daughter of a wealthy land owner; and Omandi married Kess, the daughter of a priest.

Then to prevent any controversy that might develop after his death, Ochieng yielded the throne to Odongo and established Omandi as chief priest. "God brought you into this world together," he told them. "Whatever happens, always stand together as one."

***

Ochieng wanted to give his sons the space to rule and to make their own decisions. He moved out of the castle to a smaller home a short walk away. He enjoyed the quiet and the company of a few animals. He had been in good health up to that point, so they were all somewhat shocked when he suddenly fell ill. Omandi's wife, Kess, offered to help care for him.

"I am a very fortunate man," Omondi said happily. "I have a wife who loves me enough to look after my father."

Kess smiled proudly. "My mother taught me how to mix herbs for healing. She learned how from her grandmother, who was a midwife and a healer." She was about to tell them more when Lakiara swooned. She looked as if she might faint.

"What's the matter?" Odongo chuckled, teasing her. "Are you feeling sick again? My son is troubling his mother even before he's born."

"I'm just a little dizzy," Lakiara answered. "It will pass in a moment."

"Maybe Kess has some herbs for you, too, brother," Odongo joked. "I'm sure there are some herbs and spices that will keep you busy at night. If you don't hurry, my son won't have a playmate."

"Don't worry about that," Omondi told him. "I'm not ready to share my wife with a baby yet. I want her all to myself."

The brothers went back and forth, teasing each other until they finished supper. Kess left the table first. Lakiara rushed after her, tugging on her arm.

"Don't go!" she whispered to her urgently. "I see an empty chair where you sit at the table. There are plenty of servants to care for our father. I can't explain how or why, but you shouldn't leave the castle."

"I'm not afraid. I'll be fine," Kess assured her. "I'll only be gone for a day or two."

"Please, Kess. Maybe you can gather the herbs here and send them to his healer."

"You mustn't worry about me, Lakiara. Rest yourself," Kess said, walking with her to her sleeping quarters. "I'll make something to help you calm your nerves when I come back."

Lakiara didn't sleep that night or the next night. Then they got the message that she was dreading. Ochieng's sickness wasn't just a fever; it was typhus. Two of his servants had been infected, and everyone who had come to the house were forbidden to go out, including Kess. They would have to remain isolated for ten days. Omandi was distraught. They practically had to tie him down to keep him from the house.

"Listen to me, brother. You know as chief priest, you are not allowed to be in contact with death or disease. Father wouldn't want you to come. Go into the synagogue and pray for your wife, for our father, and for the people. That is what you are supposed to do."

Omondi fasted and prayed for seven days. He was prostrate on the floor when they told him that his father had died and Kess was sick with the fever. Many days, Omondi contemplated crossing the line into his father's house. He didn't care if he lived or died. He wanted to go to Kess. She had put herself at risk to help his father. It was Odongo and his continual guidance and support that kept him from joining her.

"She is in God's hands," Odongo said. "He has the power to spare her life. You still have an obligation to the people."

"And what of my obligation to Kess?" he asked. "Doesn't she matter?"

"Yes, of course, she does. And it is God who will deliver her one way or the other. You have always found comfort in the Scriptures. Read of Ezekiel's heartache."

Omandi didn't want to read any Scriptures, and he was tired of prayers that never seemed to be answered. There was nothing to do but wait. For days, he lay in bed, weak from fasting. The pain of his grief was agonizing. When he got word that Kess had died, he picked up his Bible. He turned to Ezekiel 24:15-17. "The word of the LORD came to me: 'Son of man, with one blow I am about to take away from you the delight of your eyes. Yet do not lament or weep or shed tears. Groan quietly; do not mourn for the dead. Keep your turban fastened and your sandals on your feet; do not cover your mustache and beard or eat the customary food of mourners.'"

The words touched Omandi. Through them he heard God speaking to him, and it changed everything. He didn't feel alone or abandoned anymore. He got out of bed, cleaned himself up, dressed in his white priests clothing, tied his turban, and headed to the synagogue to teach.

***

Lakiara confided in Odongo about seeing visions. She told him of a vision where she saw him with both his arms held high, which was a sign of victory. Odongo was elated. This was confirmation of what he already felt was his destiny. As soon as he was declared king, he quickly initiated his plan to strengthen the army. One son from each family was required to join the military, and each family would pay a tax to supply the army with weapons and resources.

Six months after being consecrated as chief priest and three months after Kess's death, Omandi was fighting his own battle. Fear of the emperor's soldiers and the pressure from missionaries were testing the loyalty of the people. It was hard to convince the people to wait for the Lord's deliverance while their lives and livelihood were constantly threatened. So even though Omandi preferred a peaceful solution to the problem, he was encouraged when Odongo suggested that they stand together and present his plan before the people.

They stood side by side on the castle terrace. Omandi spoke first.

"Children of Israel, your petitions have been heard. 'The eyes of the LORD are on the righteous, and his ears are attentive to their cry; Evil will slay the wicked; the foes of the righteous will be condemned,' Psalms 34:15, 21. We have been patient and have waited on the deliverance, and the time has come. I know many of you have been frustrated and discouraged. Others have been tempted to turn away from their beliefs. What I want you to understand in your heart and in your head is that we are stronger together."

Omandi stepped aside, and Odongo stepped forward. "People of Simien, many of you know of the time before our land was invaded. You remember the years of freedom from the oppression of the emperor and his army. I don't have those memories. I've only heard stories of those wonderful days, days where the crops grew tall and wide, when we fished in the seas, and we traded fine goods with people from foreign lands. I want to know those times. I want to live in those days. We must rise up. We are not a fearful people; our faith has brought us across deserts and seas. The time has come for us to fight our enemies. As my brother has told us, we are not alone. God will help us take back our land."

The sight of those two strong young men emboldened the people. They dared to hope that after more than two decades of the Ethiopian emperors ruling over them, things could be different, that they could possibly win against Zara Yaqob. On this point, they were all united. More men, and even women, bravely stepped forward to fight against the invaders.

***

Odongo was a warrior before he was a king, so there was no question that despite the demise of other kings in war, he was going to lead his men into battle. His tactic was to do small attacks to slowly diminish the strength of the emperor's defenses. It began with a revolt against the governor of their province. The element of surprise worked in the Beta-Israel army's favor. The emperor's security forces had grown smaller and more complacent over the years. In their first strike, the commissioner over their city was killed. The other two governors, fearful of reprisal, renounced their positions.

Odongo celebrated his victory and invited all the people to a huge banquet. The Jewish kingdom experienced a level of rejoicing that most of them had only heard about. They danced, sang, feasted, and drank honey wine for days. He stood on a platform before the people to make a formal announcement.

"Beta-Israel, we have much to be thankful for today," Odongo exclaimed with his arms held high. "Twenty-five years after the emperor divided us and took our land, we have taken it back. We have regained what belongs to us."

Lakiara stood to the side just behind him, holding their baby son, Joram. In the midst of ruckus, applause, and cheers, Odongo was crowned king and declared Gideon V.

"This isn't the end, brother," Omandi cautioned, leaning toward him. "You know that Zara Yaqob will come back with a greater army."

Odongo kept his eyes on the people and never stopped smiling. "I'm sure he will. Our soldiers are not resting. We are preparing ourselves to fight the emperor's army."

"There's a chance that we will all be killed," Omandi said solemnly.

"Let the people enjoy themselves," Odongo said, totally composed. "I have a plan. We'll talk about it after the celebration."

Later, after the great meal had been eaten and the crowd had dispersed, Odongo sat alone with his brother.

"I have decided that we must split the kingdom into two groups. The stronger will stay here in Ethiopia to fight. You take the old, the women and children, the priests, and the farmers with you and travel south. There, you will find 'God's resting place.' When we have secured our territory, you can return."

***

Omandi made no argument to Odongo's plan; and after the exhilaration of their victory passed, he organized the trek for any of the people who were willing to pick up their lives and journey to another unknown place. Omandi had his reasons for wanting a fresh start away from his painful memories, but it never occurred to him how many others would line up to leave. More than 10,000 people, with all their possessions, trailed him out of Sena. He presumed that fear of Zara Yaqob and his army was the main motivation.

The plan was to lead the people south along the east coast. Omandi wasn't sure how far they would travel, only that they would walk for 40 days, one day for each of the years they wandered in the wilderness. Omandi thought about all the journeys that the children of Israel had taken, from Egypt to Jerusalem to Babylon to Saba to Axum and down through

Ethiopia. God had guided them, and they found places where they prospered and grew in number. He hoped that this journey would be as successful; and at the end of each day, he prayed himself to sleep, asking God to grant them another land where they could live in peace.

On the fortieth day, Omandi found land for his followers on the interior, near Mombasa. There was grazing land for the sheep, and the cattle would provide plenty of meat, milk, and butter. There was an abundance of food, fowl, and grain. There was rice, fruit, and vegetables. They set up a camp, negotiated over land with the native people there, and began building their new city. Omandi walked their land every day except the Sabbath, blessing the people and lending his hands wherever they were needed.

On one of his long walks, Omandi ventured near the harbor where the merchants traded their goods and conducted business. There was an abundance of grains and fruits growing there. It reminded him of the coast his grandfather used to talk about. There were tall houses of mortar and stone with wooden windows. The people were light, dark, and every shade in between. They moved about on horses. The women dressed in fine garments of silk and wore lots of gold jewelry. No one there looked as if they lacked for anything. Silently, he repeated his last unanswered prayer, that they could find more gold mines so the people could prosper again.

***

It took nine years of battles for the Jewish kingdom to take back all the land they had lost to the Christian kingdom.

Odongo basked in the glow from his victories, while Lakiara was troubled by his eagerness to stage yet another attack. She thought he was being overzealous in his ambition to defeat Zara Yoqab, that they should let peace find its place. Still, Odongo was driven to continue the war. Many nights when he couldn't sleep, he would spend hours disparaging the emperor.

"Zara Yoqab is a fool," Odongo ranted. "He isn't fit to rule Ethiopia. He is paranoid. They say he even fears his wife, and his children are plotting to overthrow him. Everyone knows that he beats all of them. A man of strength doesn't need to put his hand to his own family. He has no honor."

"We have the land. Rest and let things be," Lakiara said, urging him to come to bed.  She was afraid for Odongo. A week earlier, she had another vision where she saw him covered in blood. "Maybe we should all follow Omandi south. Here we are like animals in the forest, waiting to be hunted."

Odongo stomped across the floor. "No, wife, I'm the hunter!" he shouted. "Hiding in fear is death. I won't sit here and wait for him to come for us again. I won't die like that."

"What about our son?" Lakiara asked, trying to bring him to his senses. "You haven't been concerned with his education; he hasn't even learned to read. Who will teach him how to be king?"

"I will teach him myself. I'm Gideon V, and he will be Gideon VI. Why do you worry? I've fought and come home to you many times. I will come back to you again."

Lakiara turned away and shut her eyes. There was nothing she could do or say that would change Odongo's mind. The next day, he summoned his general and ordered him to prepare his army with exercises and new weapons.

For nine years, there were skirmishes between the Beta-Israel forces and the Ethiopian Empire, and another decade passed before Odongo decided to lead his army in a full-fledged attack to defeat Emperor Yara Yaqob's army. It was 1462 when they finally invaded Ethiopia. The clash of the two armies was brutal. Not only did Odongo lose much of his military forces in the battle, he received a severe wound in his right leg. Lame and unable to ride a horse with his injury, Odongo could no longer lead the army.

Having already conquered the Muslims and freed themselves, the Christian Ethiopian Empire again declared war on the Jewish kingdom. For the next seven years, the emperor conducted a massacre of the Jews in the region, pushing them back and shrinking their territory. Then Zara Yaqob directed another military invasion on Beta-Israel in the northwest region. Beta-Israel fought back and was gradually able to restore their mountain kingdom.

Odongo was furious that all the gains he had made were taken back and his people had been pushed further into the mountains. In a meeting with his general, he raged over their losses.

"Many of our people in Begemder have been massacred by the emperor for seven years now. He boasts about how many of our people he has killed. He calls himself the 'Exterminator of Jews.'"

"Our people are safe here," the general said to calm him. "These mountains are our refuge. They are at a disadvantage in attacking us here."

That didn't satisfy Odongo. He wanted revenge for the devastation the emperor caused.

"He will have to pay for what he has done. When it's time, we will come down and claim what's ours."

Odongo stood on the plateau outside his home on the highlands, leaning on his walking stick. On most evenings, you could find him there at sunset, staring out across the land in the direction of his castle. He was sure the emperor was housed there, the place he once took comfort in. It filled him with regrets. This wasn't the life he was born to live. He would have preferred to die with honor on the battlefield. Instead, he would have to settle for the quiet death of an old man. Joram took his place as king of Beta-Israel on the highlands, and Joram had a son named Radi.

***

The other half of Beta-Israel made a life for themselves near Mombasa. Omandi took another wife, and they had a son they named Magana. When Omandi died, Magana became the chief priest and king for the people. His life was different than his father's. There was no castle filled with servants to cook or clean, and he and his mother lived in a stone house with a flat roof. Although Magana was king and chief priest, he didn't dress in fine silks. He only wore the priestly clothes his father wore on the Sabbath. Nor was the bulk of his time spent studying or praying. Through the week, he raised cattle.

His mother chose a wife for him named Amelia. In 1470, their oldest son, Dagna, was born, 14 generations after Beta-Israel ruled Axum with Judith as queen, and the same time that the slave trade engulfed the East African coast. Two years later, their daughter, Olivia, was born. After three more years, they had another son named Jasper.

Even though Magana's sons were born to lead and rule, he raised them without special privileges. They had to work and hunt like all the other young men. He gave them instruction at night by candlelight. He taught them how to read, he taught them the history of their people, and he taught them the rules that governed Israel. He avoided long lessons on the Scriptures, believing they were political and divisive. Instead, Magana thought it better that his sons didn't form opinions until the wars subsided. Jasper had difficulty reading, so he didn't mind that their education was limited; but Dagna read every book he could get his hands on.

Amelia spoiled Olivia. She went to the coast and bought expensive fabrics to make her daughter's clothes and spent hours braiding her hair in elaborate styles that she decorated with beads. Amelia told Olivia, "One day, you will marry a king, so you must look like a princess." When Olivia was older, she joined Amelia on her visits to the coast. They bought gold and silver jewelry and dresses from around the world. It was on one of their buying sprees that Olivia met the son of the sultan, and he gave her a gift of pearls.

When Magana heard of their acquaintance, he ended all their visits to the coast, stating that they were selfish and wasteful. Olivia was strong-willed and wanted the life of wealth and riches that the sultan's son offered her. During worship on the Sabbath, she slipped away and headed to the coast. Magana grieved as if Olivia were dead when he heard that she had married the Arab son of the sultan, an adversary of their people.

Afraid of another betrayal, Magana arranged Dagna's marriage to the daughter of a Levite. Her name was Winta.

She was the perfect complement to Dagna. She was tall and lean, and he was short and stocky. She was calm and easy-going, while he was volatile and moody. The only thing Winta requested was that they have a house of their own, to which they all agreed.

## Chapter Thirteen
# Dagna

In 1498, a giant ship from Portugal landed on the east African coast. It was an ominous sight resting in the harbor. Dagna stared at it for hours, wondering what horror it would bring; and all his premonitions told him it would be more horrible than any other he had seen. For a month, when he woke, his head ached from the frightening scenes that filled his dreams, and he was too sick to get out of bed. His anxieties eased some when the sultan of Mombasa grew suspicious of the foreign vessel and its occupants and ran them off the island. However, on this morning, his feet were jolted to the floor when he heard the booms that sounded as if the earth were cracking beneath them.

In a frenzy, Dagna yelled for his wife. "Winta!" But she didn't answer. Clumsily, he pulled himself up and stumbled outside. "What is going on?" he yelled to the young servant boy sitting oblivious to the noise.

"It's the ship of white men the sultan rejected," the boy replied. "They are shooting back at the harbor."

"It's started!" Dagna said, certain that the evil he dreaded was upon them. "Who are the white men aiming for?" he asked the boy.

"They're attacking the Arab merchant ships on the coast."

"Why would they attack a trading ship? They are unarmed." he mused aloud. "They must be European pirates."

It was no secret that the Muslims had prospered greatly because of the gold on the coast. He figured that they probably came to loot the port of Mombasa for gold. "Have you seen my wife?" he asked, looking around the courtyard.

"No, my priest," the boy answered, scraping a drawing in the dirt.

"Pay attention," he said, waiting for the boy to look up. "I want you to go and get the general. Tell him I need to see him."

The boy jumped up and ran swiftly out of the courtyard, stirring the dust under his feet. Dagna stood and watched him until he was out of sight. Then he sat on a stool in the doorway, listening to the sounds of thunder and lightning that brought no rain. When the bombing ended, he went inside and fell back into bed with a cool cloth on his head. He was sure this wouldn't be the end of the assault, this was only the beginning. No doubt, it was the immense wealth that the coast generated and the gold mines that attracted the foreigners to the area.

***

"Why are you still in bed?" Magana asked, shaking his son out of his sleep. "Are you feeling bad again?"

"It's these awful headaches, Father. And when I do sleep, I have terrible nightmares."

"Well, get up. I suppose you know that the port is under attack."

"Yes, I heard. I thought the Lord was done with us," Dagna said, dragging himself out of bed.

Magana laughed. "Not yet. Winta and my granddaughters aren't here, but she has made some food for you to eat."

"Where are they?" Dagna asked. "I haven't seen them this morning."

"Her sister is in labor, so they are waiting to see the baby. Pull yourself together. Jasper is already with the general, and they are waiting for us."

Dagna ate porridge and eggs and drank some milk before they left in a rush. He struggled to keep up with his father's long strides.

Jasper and the general, Milo, were sitting at the long table in the governor's house when they got there. Being a humble man, Magana had no need or desire for a castle or a palace. He didn't want to rule over his people; he wanted to lead them. Besides, with wars raging all around them, what use would all the time and investment be if they were ultimately pushed off the land.

"What is the situation on the coast?" Magana asked Milo, taking a seat at the head of the table. "Should our forces be alerted?"

Milo leaned forward and folded his hands. "From what I can tell, things have quieted down. The white men were Portuguese. The Sultan denied them entry. In retaliation, they fired on the unarmed Arab merchant ships with heavy cannons and then looted the vessels. For now, it seems they are sailing away."

"You know why they came here, Father," Dagna said tensely. "They want the gold."

"And then they'll want the land," Jasper added.

"The sultan was able to hold them back," Milo said. "Maybe that will be the end of it."

"No," Magana said. "That was a test of the Arabs' strength. The Portuguese will return."

Dagna balled his fists. "Then we must be ready if they come back with reinforcements!"

"Don't be foolish, son," Magana said. "We have no weapons to match theirs. We must wait. This is not our fight. We can only hope that they destroy each other. Your job is to make sure the people look to God and not themselves until we know more."

"And if we can't fight them, should we just sit still and be their slaves?"

"We'll pray together for the answer, son, because I don't know," Magana said sadly.

***

"Why didn't you tell me you were leaving this morning?" Dagna asked Winta when he teetered back into the house in the evening. His head still ached, and she was humming a tune as if nothing had happened. "I was worried sick."

"You hardly slept through the night. I wanted to give you a chance to rest," she answered sweetly. "I took Eleneh and Chuki with me so you wouldn't be disturbed."

"How could I not be disturbed with all the loud rumblings going on? I didn't know if my family had been blown away."

"There you are, exaggerating the danger and being theatrical again!" she said, laughing.

"You don't have to carry my burden, so you can laugh," Dagna said. "Anyway, where are my dear daughters?"

"They wanted to stay with their aunt and help her with the new baby boy."

"Is the child healthy?" Dagna asked.

"Yes, he is beautiful. They have been blessed. Seeing him made me want a son of my own."

"I'm sure the Lord will bless us again," he said, sitting down at the table.

"Certainly, but He must stop your headaches first," she said, teasing him.

Dagna looked over at his wife. She was as beautiful as the day of their wedding; but with all the stress of the fighting and turmoil with the Arabs, he had neglected her. He was always tired from his restless nights that were full of bad dreams. Though she never complained, he wanted to be a better husband.

"Pour me a cup of wine, and rub my head for a while," Dagna said, sounding more relaxed. "I think it will help us to prepare to receive the Lord's blessing."

Winta chuckled as she poured the wine.

***

Two years later, Winta and Dagna were blessed with a son they named Tamru. Before the boy's third birthday, Dagna's headaches started again. The Portuguese had returned to the East African coast to take over the most prosperous port, Kilwa. Magana, Dagna, Jasper, and Milo sat in the governor's house having the same discussion they had had four years prior.

Although Magana sat at the head of the table, he had stepped down as chief priest and leader of the people. With failing health, he had passed most of the responsibilities to Dagna; and Jasper had also taken over more of the duties of the general in heading the military.

"What information do you have for us, Milo?" Magana asked, his voice straining.

"The Portuguese have stated that they are here for their religious principles," Milo answered. "They want to defend Ethiopia from the Islamic Empire."

"I don't believe that!" Dagna snapped. "What they really want is to take control of the gold trade and Christianize the coast."

"How big is their army?" Magana asked.

"Twenty fast ships, with an army of over 1,000 men to capture and loot Kilwa," Jasper reported. "They are well-trained soldiers, protected with body armor and helmets, and equipped with muskets and pistols."

"Will the Arabs be able to hold them off this time?" Magana asked wearily.

Milo answered. "From what we hear, the Arabs shot arrows from bows that reached their mark but were still at a disadvantage. The Portuguese had the canon. With it, they could launch attacks from a distance. Using them, they shot fire into the city and burned more houses than the spies could count."

"The question is, will the Portuguese be satisfied with Kilwa, or will they expand their invasion," Dagna interjected. "We are here in the interior, and there are many other valuable cities along the coast."

"We are in the same position we were in four years ago," Magana said. "If the Arabs can't push them back, what can we do?"

"The Arab sultanates of the coastal towns are weak because of their rivalries and disputes among one another," Milo said.

"The fact that they fail to come together in a united defense works in favor of the Portuguese."

"There is no reason for us to get involved at this time," Jasper said. "The Arabs haven't come to us for help."

Dagna held his aching head in his hands. "If the Muslims don't fight as one empire, these foreigners will take them down one after another.

***

Dagna was right; the Portuguese systematically attacked the city-states along the Swahili Coast with superior military and naval skills. They offered no treaties to the sultans. Instead, the Portuguese captains demanded tributes to the king of Portugal. In 1503, more attacks came to exact Portuguese control and order more tributes. They began with Zanzibar. City after city were attacked and burned, and the people were run off, killed, or enslaved.

In 1505, they pillaged the city of Kilwa, burning it, driving the people away with arrows and bullets, and leaving it in ruins. Only camels and stray animals were left roaming the narrow streets of the town. Between their destructions and pillaging of gold jewelry, silver, copper, precious gems, and pearls, the soldiers abducted dozens of Kilwan women, who they used for their own pleasures. The women refused to return to shore, afraid of retribution from the emir. They were assured that they wouldn't be harmed by him, but they were not guaranteed that they would be accepted by their families if they had been baptized Christian.

The Portuguese built a fortress in Kilwa and another at
their regional headquarters in Sofala. Arab merchant ships were
seized on the coast and ransomed for gold. One by one, the
city-states submitted to the Portugese; and in only eight years,
they dominated the Swahili Coast and the trade routes from
there to India. They crushed most of the resistance until they
got to Mombasa, where the sultan refused to pay tributes. The
Portuguese punished the city; but when they were not able to
colonize it, they burned through it, taking 200 slaves of mostly
women and children.

Jasper and Milo delivered more reports to Dagna about all the
violence and treachery acted on their nemesis along the coast. It
was reminiscent of the torture Beta-Israel had suffered when the
Arabs had invaded and had taken the coasts from them. It would
not have bothered Dagna, except trade on the port had declined
and his own people were miserable and hurting financially. He
hadn't traveled to Mombasa in years, but he decided to ride there
with Jasper to see the extent of the damage done.

Dagna's head hurt to see what had happened to the
prosperous city that used to be bustling with people and trade.
The once-sturdy streets and single-storied terraced houses
made of coral had crumbled. Like many of the other prominent
coastal towns, Mombasa was reduced to ashes and debris.
There was no food or crops, and the few people left living there
were starving. Oppressed by the cruel Portuguese, they called
them Afriti, meaning "the devil."

Dagna bowed his head and prayed, "'Jabez cried out to the God
of Israel, "Oh, that you would bless me and enlarge my territory!
Let your hand be with me, and keep me from harm so that I will be
free from pain." And God granted his request,' 1 Chronicles 4:10."

***

Over the next 20 years, Dagna and Winta had the joy of seeing their children grow, marry, and have children of their own. They also had the sorrow of burying Magana and Jasper. Tamru, who was more like Jasper than his father, was a soldier in the army. When he learned that his father's great-uncle Odongo's half of Beta-Israel, the Simien kingdom near Lake Tana, was in a perilous position, he wanted to join them in the fight. He broached the subject in the next council meeting.

"We gather here as the leaders of Beta-Israel," Tamru said, beginning his argument. "As you all know, our brothers in the Simien kingdom are vulnerable; they are caught between two pillars of fire. As we are one people, should we not support our brother?"

"Are you suggesting financial resources or military assistance?" Milo asked.

"It doesn't matter. We have barely recovered from the chaos brought across the sea by the Portuguese," Dagna remarked in his attempts to discourage his son.

Tamru ignored his comment. "The iman of Adal declared an Islamic holy war on Christian Ethiopia. Dawit II's military is weak right now. If the Christian kingdom is conquered, there would be no barrier between them and the Muslim invaders."

"That has been the situation for a long time, son," Dagna offered. "What is your point?"

Tamru couldn't believe his father's lack of interest. "How can you expect me to do nothing while our people are being pitted against their two adversaries, the Abyssinian Christians and the Abyssinian Muslims?"

"You remind me of myself before you were born," Dagna told him with a sigh. "My father had to subdue me as well."

"This may be the time for our people to reunite as one while your cousin Joram is king," Tamru pressed. "The Ethiopian military is weak right now. Their intense religious war with the Muslims has them landlocked. Since they cannot trade freely, they don't have access to modern muskets and shields and have not been able to improve their military skills."

"Maybe it's time for our people to choose a new alliance," Dagna said to Milo. "For almost 50 years, they have had a pact with the Ethiopian Empire, declaring our independence in the Simien Mountains and around Lake Tana. It is obvious that the emperor's military cannot stand up to the Islamic attacks. I think it would be in our best interests to align ourselves with the Muslims."

"Are you proposing that we join them in the fight against the Portuguese?" Milo asked. "That would be suicide!"

"The Portuguese are pushing the Arabs closer to our territory," Dagna responded. "They stand between us and the foreigners. We should make some kind of treaty with them."

"And how do we do that?" Milo asked.

"First, we could offer our support to the Islamic Empire," Dagna told him.

"It probably won't mean much. Without cannons and pistols, what will our help amount to?"

"Get a message to Joram, and extend the offer," Dagna said.

Milo and his entourage traveled back to the Simien kingdom and spoke with Joram's general. They agreed to request an alliance and propose support to Ahmad in the war, except the sultan rejected their offer and attacked their troops. Many of the soldiers were killed, and Milo was wounded.

Two years later, Ahmad Gragn and his army marched across Ethiopia, destroying churches, ransacking riches, occupying cities, and sowing chaos. They invaded the highlands, burning monasteries and converting Christians to Islam by force. Muslim governors were put in place to rule the countryside previously under the Christian kingdom. In turn, the Ethiopian Empire continued to fight and press against Beta-Israel, and the Jewish kingdom suffered substantial losses in their economy and territory.

***

Dagna and the rest of the Beta-Israel province near Mombasa were disheartened to hear the fate of the Simien kingdom. On the Sabbath, Dagna did his best to lift the people's spirits.

"Children of Israel, God has blessed us in this place. We were compelled to leave Lake Tana and the resources that sustained us there, though the ground is soaked with our blood. They built monasteries and then mosques on our land, but the Lord provided another place for us, and we have prospered here. Yet evil abounds in this world, and the peace and prosperity we have found is in danger. There is a new enemy coming to invade our land. Foreigners rule on the land that once belonged to us. There is always a thief lurking about, ready to steal your blessing. We have seen them take over the island city of Kilwa from the sultan. They tore it down to nothing, and they've built a fortress on it. Now the Arabs have brought them here. We know what they want. They say they want to bring Christianity here, but Christianity has been here for 1,000 years. What they really want is to take control of the gold mines and trade. The Arabs push us, but we refuse to be pushed aside again. We will watch them fight against the Portuguese as we stood aside and watched Islam fight against the Christians. We have run for the last time. If they force our hands, we will fight, and we will be the victors."

The people cheered and rejoiced. Dagna sang and cheered with them; but on the inside, he knew this moment of joy would not last. There was a lot at stake.

That evening after supper, Dagna laid in the bed, his head pounding like drum.

Winta did her best to try to comfort him. "As you said, we have been blessed here, and we are at peace now. There's no reason to spoil today worrying about the trials of tomorrow."

"The Jewish kingdom is diminished, dear wife. They've taken our land on the mountains, and we're pressed here away from the coast, unable to trade."

"That's the results of war, my love. Both sides suffer in the fight, but one side gains, and the other loses. In our history, we have been the victor and the conquered. We also killed for territory and resources when we went into Jericho."

"We must win at all costs!" Dagna said, deaf to her reasoning.

"We don't have the army that your cousins had in Ethiopia, and they were defeated," Winta told him. "You don't have the right to sacrifice your people!"

"Why would God begrudge me to bring down those who wrong me if He does the same?" he asked.

"You can't put yourself on God's level," Winta replied.

That night, Dagna had another dream of his people laid out head to foot, side by side, wailing and writhing in misery. When he woke, he frantically recounted his dream to Winta, determined to do what so many of the other kings and chief priests did: multiply and raise an army.

"You're an old man now, Dagna," she said, shaking her head. "Our time is almost done, and you have done nothing to prepare Tamru to do anything but fight. He has a son who is following in his footsteps. The people barely worship anymore. If you go back to the Scriptures, you will see that Israel suffered when they were disobedient. Your legacy is to protect and to teach the word to the people. We only have the remnants of the original ark, but the word is still complete. Teach Tamru, and teach his baby son, Theodore, so that our people will be blessed."

"You're right again, Winta," Dagna sighed, closing his eyes.

***

Dagna did his best to do what Winta advised him to do to prepare his son, though Tamru, more often than not, found excuses not to be present. However, Theodore was a good student and promised Dagna that he would protect the precious pieces of wood that were left from the ark. He assured Dagna that one day he would rebuild the ark and place it in a magnificent temple. Dagna would never see that day. A few weeks later, something burst in his head. He fell into a hard sleep and never woke up.

In that same year, 1543, the people learned that Joram, king of the Simien kingdom, had been killed in his bed by Ethiopian troops led by Gelwadewos, the son of Dawit II. Joram's murder was in retaliation against the people of Beta-Israel for switching their alliance in the war.

Joram's son, Radi, was a soldier in the Jewish army. Always surrounded by war, he had never known what it was like to live in peace. He was away leading troops in the defense of the Simien Mountains when the region near Lake Tana was attacked. When he heard of his father's death, he cursed Gelawdewos.

"What is Gelawdewos thinking?" Radi ranted angrily. "He spills the blood of his own people because of Christ. That doesn't make any sense. He should know that this is about gold and resources. What kind of courage does it take to kill an old man in his bed? They could have let him die in peace. For killing my father, I promise you that they will pay a high price."

The Ethiopian Empire did pay a high price, but it wasn't from Radi's hands. Gelawdewos, exuberant from his conquests, followed up with a six-month attack against the Abyssinian Muslims. Gelawdewos was shot down by a bullet; and while he laid helpless, the mounted troops gored him with their spears until he died, severed his head, and sent it to the sultan of Ifat.

Radi was crowned king of Beta-Israel; and as he promised, he sought his revenge against the Ethiopian Empire, now ruled by Gelawdewos's brother, Menas. He strengthened his forces in the Simien Mountains and battled against Menas's troops in the region south of the kingdom. Accustomed to the rough and rugged mountains, they benefited from their position and defeated the Ethiopian Empire military. With a recovered army, Sarsa Dengel, the son of Menos, waged a 17-year crusade against Beta-Israel, invading their stronghold in the Simien Mountains.

In the first attack in 1580, Beta-Israel was overwhelmed but survived. Radi was taken prisoner. The emperor gave him the choice: "If you convert to Christianity, we will spare your life."

Radi refused to submit. "No, I have no reason to bow to you. You're not my God. If it makes you more holy, then kill me."

Radi had a brother, Caleb, who escaped capture when the family was sent into exile in Waj. Caleb led another insurrection. Caleb's forces rolled stones down on their enemies, who tried to climb the mountain. The king had to delay their advance up into the highlands. They opted to fire cannons up into the peaks. Caleb's army was attacked on all sides, and none were left alive,

Sarsa Dengel returned to the Simien province in 1585. At the end of the assault, their beloved king, Goshen, was executed. Crushed and downcast, many of his soldiers and Israelites committed mass suicides.

***

The only thing Winta's intuition was wrong about was Theodore following in his father's footsteps. He had no desire to be a warrior. He refused to train in the military and hated everything about it. As a boy, he saw it as a rival to his father's attention. Whenever Tamru was away fighting in some battle, Theodore was so nervous that he would be killed that he could not speak without stuttering. Ultimately, Tamru was killed; and when Theodore became king and chief priest, he sent the soldiers home to their families.

"The time has come to strengthen our faith instead of the military," Theodore admonished them. When his son, Jabori, was born, he raised him to value preservation over confrontation.

There were numerous objectors and detractors who disapproved of Theodore's leadership and his opinion that building up their army kept them at war, and his assistant priest was one of them. He and a growing number of supporters believed a sovereign nation must always maintain a strong army.

Over the next three decades, Beta-Israel was able to maintain their independence, but they didn't have peace. There was a restlessness that surrounded them, and it kept the people on edge and uncomfortable. It was a constant state of anxiousness, the feeling that something, most likely bad, was going to happen. It's during those times of uncertainty that survival instincts came to the forefront. Neighbors turned against one another, worshipers turned against their spiritual leader, and subordinates ceased to be loyal to the king. So, when Theodore disappeared, there was much speculation and many suspects relating to his plight, including his assistant priest, Wasaki.

# Chapter Fourteen
# Jabori

Jabori was not yet 20 when he had to step into his father's position, but he was mature beyond his years. Despite his suspicions, and partially because of them, he chose Wasaki's daughter, Gasira, for his bride, noting the African proverb that said, "Keep your friends close, but remember to keep your enemies closer." So even though his intentions were more strategic than sentimental, he fell deeply in love with Gasira.

As far as a ruler of the people, Jabori considered himself to be more of a spiritual leader and protector than a king, and it saddened him to watch the lives of his people deteriorate. The Jewish kingdom had been destabilized with trade cut off and their territory diminished. But the most dangerous threats to them were from Christians and Muslims proselytizing among the people. He was certain that the answer to their predicament wasn't a military one. They needed more than the strength of an army to battle all the enemies. They needed the help of almighty God.

For long hours each day, Jabori searched his Bible for the words to deliver to the people to keep them encouraged. And through the night, with only the sound of his wife's breathing while she slept, he prayed for deliverance.

"Come to bed," Gasira whispered, when she woke from his stirring. "Nothing is going to change between now and the morning."

"I'm on my knees, dear wife, because everything can change at any moment. The Muslim assaults against the Portuguese are becoming more intense. There will be a shift soon, and we are not prepared for that."

Gasira pounded the bed with her heel in frustration. "The Muslims haven't been able to get rid of the white foreigners; they still control the coastal cities. How long do we have to wait for these invaders of our land to kill each other and leave us in peace? We have been trapped in this quicksand for too long. Sometimes I agree with my father. Maybe it would be better to fight than to sit here and pray for the Lord to give us the victory."

Jabori didn't respond, except to pray Psalm 3:

"Lord, how many are my foes! How many rise against me! Many are saying of me, 'God will not deliver him.' But you, Lord, are a shield around me, my glory, the One who lifts my head high. I call out to the Lord, and he answers me from his holy mountain. I lie down and sleep; I wake again, because the Lord sustains me. I will not fear though tens of thousands assail me on every side. Arise, Lord! Deliver me, my God! Strike all my enemies on the jaw; break the teeth of the wicked. From the Lord comes deliverance. May your blessing be on your people."

Then he got up from the floor. But before he got into the bed, he said, "Gasira, you must think of yourself as my wife more than your father's daughter. I don't want to hear his opinions in the room where I sleep. As king and chief priest, I can't think of what would be better for me or you. I have to think of Beta-Israel. When we fought against the emperor, we were nearly destroyed. If we are to survive as a people, we can't suffer an attack like that again."

"Forgive me, husband," Gasira said, sliding over to allow him more room.

***

Six months later, in 1585, Somali Muslims and the Turkish Empire joined forces to liberate Mombasa, along with other coastal cities that had been colonized from the Portuguese. Unwilling to give up easily, the Portuguese military rained bombs on the city in their attempt to regain control. Jabori was more worried after the battle.

"You have been a fool!" Wasaki said, berating him. "If you hadn't kept us from creating a ready military, we would be able to take advantage of the weakness of the Muslims. This will be a missed opportunity for our people to reclaim our land and to control the port."

"I'm no fool!" Jabori shouted, standing his ground. "This war has raged for nearly a century; and if you think it's over, then you are the fool! Don't forget that there is always pain and suffering when the enemy is attacked. And even if you defeat him, there will be damages."

Wasaki stormed out more angry with himself than Jabori. He should have eliminated the son as well as the father. He was as weak as Theodore or worse. Yet the more he thought about it, he realized that the situation had worked in his favor. Jabori was well-loved by the people, and if anything suspicious happened to him, the people might reject another leader—except for possibly the father of his grieving widow. The only question that remained was when and how.

Wasaki's first thought was to put poison in Jabori's food, but he was fearful that his daughter might inadvertently be affected. Then he considered an accident while hunting, but that wasn't feasible. Jabori never hunted. Wasaki knew that there was no one else to assist him. He had no allies or anyone he could trust. Still, the biggest challenge of his plan was to get Jabori out of his areas of protection and away from witnesses. For months, it seemed an impossible task, and Wasaki was growing impatient. Then on a hunt with his brother, he discovered the perfect mode to get what he wanted. Although, the groundwork would be a bit risky, in the end, it would be simple and unquestionable.

For two days, Wasaki scoured the woodlands to find a bush viper among all the vermin in the forests. He used a fishing net to trap it, and then he stuffed it into a sack. The next challenge was to bring his weapon of choice past all Jabori's safeguards at the synagogue. A creature of habit, Jabori always went into the synagogue alone for prayer after he was finished teaching his students. That would be the perfect opportunity to bring his plan to fruition.

Wasaki's heartbeat quickened from the adrenaline rushing through it as he eased along the side of the synagogue, slipped inside, and tossed the open bag onto the floor near the altar. The cloth of the bag moved just as Wasaki crept out and closed the door. He strolled home, satisfied that he would soon be the leader that Beta-Israel required to regain its standing.

Too excited to eat, he skipped supper that evening and sat outside his house to wait for the wailing. But hours later, the night sounds remained hushed. He sat there all night until the sun rose into the quiet. What could have happened? Hadn't

Jabori's dead body been discovered? Could Jabori have perhaps gone home without saying his usual evening prayers at the synagogue? Wasaki took a deep breath to gather himself and waited a few more hours until the suspense became unbearable. With swift long strides, he headed to the synagogue.

Wasaki slowed his pace as he passed the students outside, talking among themselves. Then he crept toward the synagogue's entrance. He saw that the door was slightly cracked. Cautiously, he pushed it open and saw Jabori lying prostrate on the floor. He smiled as he turned to run for help. But, out of the corner of his eye, he saw something move. It sprung on him and bit him on the leg behind his knee. Wasaki screamed, and Jabori jumped up from the floor just in time to see the yellow and black-speckled snake writhe and slither out the door.

"Wasaki!" Jabori yelled, rushing over to his side. "Have you been bitten?"

"Yes, you fool! Can't you see I'm bleeding?" Wasaki shrieked. "Get the mganga!"

Jabori ran out to summon his students and send them off to find the witch doctor. Back inside, he tore his robe and used the strip of cloth for a tourniquet to cut the circulation off above Wasaki's knee.

"My head is bursting," Wasaki cried out from the pain. Perspiration soaked his robe.

Jabori began to pray for him, asking God to be merciful. The mganga came, and the men carried Wasaki to Jabori's home, where the mganga worked on him for two days, with Gasira at his side. It was no use. Wasaki died an agonizing death.

Gasira was distraught over losing her father, mourning for months, but Jabori was subdued. He was disturbed by some of Wasaki's delirious rantings as he drifted in and out of consciousness. Though he never mentioned it to Gasira, Jabori was convinced that Wasaki had killed his father, Theodore, and had planted the snake in the synagogue to get rid of him, too. Just when they reached the point when Gasira's weeping over the "great man" her father had been and her resentment over Jabori's indifference threatened to tear them apart, Gasira learned that she was pregnant.

***

Meanwhile, Jabori had been right about the damages that war leaves. The defenses of the port cities were weakened by the attacks against the Portuguese, leaving a breach for the Zimba to gain entry. Driven by drought, disease, and famine, the Zimba were marauders, bandits who rambled from one place to another, raiding and plundering. Not only that, they were cannibals. Over the next two years, 5,000 to 10,000 Zimba made their way up the east coast. Port after port suffered the same fate. When they reached Kilwa, the sought-after village was completely destroyed, and the Zimba ate 3,000 people who weren't fortunate enough to escape into the forests.

Seven months passed, and Jabori felt the pressure of his position to an extent he had never experienced before. The hazards they faced were no longer hypothetical; they were real and moving closer every day. It would only be a matter of time before the Zimba made their way up the coast into Mombasa. He couldn't just be still; he had to lead the people. He stood outside the synagogue before his congregation and read 2 Chronicles 7:13-14.

"Children of Israel, these are the words of our Lord, 'When I shut up the heavens so that there is no rain, or command locusts to devour the land or send a plague among my people, if my people are called by my name, will humble themselves and pray and seek my face and turn from their wicked ways, then I will hear from heaven, and I will forgive their sin and will heal their land.'

"Today we are in the path of human locusts. They will devour us and all we have. If we are to survive, we must move to the hinterlands for safety. Some of you might be determined to stand tall and defend what we have, and I admire your resolve. The reality is that we don't have enough men or weapons to fight the Zimba. It is your choice to decide. I can't force anyone to believe me or to follow me.  My trust in is the Lord; He is our deliverer. All He asks is that we be obedient to Him and the laws He has given to us. He has always provided us with a place where we can thrive. There is no reason to doubt that will continue. We must migrate south and inland away from the coastal clashes and Islamic influence. Those who trust in His word, prepare yourselves and your families to leave this place in three days."

The crowd was stunned into silence. They were tired of wandering like lost sheep. Even so, they knew Jabori was a righteous man who spoke the truth. So the process for them to migrate again began.

***

On the third day, Gasira was more anxious as she watched Jabori sift through things they would need and things that would be left behind. The birth of their baby was close, and she was terrified of having her labor begin in the middle of nowhere. A fear of snakes had gripped her after watching her father suffer and die after being bitten.

"Can't we wait until the child is born?" Gasira asked, grasping her heavy belly in panic.

"No, we can't," he answered calmly. "We must move now, united as one people for protection."

Gasira shook her head. "I don't think I can make it. Leave me here with the midwife, and we will find you when the baby is here safely."

"I could never leave you. I'll be beside you, Gasira. There's nothing to worry about."

Her head fell back as her eyes rolled. "If there wasn't anything to worry about, we wouldn't be running away with our belongings on our backs."

"I'll say it again for the hundredth time: Trust God, and trust me."

Jabori tucked Gasira in a small cart packed with all the things precious to them, including the broken pieces of wood from the ark. Pulled in the cart by a donkey, she trailed behind her husband, who rode high on his horse. She looked around at the mass of men, women, and children making this journey. Some rode on donkeys, some in wagons pulled by oxen, and others on horses. Most walked burdened down with all they could carry. The stench of livestock thickened the air around them.

It was a treacherous march as they moved further away from Mombasa, most done in the early morning hours and the evenings until the dark of night. The earth below their feet turned from moist to dry as they moved through the forests to the rangeland. On the ninth day of their trek moving through the wilderness, Gasira's pains began.

"The baby is coming!" she yelled to Jabori. "We have to stop!"

They were in an expanse of bushland inhabited by wild animals, and the sun was beginning to fade. Jabori stopped and scanned the area and kept moving for another mile. Then he instructed his cousin to keep going until they reached the clearing. He guided the donkey up a small hill, with the midwife and her daughter beside them.

Gasira's labor wasn't particularly difficult. It was her fear of being in the open elements that magnified her pain. She was so horrified that something crawling in the darkness would harm her baby that she refused to push.

"I promise you that I won't let anything happen to you or the baby," Jabori said to coax her. "If you don't listen to the midwife, you are going to make things worse."

She calmed down some and began to push; and before midnight, she gave birth to a son. Jabori wrapped their child in the cloth from his turban, and they named him Chilemba. Early the next morning, they came down the hill to join the people who waited a few miles ahead.

They traveled four more days and stopped on lowland that was scarcely populated with nomads raising cattle and goats.

"This is where we will camp," Jabori told them, hesitant to declare this as a permanent home for the Israelites. "Only God knows how long we will be here. Make it your home as best you can. As the Lord said, 'The land shall not be sold

for ever: for the land is mine, for ye are strangers with me,'
Leviticus 25:23."

***

Sitting inside their makeshift hut, Jabori watched Gasira
nursing their baby and contemplated how they had come to this
point. Her clothes were tattered, and she looked thin. She was
his queen, and she should have been dressed in fine silks, with
her hair adorned. She and his son deserved a soft place to lay
their heads. He looked down at his worn-out shoes and dirty
feet. They were the shoes and feet of a wanderer, not the chief
priest.

"We can't stay here, Gasira," he said loudly, startling her.
"The ground is too dry to put down roots. This earth will never
give us enough food. A tree without strong roots is weak and
easily toppled. I pray every day that we can go back."

"You have forgotten the place we left. We were surrounded
by invaders and war. At least we are at peace here."

"There is nothing here for us. How can we thrive? We were
a prosperous nation; we generated great wealth for ourselves.
We lived in castles and homes or coral and rock. This is not the
place for God's chosen people."

"It seems we were chosen to suffer. How many times have
our people had to flee the lands that have been promised to
us?"

"I'm the chief priest, so I must look to the Scriptures.
Joshua tells us that the sons of Israel walked 40 years in
the wilderness until those who refused to listen to the Lord
perished."

"It's been 40 generations or more, and we are still walking in the wilderness."

"There are reasons for our suffering. The Scripture tells us, 'We have not obeyed the LORD our God or kept the laws He gave us through His servants the prophets. All Israel has transgressed Your law and turned away, refusing to obey You. Therefore the curses and sworn judgments written in the Law of Moses, the servant of God, have been poured out on us, because we have sinned against You,' Daniel 9:10-11. We haven't worshiped in the way God commanded us to. We have broken His commandments. For us to receive His blessings and protection, we have to renew our commitment to being obedient to God's laws."

"And how do you plan to do that?" Gasira asked, kissing the baby's hand. Many before you have tried and failed."

"We priests have tried to adjust to the people's wishes to entice them to worship and tithe. Now we must try to please God. That means we must go back to our beginning, the word given to Moses on that mountain. That's how I'm going to raise Chilemba to teach and lead."

"I can't think that far. Just get me to a place where the rain won't refuse to come."

"That I can promise, dear wife," Jabori said, staring down at his son.

***

The Zimba made their way to Mombasa in the spring of 1589. A multitude of 20,000 ambushed the coveted town and hunted down and ate everything that walked, crawled, or slithered in their path: men, women, children, oxen, cows, goats, dogs, cats, lizards, and insects. They killed every living thing that didn't escape into the woods or take their own lives in the sea, including Turks, Muslims, and natives. Then they continued north on their murderous rampage.

They met strong resistance in Malinda. It was the Segeju tribe, Bantu-speaking warriors, who put an end to their storm of slaughter. Only 100 or less of the Zimba survived. In the midst of the devastation, the Portuguese took over Mombasa for a third time.

The annihilation of the cannibals cleared the way for Jabori and his people to return to the place they called home. Even so, he wanted to preserve the identity of the group that journeyed with him. He decided they should use the name *Lemba* to refer to themselves.

Jabori addressed his people before they began the trek back. "Lemba people, there isn't much for us to go back to. Most of our city has been destroyed, but we are strong, and we can rebuild," he told them. "The Portuguese invaders still control Mombasa, along with the East African coast, so we will return to the same obstacle to our growth and stability, but we will not be dissuaded. The Lord will deliver us from that adversary as well. And more important, we must be obedient to God's word. We must keep the commandments and laws given to us."

There were no objections. The people's faith in God and Jabori had grown strong through their ordeal. For nearly a year, they had little else to hold on to.

***

The journey was much easier on the return because they knew their destination. But for some reason, Jabori was more worried about Chilemba being carried on Gasira's back than he did when she carried him in her womb. It was probably because the burden of his safety was on him now. After 14 days, they were back on the hinterland near Mombasa. Seeing the devastation of their city was disheartening, but the land was a foundation for them to rebuild their nation economically and spiritually.

Determined to obey God's laws, hold onto their identity, and remain independent, Jabori discouraged intermarriage. They celebrated Passover, and all males were circumcised. He insisted the Lemba maintain their strict laws of purity and refrain from eating pork and that they only eat meat slaughtered by a Lemba priest.

Nevertheless, violence surrounded them. Jabori cautioned his Lemba people to stay away from the coast. They were to hunt in groups and not allow anyone to infiltrate their territory. When Jesuit missionaries came to their territory to Christianize them, the Lemba were suspicious of their intentions and killed them.

The years went by quickly, and Jabori did his best to prepare Chilemba to lead the people. They studied Scriptures together and performed the rituals of high priests side by side. Although Chilemba acquired his father's commitment to the laws handed to Moses, he embraced the whole Bible, not just the Old Testament. He did not rebel or make it a point of contention between him and Jabori, understanding the importance of the people being on one accord. He became fond of a girl named Hamisi. Jabori and Gasira gave him their approval of her as his wife. The wedding was an opportunity for the Lemba people to celebrate their survival. Chilemba and Hamisi were blessed with a son in 1617, and they named him Faraji.

Chilemba held his son in his lap and looked into his eyes. He wondered if his life would be any different from his own—born in a time of war, never lived in a house of stone, or knelt in a place of peace. Only time would tell.

# Chapter Fifteen

# Chilemba and Faraji

Power and control over Mombasa had passed back and forth between the Portuguese and the Arabs for 30 years, and neither of them bothered to disguise their motives behind religion along the Swahili Coast. They openly battled over control of the slave trade. Several times, after Jabori died, Chilemba considered leading the Lemba people away from the coast, returning back to the Simien Mountains and reuniting with Beta-Israel. But each time, Hamisi would announce that she was expecting a child. Gasira fretted and badgered Chilemba with the story of how she had had to give birth to him on a hill in the wilderness. Only then would he back away from any plans for migrating.

Chilemba dismissed the idea entirely after he learned that the Portuguese were colonizing in the Simien Mountain region as well with the same ruse: preaching the religion of Catholicism while they exploited Africans. They offered them cloth, copper, and cowry shells with one hand and stole their resources with the other. When Emperor Susenyos declared Roman Catholicism as the official religion of the state and all other religions were condemned, Chilemba knew that the Lemba people could never return to Ethiopia.

Regrettably, Chilemba later realized that it would have been best for the whole Jewish kingdom to have migrated south after the emperor's forces attacked the Simien region and crushed the remaining people of Beta-Israel in 1624. Susenyos ordered all Israelite men killed and their wives and children sold into slavery. Some were forcibly baptized. He confiscated their land, burned all their writings and religious books, and forbade Judaism to be practiced in Ethiopia.

Nevertheless, time brought more changes to all of Africa. Slave-trading posts ran along the whole Swahili Coast of Africa. With more years behind him than in front, Chilemba prayed for the knowledge and insight to prepare Faraji to lead the Lemba amidst all the fluctuations that encircled their city. For more than 1,000 years, religious wars had been the greatest threat to most of the tribes; the new danger was from the burgeoning slave trade.

Why were they continuously prosecuted or victimized? Chilemba did not understand how, when, or where, but the Israelites must have been disobedient, and the punishments of the Lord were upon them. It had been written in the Scriptures he read over and over, Deuteronomy 28:68, "Then the LORD will ship you back to Egypt in ships, a journey I promised you would never need to make again; there you will offer to sell yourselves as slaves—but no one will buy you." There was no question Egypt had been slavery for his people.

Chilemba spent hours each day wondering what kind of leader the people would need in order to escape the fate he feared. Would they need a deliverer like Moses, a conqueror like Joshua, or a king and defender like David? But these times were like no other. There was nowhere to escape the cataclysm that engulfed them; Africans of every tribe were being taken as prisoners from Kenya, Tanzania, Mozambique, and the island of Madagascar. The Lemba needed to be prepared for the onslaught of evil. It became clear to Chilemba: He and Faraji would have to be like Jeremiah.

***

After the sun rose and Chilemba finished his morning prayer, he shook Faraji from his sleep.

"Wake up, son, we have much to do today."

Faraji sat up and rubbed his eyes. "Where are we going, Baba?"

"We are going to the synagogue. It's time you learn how to care for your sheep. A good shepherd rises at dawn."

"We don't have sheep, Baba," Faraji replied, confused.

"Yes, we do son," Chilemba said, taking him by the hand. "There is no time to waste."

Outside their hut, Hamisi was preparing bread for the morning meal. She was surprised to see Chilemba pulling Faraji behind him so early in the day.

"Why have you wakened the boy?" she asked, slightly annoyed.

"From now on, he will go with me. He will begin his lessons to be the Lemba leader."

Hamisi got up from her knees. "Faraji is only seven years old. Let him be a child for as long as he can. That's the only indulgence we can provide him."

"Unfortunately, there is no time for him to be a child; he must be ready for whatever tomorrow brings our people."

"Chilemba, let the boy be! You're going to scare him with all that talk."

"I'm not the one for him to be afraid of. Terrible things are happening around us, and we cannot protect him."

Hamisi's shoulders dropped in resignation. "Give your mama a kiss, son." She bent down to give him a hug and brushed her cheek against his lips. "The child is hungry," she said. "Give him a minute to eat."

"I'll get him something at the market," Chilemba said, steering Faraji out of the courtyard.

Faraji skipped to keep up with his father's long stride, taking in all the sights around him. It wasn't often that he got to leave the security of their home. At the market, he stared at all the foods and absorbed the noise of the people and animals bustling in the square.

"These are our people, son. One day you will be the father of all of them. You must make sure they listen and obey God's word."

"I don't think I'm old enough to do that much, Baba," Faraji said, wide-eyed.

Chilemba stopped walking and squatted down in front of his son. "Long ago there was a very special prophet in Jerusalem. He was the son of the high priest, Hilkiah. When he was just a boy, God spoke to him and told him, 'Do not say that I am too young.' He told him that He would put the words the people needed to hear in his mouth. Those words were to warn them of the hardships that would come to them. And then in His mercy, those words explained to them how to survive those rough times. That's the work we have before us."

"I will do my best," Faraji said, holding tightly to his father's hand.

***

Ten years passed, and still there was no peace on the Swahili Coast or in the interior. Tribal and religious wars escalated with the desire for guns. More guns meant more protection. Prisoners of war were captured during tribal conflicts, and those kidnapped by black slave traders were taken from the interior and marched to the coasts, where they were sold for more guns. The trek was hundreds of miles, and countless Africans died before they even reached the port.

Trading slaves became a lucrative business among the tribes, even African kings and merchants participated. They craved the merchandise of the Europeans that included guns and ammunition. To satisfy their desires, they captured and sold their subjects, nobles, and even members of their own family.

Chilemba did everything he could to discourage the Lemba from succumbing to the temptation. He warned them from the Scriptures each Sabbath, "'If someone is caught kidnapping a fellow Israelite and treating or selling them as a slave, the kidnapper must die. You must purge the evil from among you,' Deuteronomy 24:7." Still, they were in danger of outsiders provoking clashes to take them as prisoners to be sold.

"I think we need to have our own military to defend the people," Faraji told his father after the worship service. "We have not had an army for a long time, but this is a different day. We may not have to fight against the Arabs and the Portuguese, but we have to be able to guard ourselves from the other tribes."

Chilemba knew the Lemba were susceptible and needed protection. "I can't argue against that logic. You have excelled in your studies and have become a wise young man. I think the time is coming for you to stand beside me as my assistant priest."

"I'm ready, Baba," Faraji said, smiling proudly.

"Are you also ready to become a husband and have a family of your own?"

Faraji cleared his throat. "I think so. There is someone I believe will be a good wife for me."

Chilemba laughed. "You have quite a bit on your mind today."

"Yes, Baba," Faraji said, chuckling. "You always tell me that there is no time to waste."

Faraji eagerly began working to build an army with one of the elders who had been a warrior. In the meantime, he married Salene, the lovely girl who had caught his eye. They had two children, a daughter, Kioni, and a son, Abdalla.

As the firstborn, Kioni was spoiled and treated like a princess by both sides of the family. Eight years later, when Abdalla was born, he received much of the attention that once belonged to her, and Kioni felt pushed aside. So, before he could even speak, Kioni resented Abdalla's existence, wishing he would disappear. As time went by, she grew into a stunning young woman; and like a fox, her comeliness belied her cunning ways.

Abdalla was nurtured by the whole community. He grew as tall and sturdy as a yellow-wood tree, possessing all the vitality and strength that his father and grandfather had gradually lost over the years. He became a great speaker in volume and substance. The people marveled at his presence and loved to hear his preaching. As their province grew, there was talk that Abdalla might be king.

When Kioni came of age, knowing she was headstrong and outspoken, Faraji and Salene arranged a marriage with an athletic young man in their tribe named Kondo, the son of a merchant. He was also a warrior in the Lemba army. They figured that he would be strong enough to tame their daughter a bit. However, they miscalculated her shrewdness. Kioni saw him as the other half of her future kingdom, where only she deserved to rule.

Abdalla married the prettiest girl in the tribe. Her family were tailors. Her name was Vatusi. A few years later, they had a daughter named Chuki.

***

For close to a century, the Portuguese had dominated the slave trade; but by the middle of the seventeenth century, other countries wanted to benefit from the free labor. Europeans hungered for the taste of sugar that sweetened their coffee and tea, and the French were buying slaves from East Africa to work on sugar plantations on islands in the Indian Ocean. The Dutch and the British established outposts on the coast and joined the East African trade on the long sea route around Africa.

Europeans pitted African kings against one another and encouraged them to sell their enemies into slavery. The Swahili tribal leaders met the demand for slaves, raiding, capturing, and exporting Bantu clans to European colonists. Bought and sold through the main center of trade on the island of Zanzibar, slaves were valuable, "black gold" and "beasts of burdens." None of the city-states near the east coast were left unscathed.

When the dreaded incursion arrived in the Lemba province, it was worse than any of them could have imagined.

Faraji's army was on guard at the perimeter of the city when the invasion started and fought the attackers long enough for most of the people to escape. Many of the elders weren't physically able to flee and chose to stay behind, including Chilemba and Hamisi.

"We can't leave you here." Faraji pleaded with his father to come with them. "You don't have to walk. You can ride on the cart, or we can carry you."

"Go on, son," Chilemba said with authority. "Take care of your family. Vatusi has another baby in her belly. We would only slow you down. It's the young and the strong they're after. Don't worry about us."

Faraji kept trying to convince them. "No, Baba, please come! We can't wait much longer."

"I'm an old man. I was born running. Go on. The Lord will take care of us. There are more lives counting on you."

Faraji grimaced in pain. It hurt his heart and soul to turn away and leave his parents there in harm's way, but they gave him no choice. He ran out to catch up with the caravan heading south toward the coast.

***

The men Faraji sent back to canvass the city returned with a gloomy report. The town had been sacked. The invaders had looted their homes, and what wasn't pillaged was burned. There were no survivors to speak of.

Faraji squinted through tears, his eyes resting a moment on each member of his family sheltered in the small tent. Salene sat beside him, holding Chuki. Vatusi sat leaning against Abdalla, and Kioni paced back and forth behind Kondo.

"Thank Adonai for his mercies, we are alive," Faraji said, his voice trembling.

"We have lost everything!" Kioni said angrily.

"No, Kioni," Salene told her. "We have each other; we have all we need."

"That's right," Faraji said. "God has blessed us. He has delivered us from our enemies. 'We are hard pressed on every side, but not crushed; perplexed, but not in despair; persecuted, but not abandoned; struck down, but not destroyed,' 2 Corinthians 4:8-9."

"Don't you ever get tired of whining and want to fight?" Kioni snapped at her father. "You sound just like grandfather, preaching that God is with us and will fight our battles. But we keep running. Why don't you tell us to stand and fight like Joshua? How can we get the victory if we don't confront our enemy?"

"There is much you don't understand," Abdalla said, interrupting her. "The responsibility of leading a group of people is a heavy burden. You can't sacrifice them like animals. The chief priest has to trust in God and allow His will to be done. Baba has to be obedient to His will."

"And who are our enemies obedient to?" Kioni spat. "They trade us for pepper and silk."

"That's enough disrepect, daughter! Hush your noise!" Faraji said, waving his hand. "We have been through too much. We are all tired."

When the Sabbath came, Faraji asked Abdalla to speak. Faraji was devoid of words to offer his people. He had poured encouragement over them for years, urged them to hold onto their faith, and repeated the trials of the Israelites and how they had always triumphed. He had convinced them that Adonai had not forgotten them and that their blessings were closer than they had ever been. Now as they were cramped on a coastal piece of land near the hinterland, on territory belonging to the sultan of Oman, he was as tired of preaching as the people were of hearing it.

"We can't survive like this," Faraji whispered to Salene in the night. She had always been the one who helped him to see the light of day through the darkness.

"That is true," she said serenely. "The people want to hear a clear solution. If you want them to fight, they will fight. But they can't sit here between the lines of fire."

"What can I tell them that I haven't already said?" he implored.

"You are the leader; it's time to lead and not speak. So many of us have died. The hope of the people burned in the flames of their homes, the synagogue, and the fields. There's nothing left there. Figure out where you will lead."

"They're tired of running, and I don't have the strength to lead."

"Think of Abdalla. He needs guidance from you."

Faraji prayed and contemplated. His people were hungry and battle-weary. They needed time to recuperate, to unite. They needed a place to come together. The next day, he told Salene, "We'll build a place of worship and build homes for the people. We will plant food. We can't go anywhere with nothing. We have to renew our faith and our strength. Then we'll go further south."

Faraji joined the men as they gathered rock and stone. With Abdalla beside him, they built a modest synagogue stone by stone and rock by rock. Abdalla learned how to measure and cut the stone and rocks and how to mix mortar. He discovered that he loved working with his hands more than sitting with his grandfather and reading the Scriptures.

"These words are stronger than rock, son," Faraji told him when the place of worship was finished. "'Truly he is my rock and my salvation; he is my fortress, I will never be shaken.'"

***

"It's time for us to take our place," Kioni said to Kondo about a year later, her impatience being driven by her envy of her brother. "We are the true leaders of Lemba. You and I understand that we must be able to defend ourselves against other tribes. We need weapons; we need guns."

"How are we going to get them? We have nothing to trade. We barely have enough to survive. The men can't even hunt. They risk their lives if they venture too far. What we need is to find work for the people."

Stone-faced, Kioni stared Kondo in the eyes. "We have plenty to trade. We have dead weight pulling us down. If they don't see our vision, they'll only get in the way and cause trouble. God had to cleanse out His people before they could go into the Promised Land. He used fire, we will be more merciful."

"What are you saying?" Kondo asked, stunned by her words.

She moved close to him. "Abdalla isn't like you," she said

softly. "He's weak. We have to be strong to survive. We can start a new nation, you and I, king and queen."

"It's not right," Kondo said, turning away from her. "I'm not ordained by God."

Kioni grabbed Kondo's arm and pulled him back. "War has changed everything. Nothing in the Scriptures says you can't be king."

Kondo stood there silent, thinking. Then he said, "We can't let the people know. They would turn against us. Faraji would have me killed."

"Then he must go, too," she said callously.

Starting the next morning, Kondo left the camp regularly under the guise that he was exploring places for them to settle. Sometimes he was gone for more than four days and returned without options or suggestions. Finally, after about a month, he brought them good news.

"Mutapa is the place we'll settle," he announced. "The people there are independent, and there is gold there that we can mine."

Faraji was pleased. "That is great news, Kondo! Well done!"

Kondo glanced over at Kioni and nodded. "First, let me take a small group and investigate, around 70 men and 23 women. If we can acquire land, we will need to do some preparation for all the people. Abdalla can go with me."

"Yes, that's a good plan," Faraji agreed. "Select those you want to travel with you, and have them ready in two days."

Kondo chose strong, young unskilled men and women with no health issues. He claimed they were best suited for clearing trees and brush for the new camp. Some argued that a few

merchants should accompany them to assist in negotiations, but
Kondo discouraged the idea, stating that Abdalla was capable
of representing them in any discussions.

Vatusi had a bad feeling about the small group going to
explore Mutapa. It didn't make sense to her. If they were
migrating to Mutapa, why were they going to investigate? They
should all just pack up and go.

"We've already been separated from our elders," she told
Abdalla, thinking of Chilemba and Hamisi. "We shouldn't be
apart."

"You take care of Chuki, Silas, and the child in your belly,"
Abdalla replied, hoping to change the subject. "A voice has
told me it is another boy."

"I want to go with you," Vatusi said to Abdalla, with worry
evident in her voice. "I'm not that big. I can make the trip."

Abdalla hugged her close. "There's no reason for you to
risk yourself or the baby, sweet girl. We won't be gone long.
When we find land for us, we'll all be together."

***

The troupe of 100 had walked for a day and a half when
Kondo led them to a clearing near the coast. Abdalla noticed a pile
of elephant tusks. Suddenly, before he could say a word, they were
surrounded by a gang of Arabs armed with pistols. It only took
him a second to realize that they had been ambushed. Then the full
horror of it dawned on him when they released his brother-in-law.

"You are my brother, Kondo!" Abdalla said in disbelief,
glaring at him. "I would have given my life for you and my sister.
Why are you doing this? I have my family waiting for me."

Kondo stared off into the hills, unable to look him in the eyes. "You stood in the way, brother. You don't have the will to fight, and our people must fight. We need weapons to go against the empire."

"Kioni put you up to this!" he said desperately. "She's malicious. Don't let her corrupt you."

"God will take care of you," Kondo said. Then he turned away.

Abdalla felt his spine curve in resignation. His life had changed. He woke up that morning as a free man, and now he would be a slave. He knew it was Kioni who masterminded this plan. That realization only made the betrayal more bitter. Further insult was that Kondo was no more of a fighter or king than he was. A king is a great shepherd. He thought of the Scripture, "He who is a hired hand and not a shepherd, who does not own the sheep, sees the wolf coming and leaves the sheep and flees, and the wolf snatches them and scatters them," John 10:12.

***

Africans were being kidnapped, enslaved, and brought to South and Central America, the Caribbean, and the New World as labor to clear the land to farm sugar, cotton, rice, and tobacco. Competition from North America was holding down the price of cotton and tobacco, so the Caribbean colonies switched to growing sugarcane on the plantations. This new industry required many more workers than the white indentured servants.

It was called The Triangular Trade. Ships came to Africa with cotton, colored beads, brass, and guns they traded for slaves. The slaves were transported to the West Indies to work on sugar cane plantations, and the profits were returned to England.

# Chapter Sixteen

# Abdalla (taken in 1676)

Abdalla's eyes burned with tears that ached to make themselves known. They were not so much for his own predicament as they were for the others who had gotten tangled up in this evil net. He felt responsible for their misfortune. He stared up into the partially clouded sky to avoid looking into their faces.

"You! Give me those fine clothes! You won't need them anymore," one of the captors yelled at him, speaking in Swahili.

Abdalla dropped his head. He felt more helpless than humiliated as he undressed before them. The Arab threw him a long, tattered piece of cloth that he wrapped around himself.

"Form two lines," the same Arab shouted.

The trapped group moved slowly, dragging their feet. Then one of the young men made a quick move to take the weapon of the kidnapper standing next to him. A shot rang out from another standing to the side, and the young man fell to the ground. Screams from the women rang out as his blood seeped around their feet.

Until this moment, Abdalla had not known the depths of his sister's hatred toward him. Tied together in two long parallel lines with chains around their ankles, more than half the group had wooden yokes around their necks. Ordered not to speak to one another, they walked in fear and silence. The men in the rear had to carry the heavy elephant tusks on their shoulders. Every now and then, there would be a gasp or a shriek when they passed the bones of the weak, who had fallen on the trail before them, or when the vultures picked at the remains of a decaying corpse.

All of them struggled to stay on their feet. Any man or woman who couldn't march was killed as easily as an insect. They marched for weeks, dehydrated and nearly starved from daily rations of a scoop of rice and a cup of water. The number of prisoners increased along the way. By the time the march reached Zanzibar, Abdalla was among 820 people, mostly men and women.

In Zanzibar, they were splashed with water, and their skin was oiled. They were given only a strip of cloth to cover themselves. The women received a larger piece of cloth and were adorned with jewelry. Abdalla was placed near the end of the line with the tallest men, and they were paraded through the market for the buyers to view. Then they were examined like cattle for purchase.

Chained, Abdalla was loaded onto a British East India Company vessel named *Expectation*, with 87 others as slaves. This shipping company was called on for urgent occasions when the Royal African Company, which had a monopoly on the slave trade to Barbados and Jamaica, was not supplying enough slaves to run the plantations. With the high mortality and low fertility among slaves and continual revolts on plantations, the demand for labor kept rising.

Deep in the ship's hold, the men and women were separated, branded like cattle, and packed naked in iron shackles like animals, lying side by side to fit in the limited space. Abdalla heaved from the smell of his burnt flesh. Some of the men cursed; others groaned in agony as hungry rats ran on top of them. Turning flat on his back, as if he were already dead, Abdalla prayed to God and cried. He hadn't shed a tear since he was a young boy. He prayed and cried for his wife, his children, his mother, his father, and for his people. The tears rolled like a river flowing into his ears. Gradually, the other men quieted down and listened to his prayer.

Without any tears left and his mouth dry, Abdalla stopped. The next words were about a revolt. That's all the men talked about whenever they were alone. In between their suffering, sickness, and disease, they concocted plans of attacking their captors and freeing themselves.

They were fed beans, yams, and corn mush from animal troughs. Days were spent like hogs trapped in their own filth. For some, they escaped through death from illness or suicide before they were thrown overboard like garbage. They never got the opportunity to fight their captors. Weak and malnourished from the torturous three-month voyage, it was all they could do to survive.

***

On stiffened legs, small groups were pushed and prodded up from the bowels of the ship. There, Abdalla's beard was shaved, his wounds tended to, and his skinned oiled. They were given a larger portion of food and taken back down into the darkness. Three days later, they were all brought to the deck. The glaring light of the sun was blinding as Abdalla peered through squinted eyes. The water was beautiful, like colored

glass. His heart skipped at the sight of the shore. The end of
the miserable voyage was near. He wondered what part of the
world he had come to. He thought of the stories of Jemal, who
had traveled to India and China. Unbeknownst to him, he had
arrived at Port Royal, Jamaica.

Under the weight of chains around their necks and feet,
the slaves stumbled off the ship in single-file. Poked with long
metal rods like livestock going to market, they were prodded
and nudged to the square, where they would be sold to the
highest bidder. The port wasn't much different than the one
in Zanzibar. The sun was bright and warm, the sky blue, and
the white sand beneath Abdalla's feet felt familiar. The beauty
belied the wretchedness that operated beyond the beach. To
him, it was a vivid nightmare. If only he could close his eyes,
open them again, and be on the shore of Mombasa.

Abdalla had seen the trade of goods many times, but never
once had he envisioned himself as a commodity to be bought
and sold. Seventy-three of the captives on the vessel were sold
to Thomas Temple, 61 of them were Lemba Israelites captured
with Abdalla. This was an unusual circumstance for large
numbers to be kept together. Normally, slaves were purchased
in small numbers, but the Temple Hall in St. Andrew Parish
desperately needed to replace slaves on the sugar plantations
who had escaped to the mountains with the maroons in the last
rebellion.

Led by two overseers on horseback, one in the front and
one in the rear, for the 30-mile walk to the Temple Hall estate,
the gang trudged on in silence, afraid to speak. With so many
of them taken together, Abdalla prayed that they would be a
comfort to one another until they found a way back home. He

pushed at the back of the slender man in front of him who drug his feet with bowed head. He reminded Abdalla of an antelope gripped in the teeth of hyenas, subdued, and sensing his doom. Still, Abdalla refused to give up hope. His faith was all he had left.

***

The most lucrative and most brutal crop to produce in British Jamaica was sugar. It was so profitable that it was considered the "jewel" in Britain's crown. The Temple estate of 1,900 acres was among the most successful sugar cane plantations on the island. In addition to slaves, there were indentured servants and Irish and Scottish prisoners of war who worked on the estate; and the sugar was exported back to England for sale.

A stout white man dressed in fine clothes met the passel of fresh slaves at the entrance of the Temple plantation. He spoke to them in a language they didn't understand.

"This here is Adam and Mercy," he said. "They will help y'all get some clothes on your backs and get settled in. They'll tell you the rules here that will keep you out of trouble. We don't want any reason to take a strap to nobody. We want you to be happy here in your new home." Then he turned to Adam and said, "I need them understanding English as fast as possible."

Adam and Mercy were Thomas Temple's most seasoned and trusted workers. They could probably run the estate themselves without supervision. Adam had been brought to the island as a boy some 40 years ago from the kingdom of Kongo, near the end of their war with the Portuguese. Mercy was his wife. She had been born on the Temple plantation.

Yes, Massa," Adam said with a quick nod.

The overseer stood watch as Adam called out different words to the new slaves. When Abdalla heard the Bantu words, he spoke up.

"What is this place?"

"This is Jamaica. You are on a sugar plantation. Say no more now, it makes the overseer nervous. We will speak at length later."

"Let's go," the overseer on the horse shouted.

Adam and Mercy led the new group about a half mile away near the sugar mill to the area where they would be housed. Abdalla winced at the sight; it reminded him of home. There were about a dozen new huts with thatched roofs clustered together around a courtyard. He could almost imagine Vatusi walking out of one of the huts with Chuki and Silas close on her heels.

The routine involved the new negroes being isolated from the rest of the slaves to ensure that they didn't infect them with diseases that they might have contracted on the Middle Passage. Three nurses were there waiting to clean and dress their sores, and two seamstresses were there to dress them in clothing. The smell of food wafted through the air. The cook had prepared them a meal of yams, plantains, and salt fish. This routine was used so the slaves could regain their strength before they were assigned to a gang.

Mercy spoke with the women, while Adam addressed the men.

"What is your name?" Adam asked Abdalla, sensing his position as a leader.

"I'm Abdalla. I'm Balemba, the assistant priest to my father, Faraji, the chief priest in Mombasa. I was betrayed by my sister and traded for guns."

"From now on, your name is Abraham," Adam told him. "It ain't as bad here as it is on other plantations. Keep your back low, and you'll stay alive. Things are kinda hard right now because of all the rebels running up to the mountains. They're joining the maroons, who fled into the mountains after the British invaded the island and beat the Spanish."

"Why do you stay here?" one of the new slaves asked. "Why haven't you run?"

Adam nodded. "When slaves rise up, so many of them are killed; and the ones who didn't run, are punished. Somebody always has to bear the burden."

"Some things are worse than death," another new slave remarked.

"When I first came here, I was a young boy taken from everything and everyone I had ever known. A man named John—he's dead now—took my hand and he covered me as a father would.

"He was a protector for all of us. He couldn't free us, but he made our lives bearable. All of us can't escape. For most of us, this is our life. I was here when the English came. The Spanish master freed all of us slaves. They wanted us to help them fight. What do you think about that? Almost the whole plantation run into the hills. Some were caught, others were killed. I'm a free man, but I stayed to do for those what he did for me."

Adam spent several hours orienting the new slaves. He explained the organization of the plantation, the great house, the overseer's house, the bookkeeper's house, the hospital for negroes, and the slave quarters. He told them about the jobs of the domestic slaves, who were housekeepers, washerwomen, seamstresses, cooks, gardeners, and waiting boys. He asked the men if they had skills to work as carpenters, coopers, sawyers, masons, blacksmiths, grooms, cattlemen, hog tenders, and chicken keepers. He schooled them on the work in the cane fields, when and how it was planted, harvested, and refined in the mill. He told them about the foreman in the main field, the night watchmen, and the rat catchers, and how all the slave workers were divided into gangs and all had foremen.

After Adam helped the new slaves get settled into their huts. He tutored them in English for a while, advising them to speak it more and more each day. Worn out from the long day, Adam stood up to leave. Then he remembered one last thing.

"The work day is from sun-up to sun-down," he announced. "At harvest time, two shifts work around the clock."

Abdalla got up to ask a question. "Do we have any time to do for ourselves?"

Adam patted him on the shoulder. "We work six days a week."

"Can you get me a Bible?"

"I'll get it for you, but you gonna have to learn English to read it. The overseer knows you're a religious man. He feels that you will be good to help calm the uprisings. Sunday is your day to do what you want, unless it's harvest time."

"Those of us who are Lemba observe the Sabbath. Are we free to worship in our own way?"

"Practicing Obeah is against the rules here, but I suspect they won't mind you worshiping the same God they do. Remember, you're not guests of Thomas Temple in the great house. He owns you now. He's not as much a devil as some, so thank your God for that. There's food to eat, but it's not enough. You might want to use your free time to grow extra provisions in your gardens."

"We are Israelites," Abdalla said. "We don't eat the pig and other forbidden foods. Our meat must be slaughtered and prepared as God has deemed."

"That will be up to you," Adam told him as he stood to leave. "You may get hungry enough to change your mind."

***

The plantation bell rang before the cock crowed, at about 4:00 in the morning. The night sky still had not given way to the sun, but it was time to get out to the field. They worked for five hours on empty bellies; and at 9:00, they got 30 minutes to eat breakfast and then get back to work. The noon hour bell rang, and they stopped to pick up grass and feed for the horses and cattle before they had lunch. They had 90 minutes to eat before the bell rang again, and they returned to work. Before the sun set, they picked grass for the animals again. Finally, they gathered small branches or dry dung for a fire to cook supper.

In less than a month, Adam had the slaves assigned to their work gangs, chosen according to their physical strength. Most of them were in better shape than other new slaves that had come to Temple Hall, having come to the island on a trade vessel instead of a slave ship. Adam showed them how to plant seed cane, how to weed the field, and how to chop the cane with billhooks when harvest came. Since they were all young and strong, the women would weed the fields and bundle the long stalks while they were isolated. It was hard work, but they learned their tasks quickly, with each day being the same as the one before it.

***

Mostly the Israelites, or Balemba, kept to themselves. Abdalla knew many of them who had grown up in the city with him. Beno and Wanja were the son and daughter of a Levite priest whose synagogue was closer to the farms outside of the city. He and Beno were educated together and played games together, and he considered him a friend. But he could not bring himself to tell them that his sister, Kioni, had been an accomplice in their kidnapping.

Abdalla prayed and gave them a word from God in the afternoon on the Sabbath day. There were moments when he stood before them, seeing the same faces looking back at him, that he felt like he was home in Mombasa. The difference was the sadness in their eyes and the slump in their shoulders from bending over planting, weeding, or hacking. He did his best to lift their spirits and to give them hope.

"Children of Israel and other tribes from Africa, our faith is being tested. Even though we are suffering in a faraway land, Adonai has not forgotten us. Nehemiah 9:27 says, 'Therefore You delivered them into the hand of their oppressors who oppressed them, But when they cried to You in the time of their distress, You heard from heaven, and according to Your great compassion You gave them deliverers who delivered them from the hand of their oppressors.' While we are captive in this place, we must not forget the laws that govern our lives. We must be obedient to the covenant. Though they try to feed us the pig, we must not eat it."

"We're starving here, man!" Beno shouted at him. "We have to eat whatever we can get our hands on."

Abdalla frowned. "You know that is against our rules."

"God wants us to survive, don't He?" Beno asked angrily.

"Yes, He does," Abdalla answered. "We all could have been killed by now. That's why we can't lose our faith. Why would He deliver us if we don't follow the laws He gave to us?"

"Then you keep praying for us, Abdalla-or is it Abraham," Beno spat, standing on his feet. "And don't forget to ask Him to forgive us for whatever we have to do to make it in this hell we have to live in." Then he walked way.

Two more men got up and followed Beno, then several more, and then a few of the women drifted behind them. About half of the people stayed, including Beno's sister, Wanja.

"There's nothing I can say to explain or minimize our suffering here on this island," Abdalla said humbly to those who remained. "The only thing that comes to my mind is the struggles of Job. Adonai allowed him to go through much grief and misery, but he remained faithful. The Lord said to Job, 'Do you still want to argue with the Almighty? Or will you yield?' Then Job replied to the Lord and said, "Behold I am of little importance and contemptible; what can I reply to you? I lay my hand on my mouth.' Then the Lord told Job to stand up like a man and prepare for battle. When he showed himself to be strong, the Lord restored his wealth and happiness. I pray that we all have the strength to endure this tribulation."

When Abdalla finished speaking, the rest of the group left, except for Wanja.

"Forgive Beno. He never could hold his tongue or swallow his pain," she said. "Don't be discouraged by the others. You are still our priest."

"Thank you, Wanja."

"Willow is my new name," she said, and then she headed toward the women's area.

***

Every night, while his body ached from a hard day's work, Abdalla's mind floated back to Mombasa. He was caught in his reveries, when Wanja ran into his hut. She was frantic.

"What's the matter?" he asked, concerned.

"I beg you, Abdalla, make a child with me!" she said, grabbing his shirt.

"What's wrong with you? Don't be crazy!" he said, pulling the cloth from her hands. "You know I have a family back at home."

She froze and stared into his eyes. "You must be crazy! I am Willow, and you are Abraham. We have died and gone to hell. This place is your home. Take me as your wife, or I'll be dirt!"

"I have a wife," he said softly, trying to be sympathetic.

"You are dead to them!" she cried.

Abdalla turned away from Wanja, not wanting to hear the truth.

"Look at me," she said, grabbing him by the shirt again. "The only way I'll be safe from the white man is with a baby in my belly. Please don't turn me away!"

Abdalla didn't want to respond to her, but he couldn't control himself. She was offering him warmth and a gentle touch. She pulled him down to the mat on the floor, and he soaked in the comfort of her arms and legs. When the respite was over, he felt guilty for his betrayal to Vatusi and turned his back to her.

Wanja slipped into Abdalla's hut whenever she could, but it was his conscience that kept him from loving her the way she deserved. She didn't care. When her belly began to swell, she thanked him for loving her. To show her appreciation, she did all she could for him. She cooked, kept his hut clean, and rubbed his aching muscles; but it all made him feel more unworthy.

Reluctantly, Abdalla took Wanja as his wife. On their parcel of land, they grew potatoes, yams, corn, okra, plantain, and mango. Because of Abdalla's elevated place as a preacher, Wanja had a few chickens and a goat. Mercy would sometimes sell eggs or goat milk for her on market day to buy household utensils because they observed the Sabbath.

***

The first chance of freedom for Abdalla and his group happened at the end of April in 1678. Word came of a planned revolt in St. Catherine's Parish. Messages were circulating that all negroes should come together in the uprising. It was whispered about on the Temple plantation, but without any weapons, they would have to wait for the other rebels to reach them.

When Abdalla got to the cabin later than usual, Wanja was at the door waiting.

"I hear all the talk going on around here," she said, breathing as if she had been running.

"What talk is that?" Abdalla asked casually, keeping his eyes above her heavy belly.

"Don't treat me like I'm stupid," she snapped.

"I don't want to die here," Abdalla said, walking around her into the cabin.

Wanja followed him inside. "I don't want to die here either, but I'm big now. This child will come any day now. I can't climb those hills. Do you plan to leave us?"

That was exactly what Abdalla didn't want. He should not have taken her as his wife. He didn't want the responsibility of someone else to think about when he didn't even have control over his own life.

"I don't know what I'm going to do!" he shouted out of frustration.

For the next two nights, Abdalla, eight other men, and five women sat outside his hut. They barely breathed, listening for a signal or a voice to call out to them. It never came. The following afternoon during the dinner hour, Adam came to talk with Abdalla.

"Abraham, there has been another uprising nearby," Adam said, eyeing him closely. Abdalla kept his eyes on the plate of food in front of him. "You know, you have to be ready to meet your God when you make that choice."

Abdalla put a big mouthful of stew in his mouth. "A man told me on the ship, some things are worth dying for."

"There's a lot of truth to that," Adam said. "Well, anyhow, it started on Captain Duck's plantation. They killed him and his wife. They destroyed several more plantations in St. Mary's parish. Some were caught and were executed on the spot. Around 30 or so got away and got some recruits from two other plantations. Looks like those 30 from Duck's and the others who joined in are all dead."

Abdalla glanced out the door toward a poinsettia tree growing in the yard and wondered how a place of such beauty could be consumed with so much evil and violence. "I pray the Lord showed mercy on them," he said, spooning up more of the stew.

"I hear tell that the militia tortured one of the rebels. They broke both his arms and legs and set his feet on fire. They say it took three hours of him burning before he died."

"Shame they can't treat a man as good as any animal."

"Yes, Abraham, that is a shame."

That night, Wanja gave birth to a baby girl they named Emma.

****

Wanja suffered two miscarriages before they had another child in 1682, a son they named Daudi. When he was circumcised, Abdalla's heart was so full with the joy of a new life, one that would give him another connection with the world. But at the same time, his heart was also full with sorrow for the world his children were born into. Some days, he feared the mixture in his heart was so tight that it would burst within his chest. Late in the night, one part of him wanted to hold them and love them; the other part wanted to turn away and spare them the pain that was certainly in store for them. It was at those times that he ignored Wanja and refused to talk.

"Why don't you love me?" Wanja would plead, lying next to him.

Abdalla shook his head. "We don't have that privilege."

"That's the only privilege we have," she muttered.

"It will only bring us more pain."

"Your son deserves more than that, Abraham."

"I don't have anything to give him."

"Teach him what your father taught you and his father before him. Tell him that he's a descendant of Aaron, designated by God to teach His word to the people. What if he gets free. He won't know where he came from or his life's calling."

Wanja's words haunted Abdalla. He was ashamed to admit that he wore his self-pity like a comfortable cloak. He had stopped trusting God. He got up from his mat, went to the back of their hut, and prayed. He begged the Lord to forgive him for his selfishness and lack of faith. He hadn't learned to read the English in the Bible that Adam had given him yet, but that wouldn't hinder him. The next morning before the sun rose, he began to talk with Daudi. He started with the story of the Hebrew people, who were slaves to Pharaoh in Egypt. Telling him about Moses and the people coming out of bondage gave him peace.

On the Sabbath, the others began to gather again to hear his stories of the covenant handed to Moses on the mountain. It was a distraction from their own anguish and gave them hope. Abdalla remembered his ancestor Aaron's failings leading the Israelites and forgave himself for his own shortcomings.

Daudi was about three years old when the rumblings of another revolt were circulating. Out of fear, many of the owners would only allow white servants in the main houses. Adam was in town when he heard about the uprising encouraged by the maroons and how they needed more slaves to join them.

"Abraham, I know you've heard about it," he said to Abdalla after the Sunday service. "It's not an easy life in the mountains, as many die up there as in the fields. Advise your people not to get involved."

"At least they won't be slaves, and there is safety in numbers."

"That's not the life you want for your family, Abraham."

"Do you think I would rather have them be slaves. If the Lord tells me to move, then I will move. My family will come with me."

***

The 1685 revolt began on the Widow Grey plantation. All the slaves there rose up, more than 150 of them. They attacked the main house, killed two white men, and took 25 arms. Mrs. Grey escaped through a window and fled to the house of her neighbor, Major Price. They killed another white man and wounded another there before they retreated to the hills. One negro, loyal to Mrs. Grey, ran into town and told of the plot. Seventy troops and foot soldiers were waiting when they returned. The rebels were chased through the mountains of St. Ann's to St. Mary's. Seven were killed, 30 were captured, 50 surrendered, and the rest escaped to the hills with the maroons.

"Things are going to get harder now," Adam told Abdalla's group when they were gathered for worship on the Sabbath. "A new law says the owners must have one overseer to every five blacks or pay a fine. That means you gonna have more bosses breathing down your necks and beating up your backs."

Adam's forewarnings came to pass. Life got rougher for all the slaves with more whites on the estate. Punishments from owners and overseers, aggravated by their resentment and fear of the negroes, intensified as the attacks on the estates continued for months. The maroons raided plantations in the dark of night, and there was little the owners could do to stop it. Regularly, they made contact with slaves on plantations, continuing and establishing relationships with them to get supplies they could not produce for themselves: cloth, pots and pans, tools, and weapons.

One of the maroon men, Shamar, snuck onto the Temple estate to recruit slaves for the next uprising, and he saw Wanja. Up in the mountains, the men outnumbered the women, and he was lonely. He came back several times, encouraging her to run away with him and be his wife. Wanja was flattered by the attention and the offer. He showed her a desire that Abdalla had never shown, and she was intrigued. She kept his affections toward her a secret.

***

Wanja suffered another miscarriage and more abuse from the presence of the white servants on the estate. She began to think more about the life Shamar offered. She was reaching a breaking point, but Abdalla couldn't see it.

"Our children are big and strong now, Abraham," she said, as he pulled on his work clothes. "We can get away from here, go up into the mountains, and live free."

"It's not everything that you hear. They are not our people. Israelites have survived thousands of years by maintaining our independence from other peoples. God instructed us not to intermarry or live with our enemy."

"They are not our enemies; these white people who make us slaves are our enemy. We can live as a family there."

"The maroons don't worship or make animal sacrifices. They eat the hog. They have many gods. They practice Obeah, Myal, witchcraft, voodoo, and communication with spirits. All of it is against the commandments God has given his people."

Wanja got angry that Abdalla wouldn't consider it. She hadn't forgotten that he was eager to do it years earlier without her.

"Maybe you're afraid that you won't have authority over everybody in the mountains," she argued. "Maybe you don't want to go where you won't be chief priest. Tell me, what has God done to help any of us since we've been here?"

"Stop your griping. You're the one who said I needed to teach Daudi of his birthright. That's what I'm doing. If I never get back to our land, maybe he will."

"Do you see all the blood running through these fields?" she asked, poking him in the chest. "Nobody is going back. I want to be free again, if only for one day, one hour, one minute."

"What about the children? Are you willing to sacrifice their lives? Do you want to see their blood flow through these fields?"

"The Israelites were slaves in Egypt for 400 years before they were freed. Is that the life you want for them?"

"No, but do you know what happens to runaways when they're caught? They are castrated, half a foot cut off, or burned to death. Do you want your children beaten through skin to the bone and pepper and salt poured into the ripped flesh? Why don't you spend more timing praying than complaining? We must remain faithful."

"You're scared! You're a coward!" Wanja shouted.

"If you're in such a rush to die, woman, I'm not standing in your way, but the children are not going with you. You've forgotten what happened in Mombasa. This is the beginnings of a war between the maroons and the whites. Back home, we knew enough not to take sides."

"Look where that got you!" Wanja snapped.

***

Four months later, in 1690, there was a rebellion on the Sutton estate in North Clarendon, one of the largest and wealthiest plantations in Jamaica. Four hundred slaves rose up, took Sutton's weapons, burned down the cane fields, and stole the cattle; but only 40 of the rebels escaped to the hills and joined the maroons. Among those runaways was a girl, Nanny, and her three brothers—Accompong, Kojo, and Quao—who had been captured in Ghana, West Africa. Kojo would become a leader of the Leeward maroons, and Nanny a leader of the Windward maroons.

Nights weren't a time of rest. All manner of trouble stirred in the darkness. However, the greatest upheaval on the island occurred in the light of day on June 7, 1692. There was no hint or warning of the catastrophe that was about to take place. The sky was clear, and the sun was in its place. It was a sweltering day, but it was still serene until a strange rumbling thundered in the hills. They had just gone back to work. Abdalla was in midstroke of chopping cane when the ground shifted beneath his feet. He paused and looked over at Daudi to the right of him. Before he could speak, the earth shook. Panic and trepidation set in quickly, and the ones in the field started to run. When the third boom sounded, those running fell to the ground as it shook.

For a while, no one in the slave quarters knew the full extent of what happened until the hordes of survivors made their way to St. Andrew's parish.

"What has happened?" Abdalla asked Adam.

"It was a mighty earthquake," Adam answered, shaking his head.

"We all felt it."

"That ain't all," Adam told them. "Most of Port Royal was swallowed up. Then a huge tidal wave rared back and came full force, washing away what was left, taking all the ships under it. It's all floating out there in the sea, with dead bodies and bones from the graves that rose up in the mix. No doubt, thousands were killed."

Abdalla fell to his knees. "It's happening. God's divine retribution. He is doing His work!" he called out, raising his arms in praise. "Hallelujah, He is cleaning up the sin and wickedness of this place. The sinners were drowned like Pharaoh's army in the Red Sea."

Adam rubbed his hand across his forehead. He wasn't sure what would become of Port Royal, but he had been around long enough to know that it sure wouldn't be anything to celebrate.

"It's the beginning of the deliverance we've waited for!" Abdalla proclaimed to the group that had gathered outside of his hut. They danced and sang in hopes that they would soon be liberated.

The stoked flames in their spirits were squelched over the next week as large numbers of survivors bringing disease and death to the parish overwhelmed them. Five fell with fever out in the field, complaining of body aches, headaches, and vomiting.

"It's yellow fever," Mercy whimpered.

Sickness was all around them. The plantation hospital was full. Misery spread across the island. Death knew no color. The water had receded, but there were no ships coming or going while the British hurried to try and rebuild the port. Food was scarce, and no money was being made. Tempers flared. Slaves were flogged for no reason. Many slaves simply walked away, some migrated to other plantations, and others fled to the hills. Most were resigned to die among family.

The turmoil went on for ten years, during which there were four more major slave revolts on the sugarcane plantations, with more runaways escaping and joining the maroons. All the same, ships brought more slaves, and life on the island continued business as usual.

***

In 1698, Thomas Temple's daughter, Susannah, married her second husband, Nicholas Lawes. Despite Susannah being the fourth widow Lawes had married, the Temple estate was still given to him as a dowry. During the wedding celebration, several maroons came to the Temple plantation. One of them was the infamous Nanny. Word of her presence reached Abdalla and his group. Wanja had also heard about her and her healing powers. Without saying a word, Wanja rushed to meet Nanny and ask for her help.

When Wanja arrived at the slave quarters, a group surrounded Nanny as she spoke in the courtyard of huts. Wanja was surprised to see she that she was a young woman, probably about the same age as Emma. She paused in the back and waited within earshot. Then Nanny was ushered into a hut, where she would meet privately with those who needed healing. Wanja got in line and waited her turn until she was waved into the hut.

"How can I help you?" Nanny asked, motioning for her to sit.

"I need a healing. I couldn't hold my last three babies, and now my womb stays empty."

"Do you have children?"

"Yes, a daughter, Emma, and a son, Daudi."

"Why do you want to give your massa more babies to work?"

Wanja looked at the ground. "It keeps the overseer and the other white foreman away from me."

Nanny gently lifted Wanja's chin and looked into her eyes. "I have the cure for you, ma'am."

Wanja took in a deep breath of relief. "Bless you!" she said, while Nanny mixed the magic potion.

Nanny looked at her and said, "I know who you are, and I know your man. You must leave this place. Your daughter will soon suffer your fate. Bring your children and come with us into the mountain. You'll be safe there."

"He won't consider it."

"Then leave him and save your babies. Here they belong to Temple."

"I don't know what to do," Wanja said, covering her mouth.

"Don't think, ma'am. Just grab your children and follow me."

Wanja trembled. There was no time think. Her mind raced. What was holding her? Abdalla didn't love her.

She jumped up, nearly tripping over her skirt. "Don't leave me!" she said.

Wanja rushed through the small gathering to find Emma and Daudi. She found Emma sitting outside their hut. Daudi was inside with Abdalla having a lesson. Refusing to risk the chance that Abdalla might change her mind, Wanja took Emma by the hand and put her finger to her lips for her to stay quiet before running back to meet Nanny and her group.

When Nanny left the plantation, 12 slaves left with her. Wanja and Emma were among them. By the time Abdalla learned of it, they were long gone.

***

It took Wanja running away for Abdalla to realize how much he loved and cared for her. It was only then that he saw how he'd robbed her in an attempt to pay Vatusi for what they lost. Now, there was no way he could make it up to her. Every morning and each night when he prayed, he prayed for the safekeeping of her and Emma. The only good left in his life was Daudi, and he wanted to be sure that they wouldn't be separated. Adam was getting old, and if he died, his influence on the plantation would die with him.

"I need to find a way to get free," Abdalla said to Adam.

"You're not the only one," Adam chuckled, chewing on a twig.

"I mean it. Can you help me? I need to protect my son."

"The overseer says that they are tired of losing their investment to them hills. He thinks kindly of you. Since Willow and the girl run off and you stayed, he thinks you're loyal. The new massa wants to try to grow some different crops here on a small field, maybe some tobacco. Used to be white man's work. It don't bring the money that sugar do, but he thinks it is more civilized. It don't take the heavy lifting of cane, but it's fussy and takes some time to learn how to grow it. Possibility you might have time to do some other things to earn money to buy your freedom."

"I want to do it," Abdalla said eagerly. "Convince him we the people to do it."

Adam rolled the stick on his tongue. "I'll see what I can do."

***

Nicholas Lawes became chief justice of Jamaica. There had been many discussions in Britain on how to deal with the problem of rebellions. One idea was to add other valuable commodities, such as cotton, that were less strenuous for women and children to work. It would improve health and allow the population to grow. Lawes was eager to experiment with that suggestion.

Lawes purchased 14 slaves from the Stokes Hall plantation in Thomas Parish. These slaves were seasoned growers of tobacco. The plan was for them to generate a crop of "sweet-scented" tobacco from yellow Orinoco seeds. In an effort to preserve his investment, Lawes agreed to assign ten of the slaves that Adam recommended to be on the tobacco gang, among them were Abdalla and Daudi. They were to keep to themselves and not delve in those ritualistic possessions that he believed were used to plot against their owners and communicate plans of escape.

"This is the field that y'all will be working," Adam said, pointing out at the 24 acres designated for tobacco. "The new folks will partner with each one of you and work side by side 'til you get the hang of what to do." There were 11 men, but only two of them were under 40. Of the women, one was older, and two were under 20. He pointed to the oldest man. "This here is Paul. He'll be the head of y'all. He knows all there is to know about growing tobacco."

Daudi couldn't take his eyes off Venus, one of the young women from the Stokes plantation. Watching her work was like a dance to him. All of his misgivings about being on this new crop instantly vanished.

# Chapter Seventeen

# Daudi

Abdalla was furious when Daudi told him about his desire to have Venus as his wife. How could they expect to find favor with God if they kept breaking His laws? Intermarriage with those outside their faith had always led to their destruction. He looked into his Bible, and it was there in Deuteronomy 7:3-4: "Furthermore, you shall not intermarry with them; you shall not give your daughters to their sons, nor shall you take their daughters for your sons. For they will turn your sons away from following Me to serve other gods; then the anger of the LORD will be kindled against you and He will destroy you."

"She was born on the Stokes place," Daudi explained to Abdalla. "Her mother was Ashanti. She was sold by her own people, like you were."

"She's not one of us!" Abdalla shouted.

"Open your eyes, Fadda!" Daudi argued. "Does this place look like Mombasa, Africa, to you? Lawes owns us! I was born a slave."

"I've taught you better than that, son. Where is your faith? God will deliver us. You must trust and believe that. How else can you be the spiritual leader for our people here?"

"Ships come to this island every day, and I've never seen or heard of one take any of us back where we came from. Adam has been here for 61 years. It's like Madda told you. We have to find whatever happiness and peace we can here."

"Haven't I told you that the Israelites were in bondage for 400 years? God will move in His own time. It was His disappointment with their disobedience that delayed their deliverance. We are directed not to marry outside of our people. Sarah would be a good woman for you," he said, naming Beno's daughter.

"Venus is the one who makes me smile at the end of the day. When I'm breaking my back out there in the field, I think about her and I can keep going. Are you saying that you don't want that for me?"

"I can only tell you what the Torah says. Believe me, Daudi, she is not the only woman who can make you happy. Follow God's word, and He will bless you."

"I have never seen or read this Torah. I only know what I feel in my heart and soul. I prayed for God to make my life worth living after Madda and Emma left, and then Venus came here. What prayers of yours has God answered?"

"You were the answer to my prayers, son. I prayed that same prayer that you did, and then you were born. I only want you to be happy. I can't give you my blessing, but I pray that God will."

***

Abdalla had no inkling of when it happened, but his thoughts of Mombasa, Vatusi, Chuki, Silas, and the child he didn't know were overcome with longings for Wanja and worries for Emma. Fear kept him awake at night when the British began military campaigns against the maroons. Somehow, he wished they would come back, even though he knew their punishments would be harsh. He needed to be sure that they were safe. More than anything, he needed Wanja's wisdom in how to speak with Daudi, who was determined that Venus would be his wife.

Daudi was weary of his father's constant objections to the woman he loved, and he was seriously considering running away, taking Venus by the hand and heading for the hills to be free. The change in Abdalla's health was the only thing that gave him pause. Something deep inside him had broken or decayed, his gut or maybe a portion of his spine. His body had begun to curl and bend, and his head hung low from his neck. Daudi knew his days of usefulness were waning, and if he couldn't pull his weight, he might be sold or worse.

"Fadda, why don't you let the Obeah-man help you?" Daudi shouted at him out of frustration. "They have herbs and brews that can revive you and give you strength."

"Don't talk foolishness to me, boy!" Abdalla scolded. "This is why we suffer. The Scripture says, 'Do not turn to mediums or magicians; do not seek them out, and so make yourselves unclean by them: I am the LORD your God.' I have taught you better."

"If you would not have been so stubborn, you would be with Madda."

"Don't you confuse my failings with my faith. One I can't control; one I can."

Daudi knew there was nothing he could do to change his father's mind, and he couldn't run off and leave him in that condition. During his free time, he began working on the hut that would be his home with Venus. Although Abdalla made no secret of his disapproval, the other men offered their help to

Daudi.

"Your fadda is lost," Beno said to Daudi. "He tries to hide in his faith, but he can't. It's best to accept our fate and make the most of our days. He believes that we are suffering for the disobedience of our people. I cannot say if that is true or not. I only know that no man deserves the cruelty that we have endured here. If that girl brings you a minute of joy, you have every right to have it. Just make sure you respect your fadda."

"I will, Beno, I will."

When the hut was completed, all the negroes gathered on Sunday for Daudi and Venus's wedding celebration. Within a year, he and Venus had a daughter, Myra. A few years later, they had another daughter, Lydia. Abdalla couldn't help but soften his tone toward Venus when he saw his sweet granddaughters.

***

Another devastating blow struck Port Royal on January 9, 1703. This time, it was fire. The flames burned quickly, leaving no time to salvage merchandise, valuables, provisions, or even cash. In less than 12 hours, buildings, storehouses, and homes were completely engulfed. The only structures left standing were the two forts. The fire didn't discriminate. None of the rich were spared. More than a few lost everything. The difference in one fateful day reduced them to paupers.

Abdallah saw it as God beginning to purify the island and destroy the evil in Port Royal, the destruction even reached the Temple estate through malaria. Their beloved Adam was among the many who fell sick. Master Lawes sent for the white doctor, but it was no use. Adam died. For weeks, the pall of grief hung over the plantation, but their mourning had to be done in the fields because the work still needed to be done.

They were up early to clean the seed beds for the next season when Kennedy the overseer galloped over to them. "Your work in the tobacco fields is over!" he yelled, interrupting their sad song. "Master Lawes has gone back to England. We need all hands in the cane field."

Several of the negroes from the tobacco fields had never worked growing cane, but they were young and strong enough to make the adjustment. Abdalla had years of know-how, but he was too old for chopping. All he could do was pray and repeat Isaiah 40:29-31: "He gives strength to the weary and increases the power of the weak. Even youths grow tired and weary, and young men stumble and fall; but those who hope in the LORD will renew their strength."

Abdalla's body curled in retreat as his back humped and his knees bent. Still, he crawled up from his bed before daybreak to meet each grueling day. It pained him to swing his blade, and the amount of work he did wasn't worth the effort; but Kennedy refused to allow him to join the weeding gang or do some other job on the plantation. He had become more vicious after Adam's death and Master Lawes's departure to England.

"This ought to help you straighten up that back!" Kennedy roared, striking Abdalla on his backbone with his whip. Abdalla fell where he laid, unable and unwilling to get up.

The gang around him was stunned. They froze for a moment and then turned their heads and went back to work. Daudi kept staring in disbelief. Then Kennedy got off his horse and kicked Abdalla. "Get up, old man! You're not even worth the food you eat."

Daudi leaped through the air like a tiger and looped his arm around the neck of the overseer, cutting his breath. Gripped in a chokehold, Kennedy writhed wildly, trying to free himself. In one brisk motion, Daudi snapped his neck and dropped him to the ground beside Abdalla. Then, Daudi struck the horse on his hindquarter with the whip, and it dashed away.

Venus, who had watched the whole scene, started screaming and running to the opposite field. "Mister Kennedy's horse threw him," she cried. "He need help."

The other overseers galloped over. "What happened here?" they asked, seeing Kennedy's body lying lifeless on the ground.

"His horse got spooked and threw him over," Daudi said. "He ran off over there towards the woods."

The other overseers didn't know whether to believe him, but Kennedy was dead. "You two, bring him up to the overseer's house. The rest of y'all get back to work."

The negroes worked in silence for the rest of the day. There was no singing or calling out. Venus and Daudi didn't speak until they reached their hut that evening. The girls, sensing trouble, sat quietly on the floor in the dim light of the candles. Abdalla lay on the bed, barely conscious, his body still curved as he faced the wall, while Venus rubbed salve on his exposed back.

Daudi was on his knees praying as he had seen his father do. When he finished, he opened the worn Bible that Adam had given his father; and for once, he was thankful that Abdalla had forced him to learn to read. His eyes had barely focused on the page, when he was interrupted by a knock on the door. Venus looked at her husband with fear as he opened the door.

It was Ezra, one of the other men on their gang. "For you," Ezra said, handing him a wooden bowl of eggs.

"Thank you," Daudi said, nodding.

"No, it's my thanks to you," Ezra said.

That was the beginning of the procession. Others brought him potatoes, butter, fruit, and fish. One woman came in without a word, lifted the salve from Venus's hands, and took her place rubbing Abdalla's back. They all wanted to show their appreciation for what had happened in the cane field. His actions had lightened all their burdens. On Sunday, they gathered outside his hut and waited for him to give a word.

"Good afternoon to y'all," Daudi said, feeling insecure about the position he found himself in. He had never spoken to them like that before. He cleared his throat and took a deep breath. "I've watched my fadda stand up and give the word all my life. I never thought the day would come that I would stand in his place. Mainly, I want to say that we have to stand together as one family and look out for each other. I'm here to do that for all of you. It don't matter where you came from or how you got here. Matthew 12:48-50 says, 'But he replied to the man who told him, "Who is my mother, and who are my brothers?" And stretching out his hand towards his disciples, he said, "Here are my mother and my brothers! For whoever does the will of my Father in heaven is my brother and sister and mother."'"

"Amen, amen!" Beno said, raising his hand high, and others joined in.

"I don't know what will become of us. All I know is that we got to believe in something." He raised the Bible. "This book here shows that God is good, that Jesus Christ is our Savior. I'm gonna put my trust in His word, and I want y'all to join me."

Shouts of amen and hallelujah filled the air, and a bit of hope filled the people's hearts.

***

Slave insurrections on the plantations had subsided for several years, but the number of runaways was steady. The tie that bound Daudi to the Temple estate was his father. They nursed him as best they could, but he never recovered from being struck by Kennedy. Daudi was sure the lash of the whip had broken his spirit. Abdalla stopped reading his Bible, ate very little, and barely clung to life. Four years later, in the early hours of the morning, Venus gave birth to a son they named Tarone. Abdalla looked into the child's face and then closed his eyes. They never opened again. His spirit was set free that night.

***

It was the beginning of the second week in September 1712. The sun was just setting when the winds started to blow. All the gangs on the Temple estate were still in the fields planting canes. Suddenly, a bolt of lightning shot across the sky above them. Venus shot a glance over to Daudi. Tarone, who was tied to her back, began to whine.

"Storm's coming!" Daudi hollered to Miller, the overseer who'd taken Kennedy's gang. "Anybody get hurt out here, we got one less to work."

Miller looked up into the sky and frowned. "Leave it be! Get on to your houses," he said, disgusted. He hated letting them get even one hour of relief.

"Move quickly, everybody!" Daudi said to his gang, grabbing Myra and Lydia by the hands.

Fierce rains began to fall before they reached their huts, coming down in heavy sheets. A powerful gust swirled around them, pushing Venus to the ground. Daudi pulled her to her feet, and with Tarone still tied to her back, they rushed down the path to the slave quarters. They got there just in time to see the tops of the hut blow away like wheat tossed into the sky. Above them, sugar cane was flying through the air like a flock of birds. Around them, trees were ripped up and toppled as if they had no roots.

"Lord, help us!" Venus screamed, and the children began to cry.

"Into the sheds!" Daudi said, flailing his arms to those behind them who couldn't hear above the loud gales.

The carpenter and blacksmith sheds were already filled to capacity with people, so the only place left to find shelter was the poultry pen. Daudi opened the door to chickens squawking in distress. Loose feathers filled the coop. The girls and then Venus squeezed inside. About ten others followed them. No sooner than they had entered the coop, the walls of the shed began to shake and leaned to one side. Then like a blanket pulled from the bed, the whole shed was snatched high into the air. The chickens were carried away in a blast of wind.

The words of his father, Abdalla, echoed in Daudi's head, "How could a place so beautiful be like hell?"

"Everybody come together!" he yelled. "Make a circle. All the children lay under your mama's skirts in the middle. Come in close, loop arms with the person next to you, and lean forward." The rain pummeled down on their backs, and the wind threw tree limbs against them. Daudi began to pray loudly. Terrified in the darkness, somehow they weathered the storm holding on to one another.

What the light of day revealed was unbelievable. All their huts had been whisked away, and all their possessions were gone or strewn nearby in the mud. The animals that survived were roaming free, their sheds also destroyed by the storm.

Half of the great house was exposed to the open, and all the windows had been broken. There were bodies lying under debris. Most everything on the plantation was lost. The slaves heard that most of Kingston and Port Royal—houses, warehouses, and half the church—were demolished by the storm and flooded by the sea. Fifty-four vessels capsized, sank, or were driven ashore. *The Old Galley*, all its crew, and 107 slaves below perished. *The Ann Galley* lost half its crew, and 100 slaves drowned. More than 400 sailors died.

***

With no sugarcane to weed or harvest, all the negroes worked to rebuild huts, sheds, pens for the animals, and the mill. There was no rest for the next three years. Reconstruction of the great house, the hospital, and the overseer's house had barely been completed when another storm came in 1714.

Once things at Temple Hall were somewhat back in order, Lydia and Myra were paired with men on the plantation. As time went on, they both had children of their own. With more ties to the island, Daudi lost his father's hope of ever returning to Africa. Then, with relative peace on the island, Master Lawes returned to the plantation in 1717 and restarted the tobacco fields.

There had been no insurrections during the years with the island in disarray, but runaways and raids had never stopped. The maroons raided several plantations of arms and food and then burned the estates. By 1720, the settlement of Windward maroons was controlled by Nanny. Called Nanny Town, it was located on a ridge of the Blue Mountains in Portland Parish. Guards were stationed at lookout points, and her troops were well-trained in guerilla warfare, using camouflage to disguise themselves as trees with leaves and branches.

The British government now viewed the maroons as a threat to their economic stability. Master Lawes, who had been passive on the issue of the maroons, had to acknowledge their significance after being a victim of a raid. Serving as the governor of Jamaica in 1722, he made a speech and referenced the maroons' capturing of slaves, seizing of arms and ammunition from the Windward and Northside parishes, and the killing of English soldiers. The escalated response from the British started the first Maroon War. But despite their increased efforts, the British couldn't gain ground on the maroons.

On August 28, 1722, a pause came in the war when another hurricane raged onto the island. Commencing at 8:00 in the morning, the violent storm wreaked havoc for 14 hours. The heavy rains were relentless, soaking the whole island. The eye of the storm passed over Port Royal, flooding it with water 16 feet above the normal level. In Kingston, half of the homes and building were once again left in ruins, the fort broken, dand canons washed into the sea. The dead toll was 400, 200 of them being negro slaves trapped on an Irish ship.

Plantations suffered the same destruction they suffered ten years earlier. Many of the smaller ones couldn't recover, but the Temple plantation was large and rich enough to survive. They rebuilt again and then again after another huge storm on October 22, 1726. Its greatest challenge was the close proximity of the maroons.

***

Tarone was now almost 17 and a rebellious young man. Daudi knew he should have tried to stop him the first time he went wandering in the mountains, but he dared to hope that the boy might find his grandmother or his Aunt Emma. Tarone had connected with other slaves who escaped from Temple Hall, but not them. He would disappear for days, running wild with the maroons, answering whenever the *abeng* horn was blown. Each time, Daudi feared he was dead.

"Son, what are you doing, up to no-good running around with those maroons?" Daudi asked, after he'd come home from one of his jaunts.

Tarone shrugged. "They're free, Fadda. We should be with them."

"They're at war with these Englishmen. It's not your fight; you're not one of them."

"We're all black men. We are the same."

"You are an Israelite; these people here are your people."

"Then we can start our own group," Tarone said, energized. "We don't have to stay here. Why can't you understand? It's a fight to stay free. That is our fight."

Tarone's words alarmed Daudi. It was dangerous talk. "What you don't understand, son, is that it's not just for you or your freedom," he said trying to get through to him. "There are families here, some old and weak, and children who are too young to protect themselves. Do you want to sacrifice their lives in this mess?"

Tarone shook his head in defiance. "I want them to know what it's like to free."

"Free like an animal without shelter or food to eat?"

"No, Fadda, you're the one who told me how God took care of His people in the wilderness. They had food to eat. Where is the faith you preach about?"

Daudi almost choked hearing the same questions he had asked of his father and then having his father's answers on his tongue. He swallowed that response and said, "My faith is not rational. It can't explain the whys that you put before me. All I can tell you is that it is the source of my strength. It picks me up and carries me through the bitterness of my life on this land. I was born here as you were, but I only know what my father told me. We are the descendants of Aaron; we are the designated ones to protect and preach God's word. I will do it to my death, as my father did. Not all of us will see freedom or the land promised to our people, but these children might."

"I don't know if that's enough for me, Fadda," Tarone said before he walked away.

***

Word came from Britain that Master Lawes would be replaced as governor. The criticism was that he had made no headway in the war with the maroons. More British troops were sent to Jamaica to aggressively squash the rebellion. They struggled to overcome the advantage the maroons had in knowing the geography and landscape. Moreover, the maroons had become adept in using their network of relatives on plantations, free blacks, and friendly traders to track movements of the British troops. They were able to communicate messages using drums, and they successfully ambushed the military on several occasions.

Over the next two years, additional colonial regiments were sent to Jamaica to fight the maroons, but they only suffered more losses in money and manpower. Tarone, despite countless warnings from Daudi, continued to run with the maroons. He would come back for a few days to make his appearance known, but when he heard the horn blow, he answered the call.

"I'm worried about you, son. They have troops all around this area. If they catch you, they'll kill you, no matter who you belong to."

"Don't worry, Fadda, I have a weapon," Tarone said, pulling it from a pouch in his pants.

Daudi's heart skipped a beat. "I beg you, forget this fighting!"

"Fadda, we're getting stronger, and we're winning. This is not the time to quit. We need your eyes and ears. If you find out anything about the location of the British, relay it to us."

That night, when Tarone slipped off, neither of them could sleep. Daudi felt as if each pistol shot that rang out went through him. The next day, Venus was so afraid for her son, that her hands shook. There were moments when she could barely tug the leaves from the plants. Daudi searched for answers in the Bible Adam had given to his father, Abdalla. He had never done it before, but he made a sacrifice to the Lord on Sunday.

"I have been torn about what we should do with this war going on around us, so I looked to the word for guidance. The Scripture Numbers 31:3 says, 'So Moses told the people, "Arm some of your men for war, that they may go against the Midianites and execute the LORD's vengeance on them."' We need to be careful, I don't want to put any of you in danger, but we may have to do our part to see that the maroons win this war. It may mean freedom for us."

Daudi learned how to tap the drum and send messages when the troops passed the plantation. He wanted to have some part in the fight, but it was more so to protect Tarone than for his people's freedom. He thanked God that the maroons were able to defend their stronghold in the mountains.

# Chapter Eighteen

# Tarone

Tarone pushed the door open and fell on the floor. Venus screamed when she saw the blood seeping from his side. Daudi rushed over to him and ripped his shirt opened. He had a hole on the left side of his lower belly.

"He's been shot! The bullet is still in him!" Daudi said.

"I'll get the doctor!" Venus said, panicked.

"No! He'll report it! They'll ask questions. That won't be good."

Venus became more agitated. "We can't let him die!"

Daudi hesitated for a second. Then he said, "Go and get Cyrus."

"No! He's a Myal-man!" Venus said, shaking her head. "We can't. It'll bring the wrath of God on us."

With a solemn look on his face, Daudi told her, "We're already feeling the wrath. Go get him!"

Venus grabbed her shawl and dashed out the door.

Daudi rolled up rags and put them under Tarone's head. "Forgive me, Lord. This is my son lying here. It is within Your power to lift him up. Please, Lord, have mercy!"

About 40 minutes later, Cyrus and his daughter, Bernice, scurried in, with Venus trailing them. Without saying anything, he threw his head back and called out in a loud shriek. Then he knelt down next to Tarone. Bernice poured a cup of rum and handed it to her father. He added the contents of a small bottle into the cup, swirled it, and poured it into Tarone's mouth.

Daudi watched as his son fell into a deep sleep. Cyrus poured the rest of the rum over the wound on Tarone's belly. Then he pulled a rock out of his pocket and rubbed it in a circle around the hole as he chanted. After a few minutes, he took a knife and cut across the circle. Miraculously, the bullet was sitting under the skin. Cyrus packed the hole with herbs. Then Bernice stitched the opening with the threads of a silk piece of cloth. When she finished, Cyrus stood up, and drums from outside began to beat. He danced in a circle around Tarone.

When Cyrus stopped, he told them, "Bernice will stay here to watch for fever."

"Bless you," Daudi said, gripping his arm. "I owe you my thanks."

"I am no different than you, priest," Cyrus told him. "My father was Akan. Our people come from the same tree as your people." Then he left.

Tarone lay in the bed barely conscious for two days. It was Bernice's skillful care that put their minds at ease enough to leave for the field in the mornings.

***

Having developed a fine grade of tobacco, and without governing duties to distract him, Sir Nicholas Lawes was interested in experimenting with another crop. He'd been given Arabica seedlings during a visit to the island of Martinique. He wanted a young slave who could be taught to grow coffee for the next generations. He sent the overseer to fetch Daudi's son,

Tarone. Daudi and Venus were petrified when the overseer rode over to him in the field.

"Where's Tarone?" Miller yelled, his eyes scanning the field.

"He's ailing pretty bad," Daudi shouted back.

"What's wrong with him?" Miller asked. "Has the nurse seen him?"

Daudi shook his head no. "Looks like bloody flux. It might be contagious."

The overseer twisted his mouth and turned up his nose. "I'll give it a day or two before I send the nurse. Master Lawes wants him to work on a new crop."

"I can go 'til he gets better. Then I'll show him," Daudi said, sounding eager.

The overseer nodded and rode on. The foreman of the gang was relieved. Nobody wanted to take a beating for keeping secrets. Things were already tense with the maroons running circles around the British troops.

***

Tarone recovered, but his injury slowed him down, containing him, at least for a while. And as Bernice nursed him back to health, he had taken a liking to her. Daudi and Venus were thrilled about the match, hoping she could settle Tarone down. They all pitched in and built the couple a hut; and when it was finished, Tarone took Bernice for his wife. Dressed in new clothes made by the seamstresses, Bernice and Tarone stood before all the negroes as Daudi presided over the wedding.

For almost six months, Tarone hadn't ventured from the plantation, despite the sound of the drums. Then he started sneaking into the mountains again. Once again, he would disappear for days. Things changed when Master Lawes died on June 18, 1731. His son, James, inherited the plantation. He lacked the civilized nature of his father, and it showed in his cruelty to the negroes. When one slave ran away, his wife was beaten to her death. That's when Tarone stopped his roaming. He couldn't let that happen to Bernice. Even when he became restless, hearing about the attacks on Nanny Town that went on for six years, he ignored the sounds of the drums and the horn until his daughter, Summer, was born.

In 1734, during a lavish party at the great house, the house slaves overheard that Governor Hunter was sending three squads of the militia into Nanny Town. They passed the word, and drums beat out the warning. The Windward maroons drew back further into the Blue Mountains. As planned, the British troops moved into their territory firing cannons. They destroyed the crops and occupied Nanny Town. The commander reported that all the maroons had been killed, including Nanny.

Obviously, those words of victory were exaggerated. Three hundred survivors were said to have marched to the west of the island to join her brother, Kojo, and his soldiers, but he sent them back to Portland. Out of alternatives, the Windward maroons raided the British settlements in their territory and retreated to the high, rocky terrain. The colonial forces suffered huge casualties from the ambushes and surrendered Nanny Town. However, the militia regrouped and regained control over Nanny Town, but the occupation was too costly in money and lives with little success of eliminating them. Vowing never to be enslaved again, the maroons refused to give up the fight.

Over the next five years, Tarone had another daughter named Winter; a son named Falcon; and another son named Adio, who was born the year that the Maroons won the war. Tarone worked most of the time growing coffee plants, and Falcon worked alongside him. Adio and the girls stayed close to their mother on the tobacco field. There were still times when Tarone wanted a taste of freedom for a few days; but the horn didn't sound anymore, and the drums never signaled a meeting. He knew the resistance was still strong though. Kojo was the leader of the Leeward maroons on the westside of the island.

In 1739, the British government realized that they would never defeat the maroons. They had cost them 250,000 pounds and the lives of 3,000 British soldiers. The new governor of Jamaica, Edward Treelawny, negotiated a peace agreement with Kojo that recognized their freedom. A year later, the Windward maroons also agreed to sign a peace treaty. Their land was returned to them, and they would govern themselves on the condition that they would protect the island from invaders. There was one regrettable concession made by the maroons in the treaties. They agreed not to harbor any runaway slaves, and they also agreed to become slavecatchers and return them to their owners.

***

"I can't believe they would betray us like that!" Tarone said to his father. "I fought beside them and risked my life with them many times. They were my brothers and sisters. Now they are worse than Massa. They're working for him against us!"

"They are not the first to betray their brothers," Daudi responded. "If not for that, half of us wouldn't be on this island. We'd be free in Africa. Remember the words of David, 'Even my close friend in whom I trusted, Who ate my bread, Has lifted up his heel against me,' Psalm 41:9."

Finally, Tarone understood the words of his father, who warned him not to trust those who weren't his own people. He turned to the Bible and began to study by candlelight every night. If he couldn't do anything else for his sons, he would do what his father had done for him: teach them the word of God. He was determined to let them know where they came from. At the evening meal, Daudi told them all stories of their ancestors far away. How they were kings and queens and priests in the Temple of God.

Peace on the island increased profits. Slaves were given small plots of land to grow more of their own food and to make money selling at the market on Sundays. Tarone worked hard, and his money slowly added up. He thought he might be able to buy Falcon's freedom. As a free man, he could work and help the rest of the family. Tarone pushed his body past the point of exhaustion. Hope was his motivation; he hadn't had much of it in his life. He had only saved a few pence when another storm blew in.

The day was October 20, 1744. It had been raining for a few days, and the word was that the sea had swelled; but the overseer insisted that they keep planting the new crop and lay out the dung to take advantage of the heavy showers. Early in the evening, strong winds began to blow from the south, and booms of thunder resounded.

"Take shelter!" Miller said, riding quickly toward his house.

"It's another hurricane!" Tarone shouted. "Nothing will be safe on this land. Follow me!"

Bernice grabbed her daughters' hands, and Tarone lifted the boys into his arms. Daudi and Venus hesitated when they saw the direction he was headed. "Come on, Fadda! I know where we can find shelter."

"We can't make it up into those mountains, son. Those trees up there are going to fall like sticks. We'll ride it out in the house."

There was no time to argue. "Those who can, come with me!" Tarone urged, speaking to the rest of the gang.

Tarone guided them on the path he had taken into the forest so many times, except the rains were coming down harder, and they could barely see their way. "Link arms!" he shouted back to the end of the line. They trekked for over an hour, until Tarone stopped in front of a hole in the hillside. It was about eight feet wide and five feet high.

"What if it collapses?" one of the men asked.

"What other chance do we have?" Tarone asked grimly.

Lightning cracked the sky, and then it dimmed. Seeing they had no other options, Tarone led the tentative group inside the cave. It was dry, but it was too dark to see.

"I'm scared, Fadda," Adio whimpered

"Can we light a fire?" Bernice asked.

"No, the fire will suck all the air," he answered.

They all sat in the darkness, frightened by the sounds of the storm. After a few hours of listening to the torrents, they felt the earth shake beneath them. Terrified, Bernice started a song, and they all joined in. When the winds whipped louder, she sang louder. In spite of their fear, the children were able to sleep. The others stayed awake all night waiting. The storm ended as daylight crept across the front of the cave.

It was an apprehensive walk back to the plantation. They were afraid of what they might find and who they might not find. By some miracle, the sick house was still standing. Daudi, Venus, and 39 others had survived inside. All those in the great house had survived, but two of the overseers had been trampled by the horses in the shed. All the cane seedling had blown away.

"All I planted for us is gone," Daudi said, sadly, feeling the loss of hope. "Thank God, we're all here."

The whole island had been damaged, and Port Royal and Kingston had been severely damaged. One hundred and four vessels in the harbor, eight military ships, and 96 merchant ships had been wrecked, stranded, or sunk; and 194 men had been killed or drowned. The docks had been swept into the sea and the warehouses washed away. Dead animals floated in the floodwaters. But that wasn't the end of the horror. With all that was lost, they were left with pestilence and disease.

Burning hot in damp clothes, Daudi tried to stand, but the world seemed to swing and turn, and he couldn't keep his balance. Overcome, he fell backwards in the field and watched the world spin above him. Adio ran screaming to his grandma.

"Oh, Lawd!" Venus said, dropping her hoe and running over to Daudi. She stooped down beside him and touched his head. "He's got the fever," she shrieked. "Help me get him to the sick house."

The whole family prayed over Daudi, nursed him around the clock, begged him to wake up, but none of it helped. Daudi died. Before they could bury him, Venus took sick and died. They were burdened with grief. Death hung all over the island. When Summer got the fever and died, Tarone cursed God. When Falcon died shortly after, he struggled to find a reason to live. If not for Bernice and the other children, he would have gone up into the hill like a wounded animal and waited for death.

***

The misery after the storm had everybody on edge. Paranoia plagued the plantations after news spread of a plan to assassinate all the whites. The 900 slaves involved in the plot were betrayed by a young slave named Deborah, who feared that the white baby she nursed would be murdered. The conspirators were severely punished, some with death.

Sick, tired, and enraged, within a year, there was another slave insurrection. It was squashed by the maroons. Dressed in military clothes and carrying rifles, the maroons patrolled the plantations as the white man's police and hunted for runaways. Resentment against them grew among the slaves on the plantations.

"I have no respect for them," Tarone said. "They bought their freedom in exchange for keeping their own brothers as slaves. They are invisible to me."

Adio spit on the ground when they walked by. "More rebels are rising up to fight, better men than they are."

"Much better," his friend Peter added. He and Adio had met with some of them near the Strawberry Hill plantation.

"Sorry to say, it's finished before it starts," Tarone lamented. "They got some new laws to punish rebels who dare to rise up against their owners."

"That won't stop us, Fadda. What can they do to us that is different from the punishment we get for next to nothing 'round here any day?"

"Be careful, son. You and Peter better watch yourselves. You don't know who you can trust around here."

Adio encouraged the slaves up in the great house to listen to every conversation between the whites. He shared every move of the troops that he learned with the rebels. He wanted to do for the rebel runaways what his fadda had done for the maroons. He and Peter trudged up in the hills during the night, carrying messages and supplies to the rebels.

***

Inhumane treatment led to slave rebellions, which led to more inhumane treatment. A powerful rebellion rose up in early April 1760, beginning in St. Mary's parish. It was initiated by more than 100 slaves of Akan heritage, led by a newly imported slave named Tacky. Before his capture, Tacky had been a chief, a king in Fante land. The irony of his predicament was that he had sold his rivals to the British to be slaves in Jamaica, only later to be sold himself after being defeated by another adversary.

The Tacky-led rebellion began early one Monday morning on the Frontier and Trinity plantations. The rebels took over and killed the masters and the overseers. They headed to Fort Haldane in Port Maria, where the munitions were kept. There, they overpowered and killed British forces and took 40 firearms and four barrels of gun powder and moved to the Heywood Hall and Escher plantations. The number of rebels grew as they marched over estate after estate, further encouraged by the Obeah man, who said they would be protected in battle.

Nevertheless, there was one slave who eased away to alert the militia. The governor sent orders that the maroons were to join the 75 mounted militia to quell the revolt. They would be rewarded for each rebel they killed or captured and were paid seven pence and one half-penny each day. When the Obeah man was killed, many of the rebels were discouraged and returned to their plantations. Tacky and his remaining men headed to the mountains but were tracked by the maroons. Chased through the woods, Tacky was shot in the head by the legendary marksman, Davy. Tacky was decapitated, and his head was hung on a pole in Spanish Town. The bodies of the rest of his men were later found in a cave, where they had committed suicide rather than return to being slaves.

Tacky's defeat didn't end the revolt. Instead, it started a war, Tacky's War, as the rebellion spread all over Jamaica. Even with the help of two army regiment, marines from a British warship, the local militia, and the maroons, it would be six months before peace returned to the island. Sixty whites were killed, 400 enslaved blacks lost their lives in the battle, and 600 were deported to British Honduras.

***

Master Howe lost considerable money in the slaves that had run away, and he wasn't about to lose any more of his investment by maiming or killing another. Those that he suspected of being troublemakers and conspiring with other runaways were sold and deported off the island.

When Peter was caught sneaking to another plantation to meet a girl he fancied, he told them about Adio sharing information with the rebels. Word from the great house traveled around the house slaves that Peter had betrayed Adio. Winter, who was helping in the great house, ran over to Adio's gang to tell him what Peter had done.

"Brother, Massa gonna send for you!" she told him. "Peter got caught and turned on you."

Adio frowned. He was confused. Peter was his friend. He would never betray him like that. Together, they had plotted against the maroons for that very thing.

"I can't believe he would do that! They must have beat him badly," he said. "Is he all right?"

Winter's faced twisted as if she had the taste of something nasty in her mouth. "He wasn't touched," she said snidely. "Folks are saying he was always jealous of you and our family. Didn't think we deserved extra status 'round here."

"Hurry on back to work before they see you out here in the field," he told Winter, wanting to keep her out of trouble. "We'll talk later."

It was still hard for Adio to accept that Peter would betray him. The words of King David filled his head: "For it is not an enemy who reproaches me, Then I could bear it; Nor is it one who hates me who has exalted himself against me, Then I hide myself from him. But it is you, a man my equal, My companion and my familiar friend," Psalm 55:12-13.

The singer-man in the gang started up a new chant. There was nothing else they could do. Adio was working in the tobacco fields waiting for his punishment when the overseer came to fetch him.

"Peter done told us what you been doing," Miller said. "Come on here. You're done."

Adio walked slowly ahead of the horse up to the great house, where two of the housemaids, the groomsman, and four others were already chained together. Along the way, as they passed other plantations, more slaves were hitched to the group as they marched to Kingston.

Tarone and Bernice didn't take notice that evening when Adio didn't show up for supper. It wasn't unusual for him to do so. The next morning, while they were toiling in the field, Miller rode by with a grin on his face.

"Your boy is gone," he said to Tarone. "He's been sold."

"Where abouts?" Tarone asked, hiding his shock.

"Off the island," he told them. "He's been sold and shipped to America."

Bernice's head rolled back and her eyes closed as she crumpled to the ground. Tarone's mouth opened, releasing a silent scream.

# Chapter Nineteen
# Adio/Adam (born in 1739)

Adio had never met his great-grandfather Abdalla, or Abraham, as most of the slaves called him; but he had heard of his capture in Mombasa, how he was forced onto a ship at Zanzibar, and of his horrible voyage to Jamaica. Now, 100 years later, Adio was just like Abdalla, betrayed by someone he trusted. Once he and the other deportees got to Kingston, they were pushed and prodded onto a ship named *Greyhound*. He lay in the bottom of the vessel like a fish out of water. First having been hooked, having struggled against the hook to be free, made weak and numb from flopping about, and finally waiting for the next horror or death.

They sailed for a matter of weeks versus the months that it took on the Middle Passage from Africa to Jamaica. The ship docked in Chesapeake Bay, at Jamestown, Virginia, in September 1761. This new place was nothing like the island. The air was still and lacked the sweet smell of Jamaica. Still in a daze, Adio found himself with clean oiled skin, standing before a crowd of white men in a public auction in front of the Raleigh Tavern in Williamsburg. He was among two other men and two women of those from the Temple Hall plantation that were sold to Mr. Benjamin Harrison V, master and owner of the Berkeley plantation in Charles City County.

When they got to the Berkeley estate, Master Harrison went into the big house. A negro man and woman were standing there waiting.

"You can unchain them, Henry," the driver ordered, watching them all cautiously with the woman's help. Seeing that they weren't violent or itching to run off, he said, "Go on and show them where they gon' be, Henry. Lucy, you take them girls. They all come from them West Indies, where they got all that voodoo. Let them know Master Harrison don't have nothing but Christians on this place."

"What's y'all names?" the one named Henry asked. Adio just stared back. He hadn't uttered a word since they were loaded on the ship. Simply, he couldn't put words to his pain, betrayal, and disappointment; it was too big. What could he say that meant anything or changed anything? Who could he take into confidence? He trusted no one.

Mark, the groomsman from Temple estate, spoke up. "This is Adio. I'm Mark."

"Can't he speak?" Henry asked, staring at him.

Mark shook his head no.

Henry sighed. "Well, Adio, we gon' call you Adam."

Following the three women, Henry and the men walked a good distance from the master's mansion and a short distance from the overseer's big house to the slave quarters. Adio noticed that they all spoke English, and most of the slaves wore shoes. They didn't live in huts like the ones in Jamaica. They had small cabins. He wasn't sure what his plan was going to be in this strange place, or if there was a way to escape. He only knew that he didn't have a home to go back to in Jamaica, and he probably wouldn't see his family again on this side of heaven.

"We grow tobacco on this place," Henry told them. "Either of y'all grown tobacco before?"

Mark answered, "No. We grew sugar cane. Adam worked on a gang growing coffee beans."

"It don't make no difference," Henry said. "It's fierce work planting and pulling anything out of the ground, especially to feed another man." Henry pointed far off at the white man sitting on a horse watching the slaves in the field. "That there is the main overseer on this place. He's Massa Harvey. He's not as brutal and cruel as some I've seen and others I've heard about. From the way he talk, he thinks he's a righteous man, better than most. He know Massa Harrison wants religion on this place. Except he got one particular sin he can't control, lust of the flesh, 'specially of the darker kind."

Adio looked without saying anything. This overseer wasn't any different from the ones he had known back on the Temple estate. They were all guilty of the same sins.

***

It wasn't long before the overseer's wife, Blanche, learned about the new slaves. Curious, she moseyed down to the slave quarters to get a look at them.

"Where're the new bucks?" she asked Henry.

"They over there, missus," he said, pointing across the field. "The lighter one is Mark; the other is Adam. He can't talk."

"I'm going to be needing one of them to do some work for me," she said, eyeing them both.

Less than a week had passed before Blanche requested Adio to work at the overseer's house. For her purposes, he was perfect, not only physically handsome, young, and strong, but he was mute. If he was dumb, he couldn't reveal her sin, which was equal to her husband's. Initially, she retaliated out of jealousy when her husband snuck off into the night to pester the fresh wenches. But after some years, she needed no excuse.

For a month, she put Adio to work chopping wood, planting in her garden, tending her horse, and driving her carriage. She noticed that he kept to himself most of the time, and she liked that. In an effort to appear coy, she wore fancy dresses and created opportunities to be near him, but he didn't seem affected.

On the first frost of the autumn season, Adio sat with his knees pulled to his chest in the overseer's shed. He hadn't experienced this chill that went all through him to his bones. Moving back and forth to keep warm, he grimaced when he heard the Missus calling for him. She surprised him with an old coat that belonged to her husband and a cup of hot broth. He nodded in thanks for her kindness. Then she told him to come into the house.

Adio was speechless when the Missus invited him to share the warmth of her bed, something he had never known. Blanche took Adio's innocence in exchange for treats of meat and sweets. He didn't care for the Missus, but he figured that he might parlay her favor into his freedom one day. Five years later, Adio had gone from optimistic to doubtful and was now indifferent. It all changed in the spring of 1766, when another passel of slaves trudging in chains walked onto the Berkeley plantation.

The slave woman's shoulders were bent from fatigue, but her lips were pursed in defiance. That's where he saw himself in her face. All the things he couldn't verbalize were staring back at him. He wasn't the only one who noticed her. In one glance, Blanche knew that her husband would waste no time in slipping around in the night to bed her. To thwart his movements, Blanche insisted that the new girl be her maidservant. She gave her a Bible to keep in her skirt pocket. "If master comes near you, lift up this book, and call Jesus."

The young woman's name was Irene. When she and Adio passed each other, she avoided eye contact. And for several weeks, he only heard her say two words: "Yes, ma'am." One day, he whispered in her ear, "You're beautiful." Her eyes widened in shock, and her chest swelled as if she was prepared to scream. He pressed a finger to her lips, she exhaled, and then she smiled shyly.

"You're the missus' boy," Irene said accusingly.

Adio shrugged. "It's like any other job, feeding the hogs or running the horses. She the one chose me. I choose you for my wife."

***

Adio courted Irene with the extras he got from the Missus. She knew where he got them, but she understood the situation. She'd seen other women pestered by Massa, even her own mama. She was comforted that he only talked to her. It was the part of him that he shared with no one else. He told her about his family in Jamaica, how Abdalla had been betrayed and captured in Mombasa. He told her about the men in his family being high priests and chief priests, a designation given to them by God. Late into the night, while she mended clothes by candlelight, he read the Bible to her.

Adio asked Henry to inquire to Master Harrison about getting approval to marry Irene. He was afraid that neither Harvey nor Blanche would agree to their union. Sharing the goodwill of the Christmas season, Master Harrison not only approved, he insisted they have new clothes for a ceremony and designated a cabin for them. All the slaves gathered on the front lawn in front of the mansion for the wedding. A black preacher officiated, waving a broom over their heads to sweep away evil spirits. Then he placed the broom at their feet, and they jumped over it.

The bed he shared with Irene was made of straw and covered with a blanket, unlike the Missus' feather bed, but there was no other place he'd rather have been. It was his place of rest, solace, and love. He discovered the pleasure and passion of being with a woman he cherished. From then on, he worked hard to find ways to avoid being alone with Blanche.

The next year, in 1769, after the September harvest, Irene gave birth to a boy. When Adio saw his son, he cried out, "Glory to God! Thank you!" Hearing Adio speak for the first time, the midwife thought she had witnessed a miracle, a healing with the baby's birth. Surely, the child must be anointed! Adio and Irene rejoiced, although they knew the baby's birth had nothing to do with Adio's ability to speak, but they never revealed the truth. They named their baby Jordan. Even as a child, all the slaves considered him blessed by God.

Blanche's jealousy of Irene festered like an open sore. She envied the position she had as Adio's wife and wanted to get rid of her. She wanted her sold, but the Harrisons frowned on breaking up slave families. Still, she did her best to make Irene miserable. She would slap her for no apparent reason, and when that didn't satisfy her ire, she ordered her out into the field.

Fuming, Adio stormed up to the big house to confront Blanche.

"Bring Irene back into the house, or I'll never touch you again!" he roared.

Stunned and insulted, Blanche hollered back, "How dare you speak to me like that! I'll have you whipped!"

Adio smirked. "Go ahead, and I'll shout out to the heavens that you are my whore."

Blanche's demeanor changed. "Why do you treat me this way? Haven't I been good to you?" she asked, pleading with him.

"How can you say you treat a man good who you keep as a slave?"

"It's not my fault! I haven't done that," she whimpered.

"You have more than anyone else," he said, walking away.

***

Blanche gave in to Adio's demand. She would have done anything to keep him in her good graces. And although he detested her, he used the arrangement for his own benefit. Whenever he was in the overseer's house, he read whatever papers he could find. He read about the unrest and agitation among other slaves in the state. He read about the divide between the colonists and the British government. What interested him most was the decision in the case of James Somersett. He was a slave taken to England by his master who had run away. He was recaptured and chained in the bottom of a ship bound for Jamaica when he sued for his freedom. Since Parliament had not declared laws in England stating slavery was legal, the judge, Lord Mansfield, found Somersett should be released. This 1772 decision outlawed slavery in England.

Adam secretly shared the information to all that he could; and in a few short months, slaves in the colonies were filing petitions for freedom, stating that the decision should apply to slaves in the colonies. By September 1773, 250,000 slaves in Virginia, including Adio, were trying to get out of the colony and go to Britain where they would be free. Plantation masters were unnerved, fearful of a powerful revolt. The royal governor of Virginia suspected that in the event of war, the slaves would align themselves with the side that benefited them.

It was the main topic of conversation on Sundays among the whites and the blacks.

"When the British troops get here, I'm joining up," Mark said to Adio. "That's our chance to get free. Whether they win or not, I'm headed to England."

"I haven't decided what I'll do," Adio mused. "Whenever our people have fought for another nation's gain, we always ended up the loser."

"Adam, your only choice then is to stay a slave."

"We're men. We can join up with the other negros and have a war of our own," Adio proposed boldly.

"Have you forgotten Jamaica?" Mark reminded him. "There's always someone who will turn against the group. You'll never know who you can trust."

***

In 1774, there was talk among the plantation owners of the "conspiracy of negroes" and that if there was a war between America and Britain, that an insurrection among the slaves would erupt. The irony of the situation was not lost on a few. Abigail Adams wrote to her husband, John, "It always appeared a most iniquitous scheme to me to fight ourselves for what we are daily robbing and plundering from those who have as good a right to freedom as we have."

A year later, as the prospect of war became a certainty, the royal governor of Virginia, Lord Dunmore, offered slaves and indentured servants freedom if they were willing to fight for the British. The drawback was that his declaration only applied to slaves owned by rebels and not those who belonged to loyalists. Adio read about a man named Patrick Henry, who gave a speech in Richmond, where he said, "Give me liberty, or give me death." Afterward, the colonists signed a resolution that would send militia to fight for their independence from British rule in the American Revolution.

"We can win with them, Adam," Mark urged. "Then we can go to England and be free men."

Adio was torn. He might have tried if it weren't for Irene and Jordan. Who would look out for them if something happened to him? He had been in this position before in Jamaica when the maroons fought against the British. His father had told him of his great-grandfather being in this predicament in Mombasa. Adio knew from experience that he couldn't win.

"How can you win fighting in a war between two of your enemies, especially when they both see you as a slave?"

"I'm going to take my chance," Mark said.

"I've got a son to raise. I'm not dying for either side," Adio said, shaking his head.

Within the week, Mark left and joined the Navy with more than 100 other runaway blacks. Within a month, several hundred more joined His Majesty's troops. They wore the uniform of the Ethiopian Regiment, with the words "Liberty to Slaves" written across their chests. By the time the Continental Congress issued its Declaration of Independence on July 4, 1776, 800 blacks had joined Dunmore's forces. Starved and sick, more than half of them died of a fever epidemic in a month's time. The regiment was dissolved, and the men were left to fend for themselves. Adio never knew what happened to Mark.

In the meantime, Congress needed more soldiers. To remedy the situation, they reevaluated their position of negroes serving in their army, albeit without arms. Virginia refused to allow slaves to be armed, so to recruit more white men, they offered 300 acres of land and the choice between a healthy black male slave or 60 pounds, roughly $200.

Free blacks were the first to be called up in the draft. "It was thought they could best be spared," the governor of Virginia stated to George Washington. In 1777, Washington limited recruits of blacks to only freemen. It was a formality at this point, with planters being allowed to send a slave to substitute in his place when he was drafted. These negro soldiers had the privilege of freezing out in the cold with empty bellies and dying at Valley Forge side by side with whites in the Continental Army.

***

In the midst of the war, Jordan gave all the blacks on the Berkeley plantation something many had lost and others never had, hope. They believed in miracles again. He had an infectious smile that brightened up the darkest day. Adio noticed the way they reacted to his son; it reminded him of the reverence paid to his father, Tarone, back in Jamaica. It was the respect reserved for brave men of God, those willing to sacrifice their lives for others, those qualified to lead. Adio didn't feel like he was that man. He had allowed himself to be corrupted by others for their own purposes, but Jordan could be that man. He decided to teach him, to prepare him, as his own father had tried to do with him. Tell him of his heritage, his designation. In that way, he could amend for his sins.

Late in the night by candlelight, Adio read the Bible to Jordan and Irene. He told them stories of the Israelites, their bondage in Egypt, and how they were freed. He preached the words to him as he had seen his father preach to the people.

"We are those same people," he explained to his son. "We must call on God to fulfill his promise."

Jordan was smart and inquisitive. "How did we get here?"

"What matters is how we get out," Adio answered.

Every spare moment he could get, Adio worked in his garden, trying to have enough to provide for his family and have extra he could sell. If God didn't send another Moses to free them, he would have to free his own.

***

Opportunity stormed onto the plantation on January 9, 1781. Word had come three days earlier that 1,500 hundred

British troops, led by General Benedict Arnold, had captured Richmond. They had destroyed the Virginia naval fleet, the foundries, supply houses, and mills, and were headed back down to the Berkeley estate, raiding plantations left and right of the James River.

Benjamin Harrison V, who was a member of the Second Continental Congress and a signer of the Declaration of Independence, was no doubt a target for the British general. Taking heed of the warning, Harrison moved his family out of harm's way, making a narrow escape before Arnold arrived at Berkeley.

General Arnold ransacked the house, taking everything of value, and wrecked the rest. Determined that no image of the family would remain, he took all the portraits of the Harrisons and made a bonfire with them on the front lawn. He freed some of the slaves and used the cows for target practice.

"What do we do?" Irene asked Adio. Jordan stood beside her anxiously waiting his direction.

Adam closed his eyes tightly and searched his mind for an answer. In a matter of minutes, the British would be gone and so would their chance to run. Where would they go? If they were caught, they might be killed; but, certainly, they would be beaten within an inch of their lives. He watched as the British soldiers threw flames into the windows of the house.

"Now is not the time," he said quietly.

"We have to leave here now, Papa!" Jordan urged. "This is our chance to be free."

"Where are we going?" Adio asked soberly.

"It doesn't matter, as long as we're free from this place!" Jordan said, bouncing in his shoes.

"Black folks are starving to death, son. Winter is here on us. Your mama is having a baby. I can't put her in danger."

"Papa, you want the baby to be born into this? Where's your faith? You said God provides for His people. The Israelites weren't afraid. Why are you scared?"

"The Israelites had a mighty leader and traveled in great numbers. We're alone."

"I have a musket. One of the British soldiers gave it to me."

"I was just like you, son, and look where it got me, separated from my family and all I knew."

Jordan kept pushing. "You were a slave then and a slave now! We have a chance to be free."

"Our time will come. God has told me to be still and wait."

"Why should we sit here like scared rabbits?"

"Because they are smart enough to know when to run."

Jordan ran off into the woods. Adio didn't know if he would ever see him again. He returned to the cabin late that night with a dead rabbit in his hand. He threw it on the table and walked back out.

"I trust you," Irene said, rubbing his back. "Jordan is young. He doesn't know what we know about the world out there."

"I don't know much about that myself," Adio said.

***

The war ended in October when the British army surrendered at Yorktown, Virginia, after a major defeat. Tens of thousands of slaves had escaped and were free. Some resettled in Nova Scotia, Canada; some in Jamaica; others to England; and some hid out in the frontier regions of the North. Still, there were a number of slave owners who manumitted some or all of their slaves after the war by will. The number of free blacks in Virginia had increased six-fold.

Benjamin Harrison became the governor of Virginia. He didn't free any of his slaves on Berkeley as some other plantation owners had done. Having been educated around Quakers and Methodists, he knew that slavery was morally wrong, but they were needed to run his vast plantation. His statement was that he wanted to protect them and provide for them, that they could not care for themselves alone. So even as America gained its independence after eight years of war, the practice of slavery was further entrenched.

A large group of slaves met at the front of the Berkeley mansion to petition Master Harrison for their freedom. He answered them, saying, "If you can make enough to purchase your freedom, then I will agree. Then I'll know that you can provide for yourself."

While Adio was working his fingers to the bone trying to earn the money to buy their freedom, Jordan had realized that he could use his influence as the spiritual leader on the plantation to organize the slaves. One thing he learned from the war is that there is power in numbers. He couldn't convince his father to run, but when the next opportunity came, he would have the support of the rest of the people.

***

Jordan had just turned 21 when he heard that there was a major slave revolt happening in Saint Domingue. All the slaveholders in the States were worried that the rebellion might spread like yellow fever. Held in high esteem for his ability to quiet fellow slaves and for being a master at growing the finest leaves of Virginia, they asked Jordan to dissuade the slaves from causing trouble.

From the information Jordan could gather, tens of thousands of slaves had united and killed thousands of whites. They were demanding the right to vote. President Washington sent aid to the government in Saint Domingue to fight the revolt. Thomas Jefferson had even come to Berkeley and privately discussed emancipation of the American slaves.

"This is the lesson you need," Adio said to Jordan. "Watch and wait. You will see how this rebellion will end. Maybe then you'll understand that the best way is to buy your freedom."

"There's no time to wait for the white man's conscience to tell him to do right," Jordan argued. "We have to demand our rights! Fighting is the only way. I hear the rebels have control over one third of that island. Already, they have proposed that all black men should have rights. They have abolished slavery in France. That is real power. We can do the same thing here."

"Truth is, there's no fight left in me, son. My prayers are for you."

Adio died before he had enough to purchase his family's freedom. Irene was brokenhearted. It was as if Adio's death took most of the life out of her. Jordan was even more determined to get free. He hid the money his daddy pressed into his hand and vowed that nothing would tie him to the Berkeley plantation—no wife and no child. He worked hard to add to his chest and focused on growing the number of people who came to hear him preach.

## Chapter Twenty
# Jordan (born 1769)

Jordan was 31 years old at the turn of the century. So far, he had succeeded in keeping his vow to remain unattached to anyone or anything that would keep him from gaining his freedom, one way or another. It was the time of the Second Great Awakening, a religious revival of Protestants in the States. So when he was offered money to go and preach to the slaves at the neighboring Shirley plantation, he agreed. He thought it might give him a chance to expand his strategy for organizing the slaves beyond Berkeley; and if not, it would surely hasten his progress in earning enough to buy his freedom and possibly enough to purchase a piece of land.

Jordan decided against a radical message for his first sermon. He wasn't sure if he could trust the people sitting there in front of him. His eyes scanned the group before he began. They were dressed in their best clothes, and all their faces had the familiar look of distress with a tiny shimmer of hope. Then he saw her in the back. She was aloof, her neck still strong, and her face proud. His mind went blank for a moment, and his throat got dry. He picked up the glass of water next to him and took a large gulp, while he searched his mind for the words he had prepared to speak.

"Brothers and sisters, the glory of the Lord is upon us. Though we struggle, this is surely the time to renew our faith. Jeremiah 4:9-11 tells us, 'This is what the LORD, the

God of Israel, to whom you sent me to present your petition says: If you stay in this land, I will build you up and not tear you down; I will plant you and not uproot you, for I have relented concerning the disaster I have inflicted on you. Do not be afraid of him, declares the LORD, for I am with you and will save you and deliver you from his hands.' Saints of God, what the Scripture is saying to us is that we don't need to worry ourselves about running away, trying to get to England or Jamaica. Our place is here. This is where He wants us to be. That might not sound good to your ears, but listen carefully. Our days of suffering are coming to an end. God has promised that, and He is faithful to his people. 'For the LORD will vindicate His people, And will have compassion on His servants, When He sees that their strength is gone, And there is none remaining, bond or free,' Deuteronomy 32:36. Those words right there are reason enough to shout and praise His name."

The people were encouraged by Jordan's words. They began to sing, clap their hands, and shout hallelujah. Some jumped to their feet and danced, while they sang songs about Jesus coming back to get them. Jordan taught them a song called "Amazing Grace," that brought tears to many of their eyes.

When the worship service was over, one of the men, who said his name was Walter, ushered Jordan to the tables placed under a large willow oak tree. The women rushed about setting food on ragged tablecloths.

"Thank you for that word, Brother Jordan," Walter said. "I'm glad you can have supper with us. The women folk have prepared a delicious spread."

"It's good to be here," Jordan said, his eyes roving until he found her. "The girl there in the blue dress, what's her name?"

"That's Talitha. She was brought here a couple months back. Word is, she was shipped here before that rebellion in Haiti."

"Does she have a husband?" Jordan asked, still staring.

Walter grunted and laughed. "No, she won't give none of us a second look."

Before he sat down to eat, Jordan walked over and introduced himself to her. "Hello there, miss, I couldn't help but notice you in that pretty blue dress. I'm Jordan, and I would like to make your acquaintance."

"I saw you looking at me, and you probably already know my name," she replied.

"Yes, that's right, but you can't blame me, Miss Talitha. You make the sun turn away from the bluebell flowers just to shine on you."

When Talitha gave Jordan a half smile, all his walls came tumbling down. He insisted that she sit next to him at the table, but he left most of the food on his plate. He couldn't focus. Everything in his life had changed.

***

Jordan rushed through the week, counting the days until he would see Talitha. He thought more about her than he did the message he would bring. Even his constant plans of escape were squeezed into the back of his mind. Not only did he want her for his wife, he wanted to have a family with her and live like one. Before he spoke to her about his intentions, he asked

Master Harrison if he would give his permission for them to get married. Master Harrison was pleased with the request. It appealed to his religious beliefs, and most owners believed married men were less likely to rise up and rebel.

Master Hill on the Shirley plantation happily gave his approval of the match, with the understanding that any children born to the union would belong to him. So, three months after Jordan met Talitha, he exchanged his vow to remain unattached for a vow to love and cherish her till death. Having been reluctant to be close to anyone, especially after his mother died, Jordan was accustomed to being alone. Lying with Talitha, he felt a peace that he had never known, a happiness he had never felt.

"I thank God for the day I came here," he whispered to her. "Before then, the only thing I cared about was getting away from here."

"Where did you wanna to go?" she asked.

"Anywhere, I just wanted to be free, out from under some massa running my life, ordering me around like a dog."

"That mean you don't wanna be free no mo'?"

"Course not, I still wanna be free. I just gotta get us both free."

"Most that get free, get caught or die trying."

"There's other ways," he said. "Anyway, I don't wanna waste my time talking 'bout that. I just wanna love on my wife."

She smiled, and he blew out the candle on the floor beside them.

***

Then the time that Jordan and a lot of other slaves had impatiently been waiting for had come. Whispers of the revolt started in the spring of 1800. An army of slaves was being assembled by a blacksmith named Gabriel and his brothers on the Brookfield plantation, 16 miles away from Charles City County. They were inspired by the slaves on the island of St. Domingue who had overthrown their masters and were battling for their independence from the French.

The next Sunday, Jordan knew what most of them were contemplating. It weighed heavily on his mind. If the revolt were successful, they wondered if they might all be freed.

"Brothers and sisters, the seasons are changing," Jordan said carefully. "The seeds we have planted have grown, and harvest time is coming. It's hard to wait for our seeds to come to fruition, but it happens in God's time. We have looked to Him. The Scripture says, 'I will take my stand at my watchpost and station myself on the tower, and look to see what he will say to me, and what I will answer concerning my complaint. And the LORD answered me: "Write the vision; make it plain on tablets, so he may run who reads it. For still the vision awaits its appointed time; it hastens to the end—it will not lie. If it seems slow, wait for it; it will surely come; it will not delay."' Habakkuk 2:1-3. So, saints of God, our patience will be rewarded. The Bible tells us that the evil will be destroyed and the righteous who trust in the Lord will inherit the earth."

The people shouted and danced with more fervor than Jordan had ever seen. He clapped and shouted hallelujah until the Spirit hit him and his feet refused to keep still.

"If you wanna join those men, I want you to go," Talitha

blurted out while they were eating their Sunday supper. "It would make me happy to know you were free."

"I don't wanna talk about that," Jordan said, getting irritated. It was a subject that vexed him, and he didn't have a solution.

"Everybody is talking about it," she said, pushing the issue.

"How do you expect me to talk about leaving you? If I join the rebellion, there's no turning back."

"You would want me to be free, even if you were still a slave wouldn't you?"

"Yes, but it's different. I can fend for myself."

"That's the way I feel. If you stay here for me, it will ruin us. We'll both be sad about it."

"You're all I have," he said, grabbing her hand. "I can't be free until we both are free."

Talitha nodded, but she wasn't convinced.

***

Late in the summer, Jordan heard the uprising was set for the last Saturday in August. Thousands of enslaved men from surrounding counties had committed to the rebellion and gathered outside of Richmond. This was the dilemma that Jordan had sought to avoid most of his life, having to choose between his freedom and his inability to leave someone he loved. Having Talitha as his wife meant everything to him, and he was certain that he didn't want to live the rest of his life without her. But how could he pass up a chance to be free? His father had made that sacrifice for him, and he died a slave. Jordan felt strongly that he didn't want to die a slave.

It started raining early in the morning on August 30 and carried on throughout the day without let up. By the evening, the rain had become a fierce storm. Jordan listened for word, unsure of what he would do. Then word came that the revolt would be delayed; the army would gather on the following night. For all the nerve-wracking, he would never have to make that critical decision about joining the rebellion. Two slaves on Meadow Farm betrayed Gabriel, alerting their master to the insurrection. The master quickly warned his neighbors and then sent a letter to the governor, notifying him of the uprising.

Jordan received word that the state militia were surrounding the area. He couldn't do anything but pray for the men who had already assembled together. News spread that most of the army of slaves had dispersed and returned to their owners. Still, around 25 of the deemed ringleaders were caught and hanged. Gabriel escaped and headed downriver to Norfolk. He sought refuge with slaves on a plantation before boarding a schooner to sail down the James River. Yet again, he was betrayed by another slave to collect the reward offered for his capture.

On September 25, he was brought back to Richmond to be questioned and prosecuted. He refused to provide any information or turn in any fellow rebels. He was found guilty and executed on the day after the verdict, October 7, 1800. Slaves whispered and mocked the one who betrayed Gabriel, saying, "You know, they didn't even give that Judas the full award."

***

The failed insurrection had slaveholders terrified. Virginia and other state legislatures passed laws restricting the movement of slaves and free blacks and abolished the traditional inheritance laws that inhibited the breaking up of families for sale. The hiring out of slaves ended out of fear of uprisings through communication across plantations. Jordan's Sunday sermons were canceled, and his visits to see Talitha were limited. He wasn't even there when their daughter, Joanna, was born, and she was three weeks old before he even got a chance to see her. After that, he was more determined than ever that he had to gain his freedom.

Jordan made a request to speak with Benjamin Harrison VII after his father died. He had been denied before, so he didn't hold too much hope for his receptiveness when he finally gained his audience. Unbeknownst to Jordan, the Berkeley plantation was on the verge of financial ruin. The land had been worked to exhaustion beyond that of the slaves. Even with rotation of the crops and planting nitrogen-restoring bean and corn, they hadn't been able to generate enough income to support the household and all the slaves. Master Harrison named the price of $500.

Jordan held his tongue and went back to his cabin. He counted all his money just to be sure he hadn't made a mistake. Adding the money his father had given him and what he had earned over 11 years, Jordan had more than the $500 price Master Harrison had agreed upon. The next day, he went back to the mansion, where he paid the cost for his liberty. He was finally a free man. Walking away with his knapsack and free papers, Jordan thought of Psalm 81:6: "I relieved your shoulder of the burden; your hands were freed from the basket." He laughed raucously as he left the Berkeley plantation entrance for the last time.

***

Once he had gained his long-awaited freedom, Jordan discovered that he would have to leave Virginia within a year or risk being sold back into slavery. There was no way he would be able to purchase Talitha and his daughter in 12 months. Leaving the state was not an option. He took the name Jordan Freeman and petitioned the state of Virginia to allow him to remain in the state near his family. Seen favorably as a man of God, his petition was approved. He bought a parcel of land in Ruthville, where many of the free blacks lived, and set about to earn the money to purchase his family. He built a log cabin, a shed to raise chickens, and planted his first crop of tobacco in his own field.

Jordan felt sick to his stomach each time he walked onto the Shirley plantation. It killed him that his wife and daughter were still slaves while he was free. He felt even sicker when he left the plantation for home and had to leave them behind. He reflected on Jacob, who worked for 14 years to get Rachel as his wife, who said it seemed like only a few days because of his love for her. He had already been working ten years, and for him it seemed like 20.

When the War of 1812 broke out and the British Royal Navy fleet arrived in the Chesapeake Bay the following March, black families desperate for freedom met them in canoes in a commitment to fight on the side of the British. Every instinct in Jordan's body wanted to take Talitha and his daughter and join them, but he couldn't risk it. He didn't trust either side to honor their word to a black man. He might end up being a slave again. He would stay on his plan, work his land, and buy their freedom.

When the war was over in 1814, there was more talk about sending free blacks to Liberia. To Jordan, that was a place he knew nothing about. He had land and was getting closer to uniting his family. Then his mounting hope was dashed. What should have been a joy for them was a huge setback. Talitha became pregnant and gave birth to a son they named Edward. Now he would have to have more money to purchase three slaves. With the price getting higher, it took him another 11 years to earn the money to buy his family, but they weren't free. They still were classified as slaves. If he freed them, they would all have to leave the state and the land.

***

It was awkward at first when Jordan brought his family to the home he had built for them. Joanna and Edward seemed nervous and uncomfortable. They had left friends and the only way of life they had known. Jordan was on edge, too. He lay awake most of the night for a week, listening between Talitha's breaths for the patrol to come and take them away.

In the early days of June, a tropical storm raged upon them for two days. The cabin shook and rocked around them. Jordan could hear God speaking to his heart, calling him back to deliver His word. He found the worn Bible that had been passed down to him and held it the darkness. He made a pact with God. "If You will surround us with peace, I will preach Your word as You have directed." When the sun rose on the third day, June 5, a Sunday morning, Jordan brought his family out and preached his first sermon.

Talitha and Joanna pulled chairs outside under the big tree, and Edward sat on a rock. Jordan held his worn-out Bible by his side. He was so happy to see them sitting there in front of him, he could have shouted without a word or a song.

"Family, God has granted us a new beginning!" he happily exclaimed. "My prayers have been answered. Our lives belong to us, and we have been born again! I'm so thankful that we are together. We have hard work ahead of us, but we can do all things through Christ Jesus. Things won't be easy, and we'll have to lean on one another; but the struggle won't be for another man and his family, it will be for our own. On those days when you get tired, I want you to remember this Scripture and repeat it, Psalm 121:1-2, 'I will lift up my eyes to the hills—From whence comes my help? My help comes from the LORD, Who made heaven and earth.' Let us pray!" Jordan led them in the Lord's Prayer, and then he blessed them.

The membership to their Sunday morning service grew slowly and steadily from people from nearby farms, and soon they had enough men to build a church in the field just beyond his home. Jordan hired other free slaves to work his fields, and he became a master at growing some of the finest leaves of sweet tobacco in Virginia. When other black farmers couldn't make their ends meet, he bought their land from them and allowed them to keep working the farms. He didn't do it to profit from them; he did it to keep the white man from making slaves out of them again. His works were blessed, he prospered, and the peace he prayed for surrounded him until the late summer of 1831, when it all changed.

A slave named Nat Turner, who was born on a Southampton County plantation five days before Gabriel

Prosser was executed, was planning an uprising. Known as "Prophet," Nat was a fiery preacher who received divine messages through visions. One of the revelations was for him to "slay his enemies with their own weapons" and to lead the slaves out of bondage. A solar eclipse in February was the sign he had been waiting for. On August 21, he and six other slaves began the rebellion. They killed Master Travis and his family, took guns and horses, and recruited another 70 slaves as they moved from one plantation to the next in a bloody rebellion, killing more than 57 whites in the two-day uprising.

Edward knew something was wrong when he saw the horse in full gallop as his father approached. They usually sauntered back onto the property. When they were close enough for him to see his father's face, he knew it was serious.

"Come on to the house!" Jordan ordered without stopping, as he passed him in the field. He practically jumped off the horse when he reached the house and charged through the door as if he would break it down.

"What's the matter?" Talitha asked, alarmed. "I thought you were going into town."

"We've got to get away from here, now!" Jordan told her, loading his gun. "White folks are out hunting black folks. They want blood for blood. They killing every negro they see off plantations cause of Nat and the uprising." Joanna's eyes got big, and she started to shake with fear. "Help your mama, Joanna!" Jordan directed. "Bring whatever food and water y'all can carry in knapsacks. Edward and I will get everything else we need."

"Where are we going?" Talitha asked, moving quickly to pack the bags.

"Into the woods," he answered, going out the door.

***

Nat's plan was to head to Jerusalem in Southampton, where they would take over the armory, but militiamen at a plantation just outside of the town cut them off. In the melee of fighting, Nat fled into the woods. All hell broke loose while Nat was in hiding. Rumors of the rebellion having spread fueled undue retaliation across Virginia and throughout the South. Vengeful white mobs terrorized the blacks in Southampton County, and close to 200 blacks were massacred, most of whom had nothing to do with the uprising.

A week later, when the revenge-crazed vigilantes were reigned in by the militia, Jordan thought it would be safe for the family to return home.

"Lord, have mercy," Jordan said when they reached the edge of their property. Half of the fields had been burned.

Then Edward hollered, "Papa, they set fire to the church!"

Jordan was overwhelmed. He roared like a grizzly bear caught in a trap. Talitha began to weep at the sound of his pain. Joanna wrapped her arms around her mother for comfort, while Edward ran ahead to check other damage on their property. The house had been ransacked, and all the chickens had been killed.

The militia searched for Nat for two months before he was found. He was tried and convicted of "conspiring to rebel and making insurrection." He was hanged and beheaded on November 11 in Jerusalem, Virginia. His head was displayed to frighten other blacks from revolting. The Virginia General Assembly passed laws making it illegal to teach reading and writing to those enslaved. Possession of firearms by free blacks was banned. Religious services were restricted without the presence of a licensed white minister present.

# Chapter Twenty-One

# Edward Freeman (born 1814)

Talitha and Joanna spent days cleaning the house and the chicken shed. Edward cleaned up the yard and the garden, while the workers turned the soil in the fields to prepare it for planting after the new year. All the members of the congregation donated time and money to rebuild the church and to repay Jordan for the kindness he had shown their families. Still, they couldn't undo what had been done. The fact that everything he had worked so hard to gain could be turned to dust without question or recourse shook something inside him, he never fully recovered mentally and began to decline physically.

Edward took over the hard labor in the tobacco fields, while his father sat in a rocking chair on the front porch, mulling over the tribulations of life between his meditations on God's word. Thankfully, they were able to reopen the church doors after Talitha heard about a white minister who lived nearby who had a license to monitor their Sunday worship services.

The man was Robert Shields. He grew tobacco on his own farm at the edge of Ruthville. Jordan found that he and Robert had much in common. The white preacher had a black wife and informed him that he had to be on guard as much as the black people. From what he told Jordan, the white vigilantes lynched abolitionists without hesitation, white or black. In a short time, the two men became good friends; and whenever the tobacco buyers tried to cheat Jordan out of a fair price at the market, Robert displayed his crop alongside his own.

Before long, there was a little money for extras around the house, and Talitha and Joanna started getting their hair styled every other Saturday by Caroline, a black woman who ran a beauty parlor in her home. Caroline had bought her own freedom with money she made doing hair for wealthy white women. Going to Miss Caroline's gave Tabitha and Joanna a chance to get away from their chores and socialize with other women.

Even so, it worried Jordan whenever they were away from the house. As a precaution, he would have Edward drive them in the wagon and pick them up. On one Saturday, when he was about to leave Miss Caroline's, Edward a saw a pretty, young lady in a blue dress, pumping water at the well. He got off the wagon and walked over to make her acquaintance.

"Good morning, miss, I'm Edward Freeman," he said with a toothy grin. "I bring my mama and sister here twice a month. I haven't seen you here before."

The girl stared at him and said, "I haven't seen you here before either, but I live here."

"Oh, I'm sorry," Edward said, a little embarrassed. "You must be Miss Caroline's daughter."

"That's right," she said, seeming unsociable.

"Well, I hope to see you when I come back," he said, ignoring her coolness.

She stopped and put her hand on her hip. "I don't think so. I'll probably be busy." Then she paused and said, "Or you could come to church tomorrow."

"I'd like to do that, but my family attends our own church. My papa is the preacher. It's God's Church. Have you heard about it?"

She nodded. "I have, but my family has always gone to Elam Baptist Church. Rev. Brown is our pastor."

Edward was disappointed. "I've heard good things about him," he told her. "Well, I'll see ya," he said, walking back to the wagon.

"We're having a church picnic next Saturday. Maybe you could come?" she hollered after him.

"Yeah, I'd like that!" Edward said, smiling, glad to have a way to see her again. "I'll surely see you next week." He was almost to the wagon when he realized he didn't know her name. "I didn't ask your name," he shouted.

She shouted back, "It's Blossom."

That's how he met Blossom, the girl who worked with her mama fixing hair, the girl he knew he wanted to be his wife.

Edward arrived at the picnic on Saturday, dressed in his best slacks, an ironed shirt, and wild flowers in his hand. He was nervous. Blossom hadn't been that friendly when they first met, but he relaxed when he saw her near the tables watching him. She piled a plate high and heavy with a bit of everything there was to eat.

"This is a lot of food?" Edward said, half-smiling and weighing the plate in his hand.

"We wouldn't want you to go back to your church and tell them we didn't feed you properly," she joked.

Edward smiled wider. "I surely can't say that." Then he asked, "Where's your plate?"

"I've eaten already," she answered, leading him to a spot under a shade tree.

"Good, then you can tell me all about yourself while I eat."

"Okay, there's a lot to tell," she chuckled. "You sure you want to hear it?"

"Absolutely," he said, biting into a hunk of cornbread.

***

Just when it seemed happy days were ahead and the hard times were behind them, the young temperance movement merged with an anti-tobacco movement, stating tobacco dried out the mouth, "creating a morbid or diseased thirst" that only alcohol could satisfy. The campaign made the fall in tobacco prices even worse, and money became tight for the Freeman family. Then a financial crisis at the banks led to the Panic of 1837 and started a depression. For the next five years, the best they could do was keep food in their mouths.

After a long, hot day in the fields, Edward practically staggered to the front porch.

"Papa, things are getting really hard around here!" he said, discouraged. "We can't make it like this much longer. I've got to get me a job."

"Trust in the Lord, son," Jordan replied firmly through gritted teeth, rocking faster in his chair. "Don't let nothing run you off this land."

"We're losing more than we make on the fields," Edward said, forcing the issue. "I want to help; I'm a man now. Plus, I want to marry Blossom. How can I take care of her if we don't got enough to take of ourselves? We all got to eat."

Jordan shook his head, being obstinate. "God has given you a job. You have to honor that."

"I need a job that puts money in my pockets and something on the table," Edward argued.

"You don't have free papers, son! If they arrest you, they'll sell you away from here. They trade slaves here more than anything else. They'll put you back on a plantation for sure. Is that what you want?" When Edward didn't answer, Jordan kept talking. "Our fathers were men of high esteem. They served King David and King Solomon, and they were kings in their own right. They lived in huge palaces with great wealth."

Edward lost his patience and pounded his fists on his legs. "I don't want to hear about the palaces we once lived in! We're here now in claps of wood barely holding together."

"Don't belittle what God has blessed us with!" Jordan said, getting angry again. "You could be back in master's house."

"What I can do is work in Richmond," Edward said, standing up to him. "They hiring blacks at Tredegar Iron."

Jordan took a breath. "Why would you do that, son? We got more work here than we can do."

"It's steady work there, Papa, making cannons and ammunition for the army and the navy. It pays good. When things get better, I'll come back."

"How you gonna help your mama and your sister if you end up back in chains? Then how you gonna marry Blossom?"

"That's not gonna happen. I promise you that."

"Promise me something else, and I'll give you my blessing."

Edward furrowed his brow. "What's that?" he asked, wondering.

"That when I die, you will step into my shoes as the

preacher in the church. It's a legacy given to us by God, for you and your son after you."

Edward sighed. "I promise, Papa."

Two days later, Edward packed his knapsack and headed to Richmond with two of his best buddies, Philip and Alfred, both free. All three of them got jobs at Tredegar and rented a room together. After he had saved a year's pay, Edward came home to get married. The evening after the wedding, he went back to Richmond to keep from missing a day's work. It took him another two years before he was able to rent a place of his own and bring Blossom to Richmond.

****

The long hours at the mill left Blossom alone at home most of the time. Gradually, she made friends with several women around the neighborhood where they lived and started fixing hair out of the house like her mama did to occupy her time. For the next couple of years, with both of them earning money, Edward and Blossom saved as much as they could. At the start of the new year in 1847, they were feeling good about their progress; and when Blossom told Edward she was pregnant, it was even better. Then in May, there was a strike at Tredegar Iron. The white workers protested against enslaved workers taking skilled jobs away from them in the rolling mill.

"Things are getting dangerous around the job," Edward told Blossom over supper. "The white men are raising a ruckus because more negros are getting hired. They don't care that we get paid half the money they earn."

"Maybe you can get a job working in the tobacco factory?" Blossom said, worried that things might get violent.

"That's harder work for less money. Anyway, to calm the fuss, the mill wants all the negro men to stay together on the property for a while."

"Do what you have to do. I'll be all right," Blossom said, confident.

"I don't know how long that'll be. What if the baby comes, and I'm not here?"

"Don't worry. There's plenty of folks around here to look after me, and there's a midwife about a mile away."

Things calmed down at the mill after a few months. All the white men who went on strike were fired, and the free negro workers were allowed to leave the property. The hours were still long, and Edward was scarcely home long enough to get a good night's sleep. In mid-September, Blossom went into labor not long after Edward went to work. A neighbor fetched the midwife; and by the time Edward got home in the late evening, the baby was already born.

"This isn't how I thought things were gonna be," Edward said, marveling at his baby son in Blossom's arms. "This ain't no place to raise no child."

"We'll be fine," Blossom said, rubbing his arm. "We have everything we need, and things are gonna get better."

The next day, Edward sent a letter to Ruthville, telling them that Blossom had a baby boy and they named him Thomas Edward Freeman.

***

Thomas was a year old when Blossom was pregnant again, and Richmond wasn't the place where Edward wanted to raise his family. Since more slaves were escaping on the Underground Railroad, more free men were being kidnapped and sold as slaves. It made Edward uneasy in the city now that he had a family to worry about. Against Blossom's objections, he arranged for her to ride back to the farm with Alfred, who was taking his new wife home to Ruthville.

"I'll feel better with you all back safe on the farm," Edward told her as they said goodbye. "I couldn't take it if anything happened to y'all while I was working."

"I've told you, I want to stay here in Richmond with you!" Blossom complained. "We've spent most of our time apart. You don't need to worry about me. I can shoot a gun," she said, pleading her case. "I can take care of myself!"

Edward wrapped her in a bear hug and then helped her into the wagon. "What I need you to do is take care of Thomas and that baby in your belly. When things settle down, I'll send for you to come back here."

Back in Ruthville, Blossom preferred to stay at her mother's house. Although she let Thomas spend a lot of time with Jordan and Talitha, she didn't want them to make a permanent place for her and Edward to live there. She planned to go back to Richmond soon after the baby was born.

Five months later, she gave birth to a daughter. Caroline rode over to give Jordan and Talitha the news, and the next day they came to see their new grandchild.

"She's like a doll," Talitha said, cuddling her in her arms. "She looks just like Blossom."

"She sure does," Caroline added.

Jordan nodded in agreement. "What are you gonna name her?" he asked Blossom.

"We decided to call her Maria."

"That's a sweet name," Jordan said, approving. "Wonder how long it'll be before Edward gets back here for good."

"Don't seem like this is the place to be," Blossom said. She wasn't attached to the land. She didn't want to come back. One thing she learned from her mama was that she could earn a living fixing hair anywhere. "Folks are escaping out of here and getting to freedom on the Underground Railroad. They say there's a better life up north," she told them.

"This is our land, and we have a good enough life here," Jordan said strongly. "This is home."

Blossom didn't feel like arguing and changed the subject. Her father-in-law wasn't the one she had to convince. "Y'all won't believe it, but there was a slave who was hired out to work in a tobacco factory there in Richmond. His name is Henry Brown. After his family was sold down south, he shipped himself in a wooden crate to Philadelphia, where he could be free. They calling him Henry 'Box' Brown," she chuckled. "He's famous now. They say he done even met up with Frederick Douglass."

"You don't mean it!" Talitha said, pressing her hand on her heart in disbelief.

Blossom laughed and said, "Yes, he did!"

They all laughed, enjoying the cleverness of Henry Brown. But Jordan didn't laugh; he was worried about the freedom of his own family.

***

Later in the spring, there was a cholera epidemic. Jordan sat beside Pastor Shields's sick bed, praying for him to get well. It wasn't a totally unselfish prayer because several of the black farmers relied on him to get fair pricing for their tobacco crops; and without Pastor Shields monitoring the Sunday service, Jordan wasn't sure if they would have a church.

"I wanna thank you for coming by and checking on me," Pastor Shields said. "You've been a good friend to me, and I tried to be a good one to you. I ain't never been stupid, so I know I ain't gonna get up from this bed. I'm not bitter about it. I don't question God's will after all I've seen in my life. My family is my only concern on this earth."

"Pastor, you know I'll look out for Clara like my own family."

"Thank you again, but it's not necessary. Clara is going north to Philadelphia as soon as I'm laid in the ground. That's what I want. What you can do for me is buy the land from her so she'll be free and clear."

"You know times are still tough 'round here, but I'll make you a reasonable offer. I'll talk about it with Edward. He's been saving to get a place for him and Blossom."

"What about you, Jordan?" Robert asked. "You aren't looking so good yourself. Have you seen the doctor?"

"I'm feeling poorly this morning, but I'll be all right," Jordan told him, staring at the floor. He couldn't lie. He was worried sick. He needed to figure out how to be sure his family would never be slaves again. In that, he couldn't trust anyone. After a minute, he said, "What's got me bothered is what would happen to my folks if I die."

"Make a will, and the land belongs to them," Pastor Shields said, matter-of-factly.

"Talitha, Edward, and Joanna aren't free. I hold the papers on them. I don't even know if our grandchildren are totally free. If I free them, they'll have to leave the state and the land."

"All you have to do is sell them to Blossom. She is a free woman, and they're her family, too."

"I hadn't thought about that," Jordan said, breathing a big sigh of relief. "I'll sell her the land, too, and then it'll belong to Thomas."

Pastor Shields died in May. Before they could bury him, Jordan fell ill. Within a month, Jordan died and Talitha soon after. Edward came back home to fulfill the promise he made to his father: to step into his shoes at the church and to take care of the land.

Edward didn't have any regrets about coming home and working in the tobacco fields again. The truth was, it was getting too dangerous to stay in Richmond. Every day, free blacks were being kidnapped on suspicion of being slaves. Ineligible for trial, they were placed back into slavery. Without free papers, he was in jeopardy, too. Thankfully, he didn't come home empty-handed. He had worked hard, had two jobs and another one on the weekend. He was determined to make his father proud. With his savings, he bought Pastor Shields's land from Clara.

He was surprised when Joanna announced she was leaving Ruthville and going to Philadelphia with Clara.

"Mama and Papa are gone now, and you have a family of your own," she told Edward. "There's nothing to keep me here."

"This land belongs to both of us," he said. "Papa wanted us to keep it."

"You keep it. I can make a life for myself up north. Clara says we can start us a business or somethin'. I might even find myself a husband," she chuckled. "All we need to do is change my papers over to Clara's name."

Blossom signed the papers, saying that Joanna was owned by Clara, just in case they were stopped. More than anything, Blossom wished she could trade places with her sister-in-law and go north. She complained to her mama.

"I have the papers that say I own Edward, but he orders me around. I can make my own money. I could even sell him."

"Hush, child!" Caroline scolded. "That's nothing but the devil talking."

"Pray for me, mama," was all Blossom had left to say.

***

On the new land Edward purchased, he planted things they could eat instead of tobacco. He wasn't particularly spiritual. It wasn't intentional. He had always been busy doing other things instead of studying the Bible. Nevertheless, he stood in his father's place at the church as he had promised, and he recited the words he had heard Jordan say all his life. It made him feel like a thief when the people gave their tithes, so he began to read and study God's word. It made him want to read other books he could get to learn about history.

Edward and Blossom had another daughter a year later, Eliza; and as soon as she was knee-high, she joined Maria and Thomas, and they worked beside Edward in the field.

Whenever his children's bodies had been pushed to the limit on the land, Edward insisted that they use their minds. With the Bible in his hands, he taught all of them how to read. Like his father, he believed in education as much as in hard work. "Folks need both to be truly free," he said reciting the words his father would always tell them. When he figured they were old enough to fend for themselves, he let them join the other children who went to school in secret in Charles City.

The teacher at the school was Jane Caldwell. She had been a slave until her master freed her just before he died. The students called her Miss Jane. She was strict with them, but they loved being there. She opened up the world to them and taught them to imagine more for themselves with books such as *Moby Dick*, *A Tale of Two Cities*, and *The Scarlet Letter*. Thomas's favorite was the *Narrative of the Life of Frederick Douglass*. That book proved to him that a slave could become a great man. School also opened up other possibilities for him. Miss Jane had five children. The youngest daughter, the only one born out of love, was named Anna Bell. She and Thomas sat next to each other in the small room.

Anna Bell fascinated Thomas with her big, brown eyes and a smile that showed every tooth. She was smart, too, with an amazing memory. He waited for the days when she would stand in front of the class and recite long passages from books she had read. She wasn't like the other girls. She wasn't afraid of toads or lizards or whatever his buddies could find to scare the other girls. Tall, with long, slim legs that could outrun all of them, boys included, Anna Bell was like a puma cat, beautiful and intimidating. Thomas got her attention after school one day by quoting the poem "On Being Brought From Africa to

America" by Phillis Wheatley:

> Twas mercy brought me from my Pagan land
> Taught my benighted soul to understand
> That there's a God, that there's a Saviour too:
> Once I redemption neither sought nor knew.
> Some view our sable race with scornful eye,
> "Their colour is a diabolic dye."
> Remember, Christian, Negroes, black as Cain,
> May be refin'd and join th' angelic train.

"Very good, church boy!" Anna Bell said, clapping her hands and nodding. "I didn't think you knew anything that wasn't in the Bible."

Thomas grinned, seeing she was impressed. "I guess that means you don't know everything after all," he said, teasing her.

"I still know more than you," she said, pushing him and running off.

Thomas chased her around the schoolhouse to the edge of the woods. He chased her for the next two years until they became teenagers. That's when she decided to stop running from him.

***

The United States was a divided country on the issue of slavery. More slaves were escaping to the north on the Underground Railroad, and the hostility between free states and slave states was growing. Laws were passed that declared all escaped slaves who were captured would be returned to their masters, and any persons aiding runaway slaves with food or shelter were subject to six months in jail and a fine.

In the November 1860 election, Abraham Lincoln, who argued against the spread of slavery, won the presidency. Shortly after he was inaugurated, the secession of the Southern states from the Union began. Confederate forces attacked Fort Sumter in South Carolina on April 12, starting the Civil War. On April 17, Virginia seceded from the Union. The Confederacy moved their capital from Montgomery, Alabama, to Richmond. Virginia, which had hundreds of factories that produced tents, uniforms, and leather goods. Richmond was the South's largest city; but, more important, it was closer to the Tredegar Iron Works, where the field guns, heavy cannons, ammunition, railroad tracks, and iron cladding for naval vessels were manufactured.

Only three months into the war, the Union realized that the Confederates were using slaves to their advantage as laborers. To eliminate the handicap, President Lincoln passed the first Confiscation Act on August 6, 1861, authorizing the seizure of rebel property by the Union. All slaves who fought or worked for the Confederate military service were freed.

Edward rushed into the house. "It's happening!" he called out to Blossom. "Where are the children? We all gonna be free! I wish my papa and mama could have lived to see this day!"

"What if the Union don't win the war?" Blossom asked dryly, doubting that this would be the end of slavery. "This is the time for us to go north. We can get away from this hard life. There are good jobs for blacks in Maryland and New York."

Edward frowned, shocked at the way she was acting. "We don't need to leave here if we're free, honey! We can make a good living on the land. Besides, I promised my papa that I would keep the church going. I'm not gonna walk away from that."

"What about the life I want?" Blossom shouted, getting emotional. "Does that make any difference to you?"

"Listen here, you said you wanted a life with me. This is my life. I never promised you that I would leave here. You're my wife, so this is your home, too."

"I know that," she said calming down some. "But I liked the life we had in Richmond. I liked being in the city. I just wanted to get away from all this dirt."

Those words got Edward riled up. "My papa broke his back to buy this dirt and to get us off that plantation! You ain't never been a slave, so it might not mean much to you, but it means everything to me!"

"What makes you think I had it easy just because I wasn't a slave? Things been hard here for me and my mama, too. I just wanted better for us and the kids."

"Trust me, and give me some time," Edward said, standing close to her. "I promise you it'll be better for us right here in Ruthville."

***

The consequence of the Confederacy's capital in Richmond being close to the capital in Washington was nonstop combat. The war brought food shortages and hard times. Crime was rampant among poor whites, deserters, and free blacks; and soldiers overwhelmed the city with drunken scuffles and shootings. The only business thriving in the city was prostitution. In February 1862, the Virginia legislature passed a law authorizing the impressment of free black labor.

Before he gave his Sunday sermon, Edward made the announcement to his congregation.

"The sheriff came into Ruthville two days ago. He says all free black men between the ages of 18 and 50 have to register for military labor. When your name is chosen from the list, you have to serve the Confederacy for 180 days. He has assured me that everybody will be paid for their work; but if you decide you don't want to work, you will be fined $50 to $150."

"Sounds like we back to being slaves again!" one of the men hollered out.

Edward felt Blossom's eyes prickling his skin from the front pew. He was sure she was feeling justified in all her efforts to get him to leave Virginia. He avoided her gaze because it didn't matter. Nothing would make him break his promise to his papa.

"The winds of change are shifting, brothers and sisters," Edward told them. "In 1 Samuel 3:11-13, the Lord said to Samuel, 'See, I am about to do something in Israel that will make both ears of anyone who hears of it tingle. On that day I will fulfill against Eli all that I have spoken concerning his house, from beginning to end. For I have told him that I am about to punish his house forever, for the iniquity that he knew, because his sons were blaspheming God, and he did not restrain them.' Saints, don't be troubled by the stumbling blocks put in our way. God will remove them all. We have to continue to be patient. God's time is not our time, but change is on the way. The storm is passing. It's in the air all around us, brothers and sisters. Breathe it in, and let it fill your lungs. It will give us life, the stamina we need to finish this race."

Edward's words encouraged the small congregation. Everybody stood on their feet, shouting, crying, dancing, and thanking God for his mercy. Edward bowed his head and prayed that his words were weighted in truth and not fancy.

***

Blossom was given more ammunition to fight Edward's decision when the second Confiscation Act was passed on July 17, 1862. This law declared that all slaves held by Confederate supporters who crossed over Union lines were "forever free." She pressured him, but he answered that they would wait on the Lord. Then on September 22, 1862, President Lincoln issued the preliminary Emancipation Proclamation, stating that all persons being held as slaves in the rebel states would be free. One hundred days later, on January 1, 1863, Lincoln issued the Emancipation Proclamation that declared all slaves in the rebel states were free.

"Hallelujah! Hallelujah! Hallelujah!" Edward yelled to the high heavens. He was filled with such jubilation that he could hardly speak. His eyes were so filled up with happy tears that he could barely see. He was in every sense of the word a free man. His life was his own.

"See, Blossom? I told you we just needed to have faith. After a while, things will be different for us black folks!"

"Some things will change, but not much," she said soberly. "I've been free all my life, and I ain't never been treated like a white woman. The hearts of these people in Virginia ain't gonna change. Up north, we can get rich. I can work as a hairdresser for white women, and you can build a big church with the money from this land."

"We raised our children here. This is our home."

"Our children are almost grown. Can we live a little before we die?"

"The Bible says, 'A man to whom God has given riches, wealth, and honor, so that they lack nothing their hearts desire, yet God does not grant them the ability to enjoy it. They die, and someone else enjoys it, this is vanity, an evil disease, ' Ecclesiastes 6:1-2. I'm content with the blessing God has given me. It makes me sad that you're not happy here."

"Don't judge me for wanting to be better and to have better."

"I love you, Blossom, and that's enough for me."

"Then you make me your slave," she said, walking out of the room.

***

It was early on Saturday morning, May 23, 1863. There was a quick knock on the door. Edward was home by himself. Caroline had been sick, so Blossom and the girls were staying at her house for a while. He opened the door, and it was Philip and Alfred.

"Have you heard the news?" Philip asked, excited. Edward shook his head sleepily and stepped out on the porch. "Yesterday the War Department said there's gonna be a Bureau of Colored Troops. They recruiting black soldiers to fight in the war with the Union Army. They saying all healthy freed men will be accepted and paid a wage."

"Are you saying you going to sign up?" Edward asked, dropping down in the rocking chair.

Philip folded his arms and sat down beside him. "Why not, at least now we have something to fight for."

"The Rebels are recruiting blacks to serve with their troops, too," Alfred added.

"Yeah, and as soon as they win, they'll make slaves out of all of us," Edward sneered. "There won't be a free black man in this country."

"Our only chance is to join the Union," Philip said. "If they win this war, we might get some equal rights."

"The Confederates are offering good paying jobs for coloreds in Richmond," Alfred said, disagreeing with Philip. "I could use that money. Most likely, we won't have anything left as it is when this war is over."

"Whatever they pay you, it won't last," Philip argued back. "They'll use you, chain you back up, and use you some more when this war is over. You see how they came up here and took over Virginia. We won't be free if they win. If we gonna fight, it got to be with the Union."

Edward watched them fuss back and forth without saying anything.

"I think I'll be a navy man," Philip said, ending the argument.

Alfred grunted and shrugged his shoulders.

"I'll hold things together here," Edward told them. "We probably too old to enlist anyway. Plus, it don't make sense for all of us to leave Ruthville. It ain't safe."

After they left, Edward sat on the porch for a while, pondering both sides of the conversation. His papa had always taught him that it was a waste of time to fight another man's battle and to save your strength for your own struggles. He was about to go into the kitchen and rustle up something for his breakfast, when he saw Thomas come around from the chicken coop.

"Morning, son," he said, still amazed that his baby boy was almost a man.

"Morning, Papa," Thomas answered, his long strides bringing him to the steps in no time.

"Have you finished all your chores?"

"Yes, sir," Thomas answered and then twisted his lips to the side.

Edward had seen the look many times. "You got something on your mind, son?"

"The Union Army is recruiting colored soldiers," he replied.

"So I heard," Edward sighed. "What about it?"

"I'm old enough to fight, Papa," Thomas said. "The money will help us get the farm running again when the war is over."

Edward shuddered at the thought. "I don't want to hear about that, son. You're too young to throw your life away."

"I just want to do what you did for the farm, Papa. You went away to earn money to marry Mama. I wanna marry Anna Bell."

"You're right, I went to get work. I didn't go to war."

"Papa—"

"I said I don't want to hear about it anymore!" Edward shouted. "Your mama is already worried enough about your grandma. She don't need you going off to kill yourself right now."

Thomas kicked an imaginary rock in frustration. He would let it rest for now but not for long. He was pretty sure that the fight to stay free with food on the table would never be over.

# Priscilla and the Stranger

"**S**ave your breath, mister!" I said, waving my hand when the stranger paused in his story. "I get it. Life is a struggle for damn near everybody. What you don't get is that I'm consumed with my own battle. I've lost, and now I want to retreat."

"We began this portion of the story with the brothers Yonas and Simeon," he said, speaking with the patience of a saint, despite my attitude. "Couldn't you see your struggle in Yonas's?"

I put my elbow on the table and rested my head in my hands. "I know where you're going with this."

"Good, Priscilla, then you already know the lesson in Yonas. He, like you, suffered a tremendous loss. And though he wasn't able to fully recover, he found a reason to keep living."

"Possibly he saw that he was needed," I told him, letting out a huge sigh. "He had his brother's children. I don't have a brother or a sister, nieces or nephews. Those who might miss me will be relieved of the burden that my being has brought them."

"You may feel you are being gracious in your actions, beloved, but it is all selfishness."

"That's from your point of view, mister. I would never have chosen this if I had known the outcome."

"You didn't choose this. You were chosen, and this isn't the end. There's always another vessel or someone else for us to pour into. Life doesn't stop."

"I've listened to you. Why can't you hear me?" I said, throwing my hands up in the air. "I have nothing left in me to pour."

He calmly replied, "Then let me pour more into you."

I shook my head wondering where this peculiar man came from and why he was so concerned with me. I was overwhelmed, and my emotions were bubbling up.

"From what you told me, Yonas poured so much into Jemal, and then he was killed in battle. It was all lost. What was the point in that?" I asked, trying to hide the melancholy in my voice.

"The point is, everything is not about you or any individual. Some things are bigger than us and our personal gains and losses. We are only one piece of the gigantic puzzle. It's not always clear where we fit in. We have to stay involved until it's finished."

I shook my head no. "You haven't convinced me yet."

"Yonas didn't give up. He poured what little hope and strength he had left into Koji. And then Koji poured into Melku and down through the generations to Mekonnen, Miruts, and then Tariku. He was one of many who suffered great loss. He had to be brave enough to lean on his faith and move to another place, another phase of life and history."

"I never professed to be brave, and obviously my faith is shattered. I tried to move forward, but I ended up back in the same place I started."

The stranger paused, stood up, and walked to the window. He looked out into the darkness. "There are times when we go full circle in our journey. But even though it may seem as if we have returned to the place we started, that circle we traveled enlarged our perspective and our territory many times."

"If that journey leads you to a bad end, why would someone want to keep going?" I asked, wanting him to see my reasoning. "And if you come full circle, there's nowhere else to go."

"That's when you remember Proverbs 3:5: 'Trust in the LORD with all your heart, and do not lean on your own understanding.' Beta Israel had to keep going. Workneh had to move the people again out of Ethiopia and into what is now known as Kenya. There are always external conflicts that complicate our internal conflicts, but we have to adapt and evolve."

"This story you have told me is awesome. I can't deny I am humbled by their struggles. I can identify with all the trials of the priests. They were courageous and persevered through their challenges. In the end, so many of them wanted the same thing I want, and that's peace."

"Your peace is within your own power. Matthew 11:28 says, 'Come to me, all you who are heavy burdened, and I will give you rest.' It doesn't mean you should lie down and give up. It means that 'when you pass through the waters, I will be with you; and through the rivers, they shall not overwhelm you; when you walk through the fire you shall not be burned, and the flame shall not consume you,' Isaiah 43:2.

"The lesson is that the struggle is continual. Many of the priests lost their wives and some of their children, and then they were made slaves. Against their will, they were brought to Jamaica and then to the States in Virginia. To fight for their freedom, they had to deepen their commitment and lean on the Holy One of Israel, your Savior, Jesus Christ."

"I appreciate that, mister, but the truth is; we all press on until we can't anymore. The will to survive is a strong motivator that I no longer have."

"This isn't only about you. The legacy is bigger than you and your sorrow. It must continue. You must give what has been given to you."

"Please finish your story, and leave me in peace."

"All right, Priscilla. I'll continue with your story. There is so much more to tell."